FIVE REASONS WHY YOU'LL LOVE THIS BOOK . . .

ELECTRIGIRL is a superhero for the new generation! A human battery, she's shockingly good!

Every time Holly becomes **ELECTRIGIRL**, the action switches to awesome comic strips!

"Electrigirl is a mind-blowing adventure . . . full of strong heroic characters. I would recommend it to my friends."
Freya, age 10

An electrifying page-turner — erfect for readers o like their stories lightning fast!

"A real page-turner! Every chapter leaves you on a cliffhanger, leaving you in suspense to read more."
Isabella, age 9

FOR MY SUPERHERO MOM
WITH LOVE
– J. C.

FOR MY SPARKY NIECE, MOO (BECAUSE SHE'S AMAZING
AND BECAUSE HER SISTER GOT THE LAST DEDICATION AND
I'D NEVER HEAR THE LAST OF IT OTHERWISE!)
#LOVEYOUBOTHEQUALLY XX
– C. B.

Electrigirl and the Deadly Swarm is published by
Stone Arch Books, a Capstone imprint
1710 Roe Crest Drive
North Mankato, Minnesota 56003
www.mycapstone.com

Text copyright © Jo Cotterill
Illustrations copyright © Cathy Brett

Electrigirl and the Deadly Swarm was originally published in English in 2016. This translation is published by
arrangement with Oxford University Press.

Library of Congress Cataloging-in-Publication Data is available on the Library of Congress website.

ISBN: 978-1-4965-5662-2 (Library Binding)
ISBN: 978-1-4965-5661-5 (Paperback)
ISBN: 978-1-4965-5664-6 (eBook pdf)

Summary: After honing her superpowers, rescuing her best friend, and defeating the evil Professor
Macavity, Holly needs a vacation. But when a mysterious and deadly swarm attacks the beach, there's only
one person who
can save the day ... ELECTRIGIRL!

Designer: Mackenzie Lopez

Printed and bound in Canada.
010407F17

ELECTRIGIRL AND THE DEADLY SWARM

By Jo Cotterill   Illustrated by Cathy Brett

STONE ARCH BOOKS
a capstone imprint

Hello!

We're back with another exciting adventure for Holly and her friends! Writing this story was SO much fun, and this time Cathy and I knew exactly how to tell it. There's EVEN MORE artwork in this story than the first, so feast your eyes on the amazingness!

Since ELECTRIGIRL was published, I've been reading loads more comics. If you're into Marvel superheroes, you MUST check out the fantastic Ms. Marvel, who is a Muslim girl with superhero powers who still has to deal with her strict parents. I've also laughed all the way through Phoebe and her Unicorn by Dana Simpson, which reminds me of Garfield, a comic strip I loved as a kid. But my favorite find is Evil Emperor Penguin by Laura Ellen Anderson, which is not only laugh-out-loud funny but also has cracking plots and a hopelessly inept villain.

Happy reading! And watch out for the DEADLY SWARM . . .

CHARACTER PROFILES

HOLLY is a perfectly normal 12-year-old who's been struck by weird lighting and can now create and control electricity. Also known as **ELECTRIGIRL**!

JOE is her younger brother, superhero and comics geek and training mentor. Not many younger brothers get to boss around their superhero sibling.

IMOGEN is Holly's best friend since forever. Resourceful and clever, Imogen's favorite hobby is drawing, and she's rarely without her sketchbook.

CAMERON lives in Polperro, where his parents run a campground. Cameron loves myths and legends and is obsessed with health and safety.

MAVERICK would like to be James Bond. He does actually work for a mysterious government agency, so he's already got some great gadgets.

PROFFESSOR MACAVITY is a technological genius bent on world domination. Beaten by Holly and her friends in their first encounter, but where is she now ...?

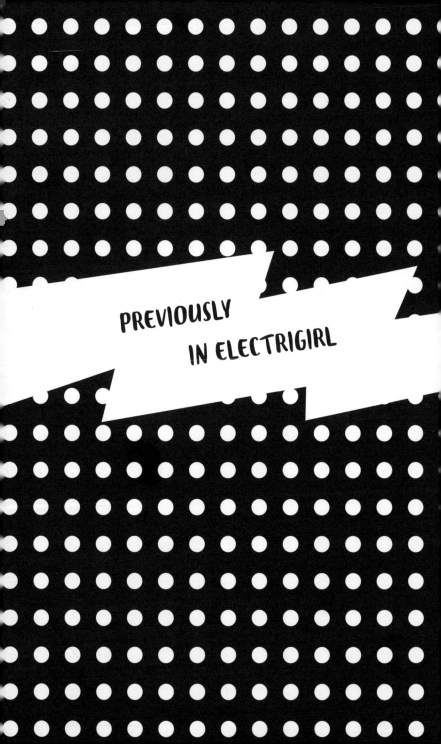

PREVIOUSLY
IN ELECTRIGIRL

HOLLY SPARKES WAS AN ORDINARY GIRL, WITH ORDINARY PROBLEMS . . .
Aren't you my friend anymore?
hmph!
BUT THEN SOMETHING *EXTRAORDINARY* HAPPENED . . .
Is that ... lightning?

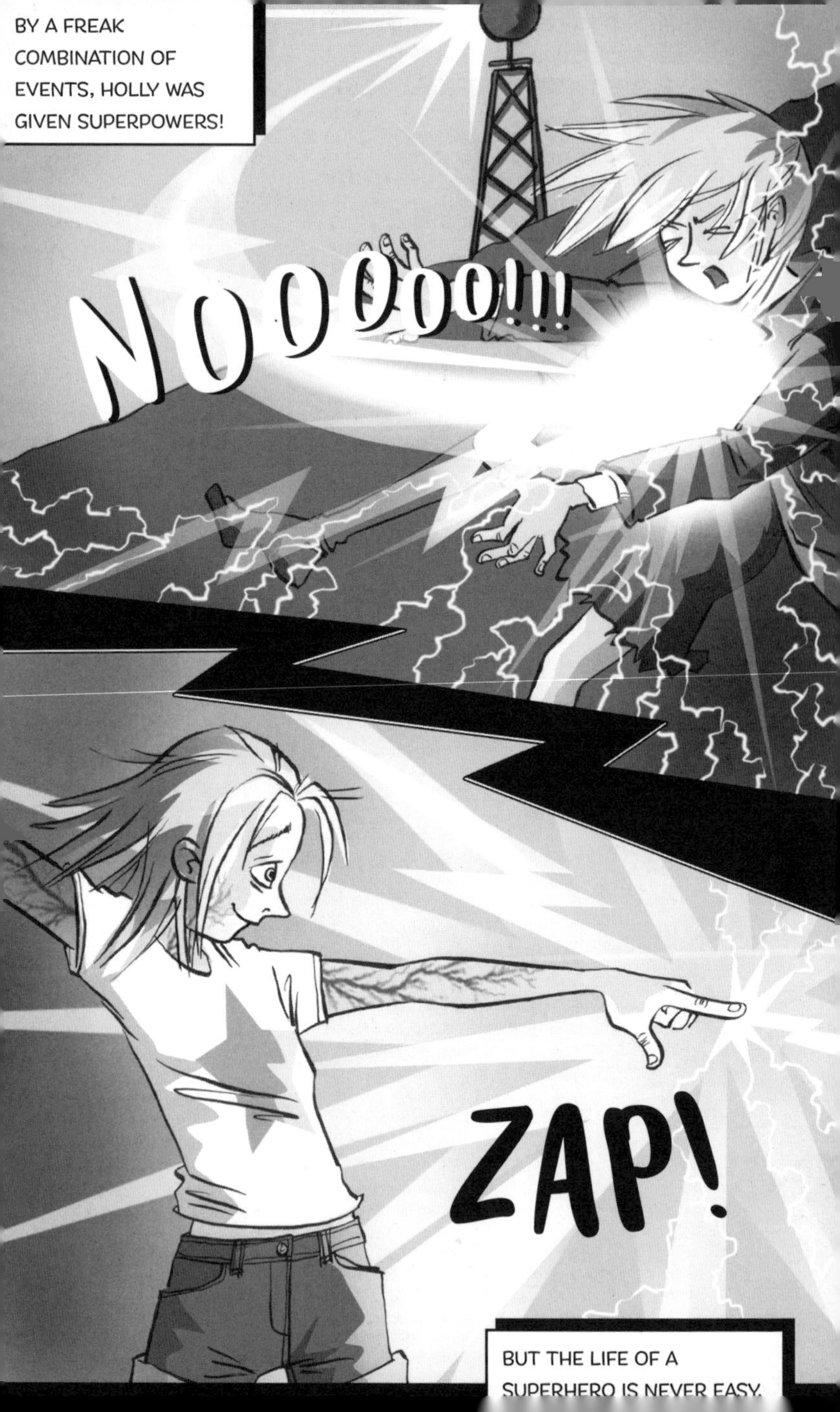
BY A FREAK COMBINATION OF EVENTS, HOLLY WAS GIVEN SUPERPOWERS!
NOOOOOO!!!!
ZAP!
BUT THE LIFE OF A SUPERHERO IS NEVER EASY.

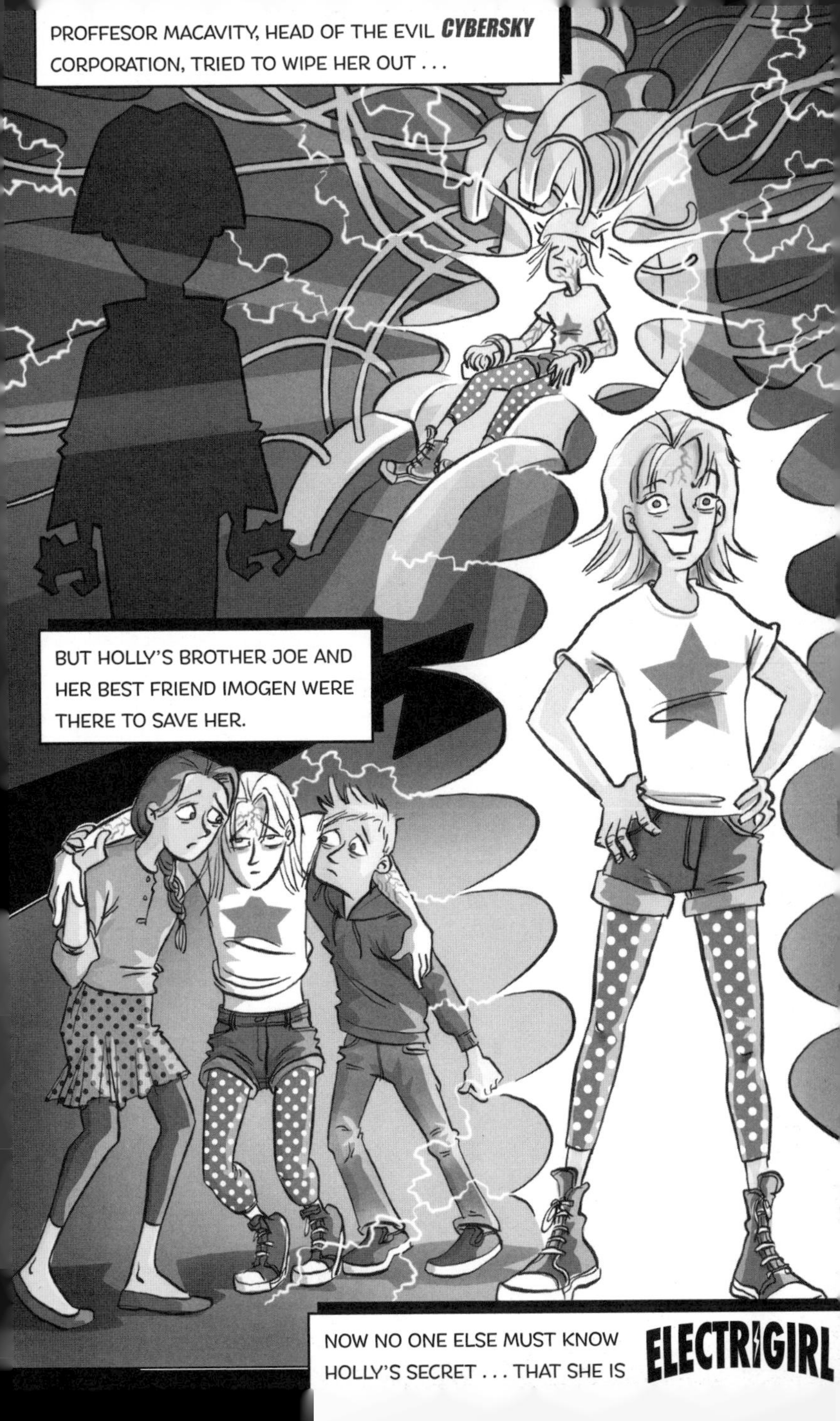
PROFFESOR MACAVITY, HEAD OF THE EVIL CYBERSKY CORPORATION, TRIED TO WIPE HER OUT . . .
BUT HOLLY'S BROTHER JOE AND HER BEST FRIEND IMOGEN WERE THERE TO SAVE HER.
NOW NO ONE ELSE MUST KNOW HOLLY'S SECRET . . . THAT SHE IS
ELECTRIGIRL

CHAPTER 1

There should be a law against rain over summer break. School finished two weeks ago, and we've barely had a single day without rain. I hate it when it rains. It means I can't get outside, and I go **BONKERS** when I'm cooped up indoors.

I've never liked being indoors for too long. But since — well — since the whole nearly-dying-in-a-freaky-world-domination-plot thing at the end of the school year, I've liked it even less. I try so hard not to think about what happened, but it's not that easy. My brother Joe says, "Don't show fear. If you show fear, the bad guys have won," which is typical of him, and all fine and dandy if you haven't got superpowers that could destroy the world . . .

I don't mean to make stuff **EXPLODE**! I've done lots of training, but when I get anxious, accidents happen. Mom still doesn't know it was me who short-circuited the TV. Joe was steaming mad because the latest Avengers film was showing that night and we couldn't watch it. He didn't speak to me for eight entire hours.

I did say sorry a lot.

But today the sun is shining at last! And so I invited my best friend Imogen over, and we went into the backyard.

"Blown anything up lately?" Imogen asked as I bounced on the trampoline. She sounded sympathetic.

I made a face (which is not easy to do when you're bouncing). "I'm trying not to. Joe's given me some more focus exercises to do. I'm training every day."

Imogen hesitated and then said, "Do you think maybe you're doing too much?"

"I can't train too much!" I exclaimed. "She could be *anywhere*, Imogen! She could be watching me right *now*! I have to be ready!"

Imogen didn't ask who "she" was. We both knew. **Professor Macavity**, insane technological genius. The one who nearly killed us all only a few weeks ago. "But there's been no word from her," Imogen pointed out. "No sign, since she sent that threatening text."

"That doesn't mean she's not about to attack," I said and felt a shiver pass through me, even in the bright sunshine. I'd ruined her plans, and the **Professor** had vowed to get her revenge. I didn't know when or where it would be, but I knew she'd be back. "Hey," I said, to take my mind off things, "look what I've been practicing."

Higher and higher I bounced, feeling electrical charges tingle through my fingers and scalp.

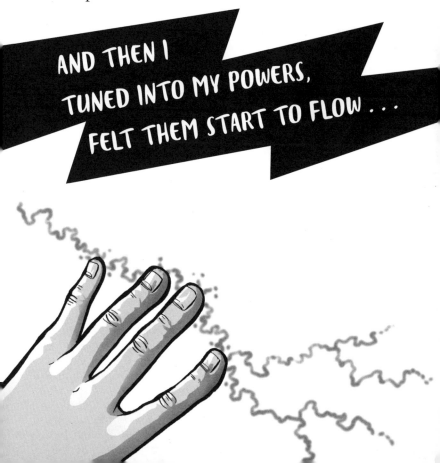

AND THEN I TUNED INTO MY POWERS, FELT THEM START TO FLOW . . .

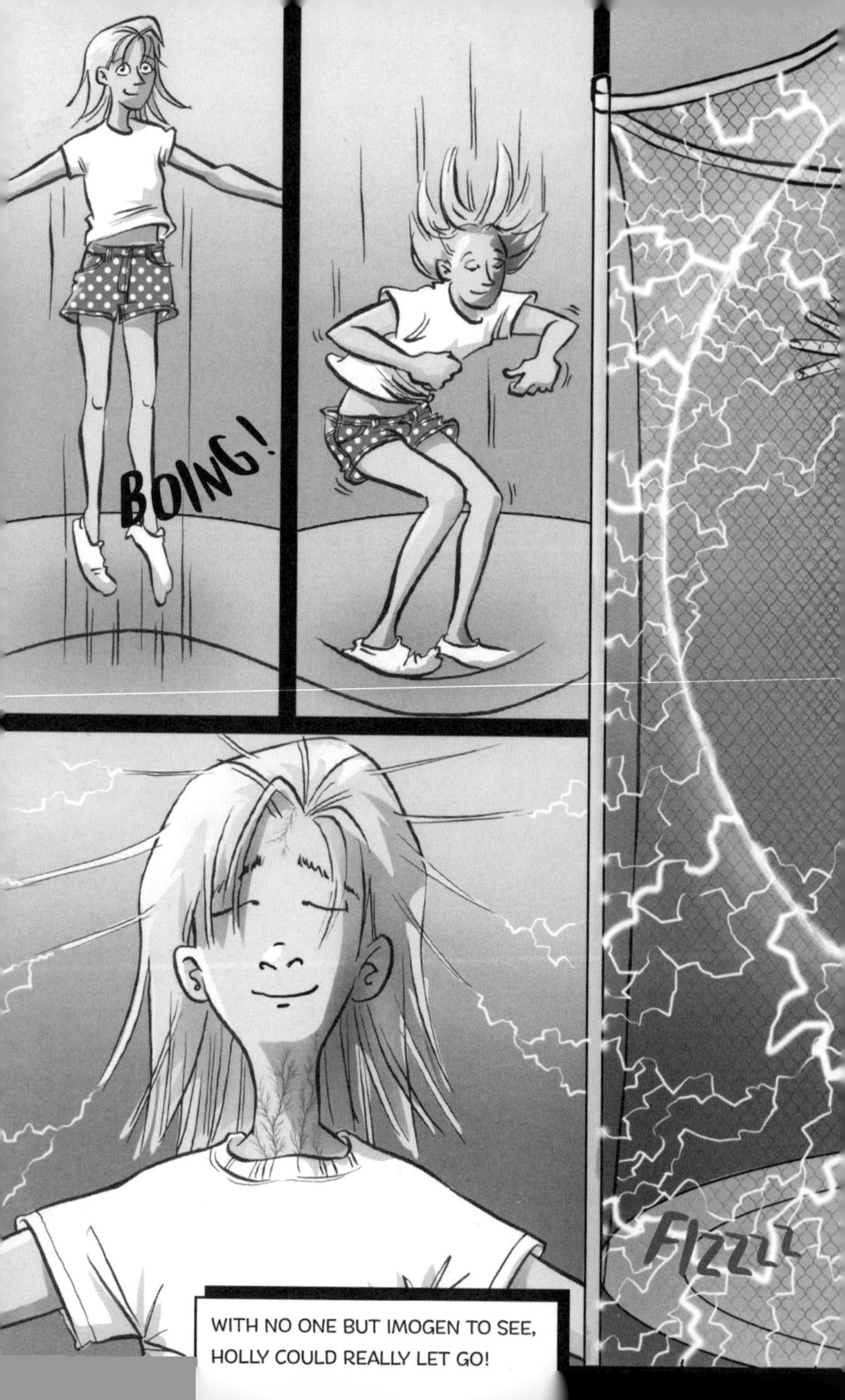
BOING!
FIZZZZ
WITH NO ONE BUT IMOGEN TO SEE,
HOLLY COULD REALLY LET GO!

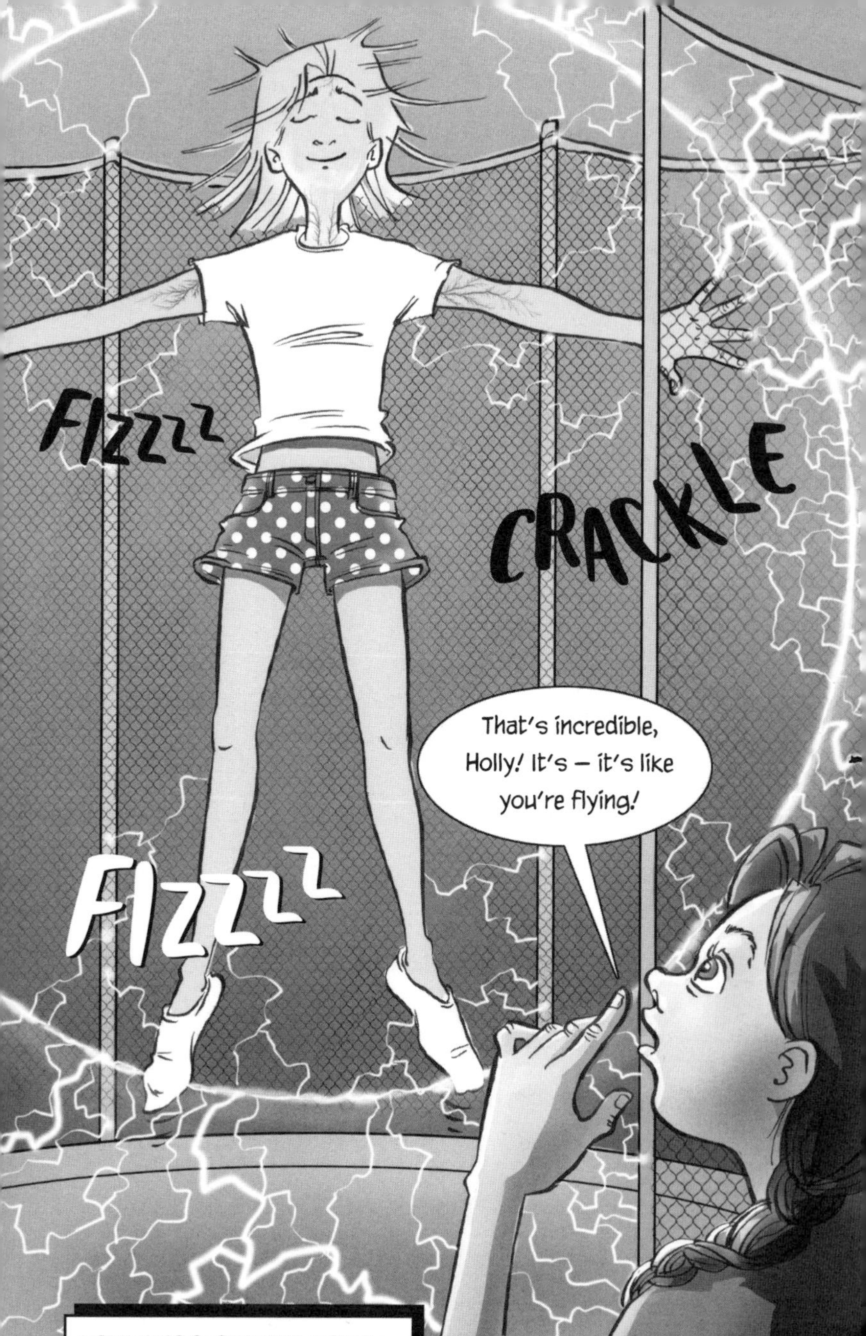
FIZZZZ
CRACKLE
That's incredible, Holly! It's – it's like you're flying!
FIZZZZ
HOLLY WAS SUSPENDED INSIDE HER VERY OWN LIGHTNING CAGE!

I released my powers and felt the electricity flow away, landing back on the trampoline with a bit of a bump. I grinned at Imogen. "Cool, isn't it?"

"How do you do it?"

I waved a hand at the poles that held up the trampoline net. "These are all metal, so they conduct electricity. Because they go all the way around, I can make a kind of electric net with me inside, and that keeps me off the ground."

"That's amazing!" Imogen's eyes lit up. "Do you think you could use it to really fly? Up there?"

I shook my head. "I need a circle of things that conduct electricity. I don't think birds or clouds would do!"

"It makes your scar glow," Imogen said.

Self-consciously, I rearranged my bangs to cover my forehead. Thin, wavy red lines decorated the smooth skin there, a result of my run-in with **Macavity** and her evil corporation, **⊛CyberSky**. "I wish it wasn't so obvious. I hate it when people notice."

"It's not as obvious as you think," Imogen said, but I could tell she was just saying it to make me feel better.

"Hey, you want one of these?" My younger brother came bounding down the yard with a handful of popsicles.

"Thanks, Joe." I took one.

"Not my idea," he said. "Mom made me. I'm in the middle of shooting a scene."

Imogen unwrapped her popsicle and folded the paper into a neat square. "What are you filming today?"

"The Hulk versus King Kong," said Joe enthusiastically. "I've made an Empire State Building for the final showdown."

My brother is *obsessed* with superheroes. He's always reading a comic, and he loves making his own films. I accidentally melted his video camera when I first got my powers, but he managed to borrow another one only last week, so he was back to building sets and designing gadgets for his superheroes and supervillains.

Imogen raised her eyebrows. "Who wins?"

Joe was scandalized. "I can't tell you that! You'll have to watch the film when it's finished."

"You might not want to be around for that," I suggested to Imogen with a grin.

"Yeah, keep laughing," Joe said. "It won't be so funny when I get my Oscar for Best Director."

"Are you going to film when you're down in Cornwall?" asked Imogen.

Joe's eyes lit up. "Good idea. Yeah — I could use the rock pools, or the sand. Sand lairs!"

I groaned. "Oh, thanks, Imogen. Looks like I'm going to be playing on my own this break."

"I wish I was coming," she said quietly.

I felt bad. "I wish you were, too; it's so much fun down there. Such a pain your dad can't get the time off. Dads should get way more holiday time. If my dad weren't in some random country doing something army-ish, he could come with us. And if you came I could show you all the cool beaches and stuff. There's rock pools and swimming and climbing and all kinds of stuff."

Imogen smiled a bit. "It's more likely I'd want to sit and draw all day."

I shrugged. "I wouldn't mind. You could draw in the morning and swim with me in the afternoon. Your parents don't even need to come! My mom would look after us."

I knew, even as I said it, that it was no good. Imogen's mom had already said no — twelve times.

Imogen sighed. "Sorry. Mom's paranoid. She thinks I'm going to get kidnapped again."

I bit my lip. Being friends with me made Imogen a possible target for **Professor Macavity**. I hated it, but it was true.

"If you were," Joe said through a mouthful of cookie, "we could get the government to help."

I rolled my eyes. "It's not the government. It's just Steve."

"*Secret* government," he said darkly. "Mysterious undercover department . . ."

"They're keeping an eye on her, you know," Imogen said to me reassuringly. "Steve said they were. If she was coming after you, we'd know."

"It's not just about me, though," I said. "She knows you're my friend. Joe's my brother. Just by being with me, you're putting yourselves in danger."

"That's the job," Joe said, shrugging. "I can't just un-brother you, can I? Plus, I'm your mentor." He puffed out his chest in pride. I'd agreed to let Joe be my superhero mentor since he read more comics than anyone I knew, but sometimes he took his job way too seriously.

Imogen looked less confident. "I still have dreams about her."

I shivered again. "Me too." I felt in my pocket for the pager Steve had given me. I took it everywhere — even into the bathroom. He'd said if there were the slightest hint we were in danger, he'd be in touch. But the pager had stayed silent for weeks now.

"Look," said Joe, echoing my thoughts, "there's nothing to worry about. If there was an emergency, we'd be told."

"Kids!" Mom was standing at the back door calling. "Can you come up here a minute? We've got an emergency!"

CHAPTER 2

Imogen's mom had come to pick her up. She looked worried. "Sorry, sweetie," she said to Imogen. "Something's happened."

I felt sick. This was it. **Macavity** had found us — and now Imogen would pay for being my best friend. I gripped the doorframe for support.

Imogen had gone pale. "What is it?"

"Your gran's sick," her mom told her. "Got a nasty bout of pneumonia. Grandad called — they've taken her to the hospital."

For a moment I was bewildered. What did Imogen's gran's pneumonia have to do with **Macavity**?

"Oh," said Imogen, and I wondered whether she too was baffled. "Is she going to . . ."

Her mom shook her head quickly. "Oh, no! No, we hope not. The hospital is looking after her — but your grandad isn't in the best of health either, and we need to go up there."

"Up?" I asked. "Up where?"

"Scotland," Imogen said. "They live in Scotland." She didn't sound pleased. "I thought Dad couldn't get time off?"

"Your dad isn't coming. Just you and me." Her mom tried to smile. "It'll be a mom and daughter road trip."

"For how long?"

"Not sure. Maybe two or three weeks."

"What?" Imogen looked horrified. "But there's nothing to do up there! They live in the middle of nowhere!"

"I can't help that," her mom said. "We'll take some puzzles. And your sketchbooks."

Imogen gazed at me helplessly. I felt sorry for her. I mean, it was awful that her gran was sick, but being stuck in the middle of nowhere for three weeks didn't sound like much fun to me.

Mom coughed. "Er . . . well, Imogen could always come to Cornwall with us."

I let out a kind of **SQUEAK** and stuffed my fist into my mouth.

Then there was a **LOT** of talking — by my mom and Imogen's mom and Imogen. And I said NOTHING AT ALL but I made my eyes as pleading and big as they could possibly be.

And finally Imogen's mom said she could come with us, and I just went "**YES!**" and did an air punch, and then Imogen and I did lots of hugging and jumping up and down until her mom reminded us that her gran was really sick and that this wasn't something to be happy about. And so we tried to calm down, and Imogen and her mom went home.

Mom smiled at me. "Things have a way of working out, don't they? And the camper sleeps four, so it's going to be fine."

"Yes, but one is a double bed." Joe looked suddenly appalled. "I won't have to *share* with someone, will I?"

Mom laughed. "No, Holly and Imogen can share. Or I can share with Holly."

"I'll share with Imogen," I said immediately. "No offense, Mom, but you snore."

Her jaw dropped. "I do not!"

"You **SO** do," Joe and I said at the same time.

My best friend was coming with us on our trip! I was thrilled — and also terrified. Because if Imogen came to Cornwall with us, would I be putting her in danger again?

Mind you, if **Professor Macavity** wanted to kidnap Imogen, it wouldn't matter whether she was in Scotland or Cornwall or Timbuktu. Maybe it was better to have Imogen close by, so I could protect her with my powers. But what if **Macavity** showed up and I couldn't stop her?

"You're panicking about nothing," Joe told me, when I confessed my fears to him later. He tapped the pager that I was gripping. "This isn't going off, is it?"

I peered at it. "Maybe the battery's dead. Maybe it's not working!"

"Stop it," Joe said. "Even superheroes need a vacation. Can you imagine **Professor Macavity** on a beach?"

That terrifying, gray-suited, gray-eyed, sharp-faced woman . . . on a beach? No, I couldn't imagine it. The very idea made me laugh.

"See?" said Joe. "Stop worrying. It's going to be **AWESOME**!"

CHAPTER 3

It rained **ALL THE WAY** to Cornwall. "It's going to be **AWFUL**," I muttered for about the tenth time.

Mom did that thing where she presses her lips together really hard to stop herself from saying something rude. There are no straight roads on the south coast, and we had to stop three times because Imogen was feeling sick. "Sorry," she said. "I usually take medicine but I forgot." After she really *was* sick — as in, Imogen puked — Mom let her sit in the front.

Joe was glued to his DVD player, watching back-to-back Spider-Man films. I watched a bit of something but then got fidgety. It's a VERY LONG WAY to Polcarrow, which is nearly off the end of the country. And being cooped up was really getting to me, which was NOT good for my electricity issues.

By the time we finally pulled into the gravel driveway of the campground, I was ready to burst and had given myself three static shocks from the metal buckle on my seat belt.

"It's raining here too," said Imogen in dismay as we got out of the car.

I was so relieved to be out in the open space again. But the weather was **DISMAL**. The sea, only half a mile away, was shrouded in gray mist. I felt bad that I'd talked-up the place to my friend, only for it to be so disappointing when we arrived. "The view is amazing when it's not like this."

"Come on," said Mom. "Let's find our camper and have a nice cup of tea."

"Hello!"

A tall boy with scrubby black hair and rain-spattered glasses was heading toward us. "I'm Cameron," he said, staring at us one at a time. "Welcome to Polcarrow."

"Thank you," said my mom, smiling.

Cameron didn't smile back. "My parents run this campground. Have you booked with us?"

"Yes," said Mom. "The name's Sparkes."

"One adult and two children, aged twelve and ten, Holly and Joseph," Cameron said immediately, his gaze flicking between me and Joe and Imogen. It was a bit weird — I mean, did he have a photographic memory or something? Did he know the names of *every* person arriving today?

"Yes," said Mom. "We've got an extra." She turned to smile at Imogen.

"She's not on the list," Cameron said.

"She could only come at the last minute," I explained. "Her mom had to go to Scotland to look after her gran because she's ill."

Cameron turned his big brown eyes on me. "The mother's ill?" he said. "Or the grandmother?"

I stared at him. What was with this kid? "The grandmother, of course."

His brow creased as his gaze slid to my forehead. "What's that on your head? Have you got a skin condition?"

Instinctively, I reached up to pull my bangs across to hide my scar. "It's nothing."

"Is it psoriasis?" he asked. "I know someone with psoriasis."

"I don't even know what that is," I snapped.

"Is your mother around?" Mom interrupted. "I'd like to talk to her about bringing Imogen."

"We have to have all the names for fire regulations," Cameron told her. "It's the rules."

I could feel my **POWERS** rising along with my temper. Honestly, Cameron was so annoying! And so rude! Asking me about my scar without knowing me at all!

Thankfully, just at that moment, a woman came into view. She had the same wild hair as Cameron and the same brown eyes, but hers were more friendly. "Hello!" she said. "Sorry about the weather; what bad luck for your arrival day! Don't stand in the drizzle — come inside while we get everything sorted out."

Glaring at Cameron, I followed Mom and the others into a small office building on the edge of the parking lot.

"I'm Julie," said the woman, "and you've already met my son Cameron."

Cameron was waiting patiently outside the cabin, seemingly unbothered by the rain. "He said Imogen couldn't stay with us because she wasn't on the list," I said.

Julie smiled. "He's very big on the rules, my Cam. Doesn't like last-minute changes. He's always been like that, since he was little." She laughed. "I never have to worry that he'll do something dangerous. He'll probably grow up to be a health and safety officer. Now, then, where's your file?" She reached up to the little shelf and took down a thick black folder. "Here we are . . . Sparkes. That's fine. Your camper has plenty of room for a fourth person. I'll just add her name to the list."

I breathed a sigh of relief, and within minutes we were trooping back outside with the key for camper number seventeen.

"I'll show you the way," Cameron said in an almost friendly tone of voice. He even gave a kind of smile. I glared back at him.

"I hope he doesn't hang around all the time," I whispered to Imogen as we tramped along the gravel path. "He's really annoying."

"He does seem kind of bossy," she agreed.

Joe came up behind me. "You could **ZAP** him," he whispered mischievously.

I was seriously tempted.

"No," said Imogen. "You shouldn't use your powers on people. It's not fair."

I raised my eyebrows pointedly.

"Er . . . unless they're evil, of course," she added. "And planning to take over the world. And I don't think Cameron fits into that category."

"He might," I said darkly. "We don't know yet." A sudden fear gripped me. Was Cameron *normal*? Only a few weeks ago, I'd seen people I knew turn into near-zombies thanks to **CyberSky**'s creepy evil cell phones. What if . . . what if Cameron was under the control of **Professor Macavity**? What if she was actually here, already, waiting for me — and Cameron was part of her trap?

My feet slowed on the path, and I looked around fearfully.

Imogen glanced back. "Come on, Holly! I can't wait to see our camper!"

I made an effort to smile. "Yeah."

"Here we are," said Cameron as we reached number seventeen. "You should find everything you need inside. There's a shop down the road for milk and bread and things. I hope you've brought flashlights because it's not safe to wander around at nighttime, and we don't want anyone to fall into the sea. Stay away from the cliff edge. Remember to turn the gas stove off when you've finished using it."

"I know how to use a stove," Mom said with an edge to her voice.

He turned his brown eyes on her. "Some people blew up their camper once," he said. "They left the gas on and then lit a match. *Boom.*"

There was a pause.

A cold fear settled in my stomach. Was he **WARNING** me? Was this what Macavity was planning? To blow us up in our own camper?

"All right," said Mom brightly. "Thanks so much, Cameron, I'll take it from here."

"There are guidebooks on the side . . ." Cameron began.

"Good*bye*," said Mom firmly, opening the door and beckoning us in.

"Oh. Goodbye." Cameron gave a shrug and headed off. I stepped back jerkily as he passed, banging my arm on the camper door. Was he going to report to Macavity right now?

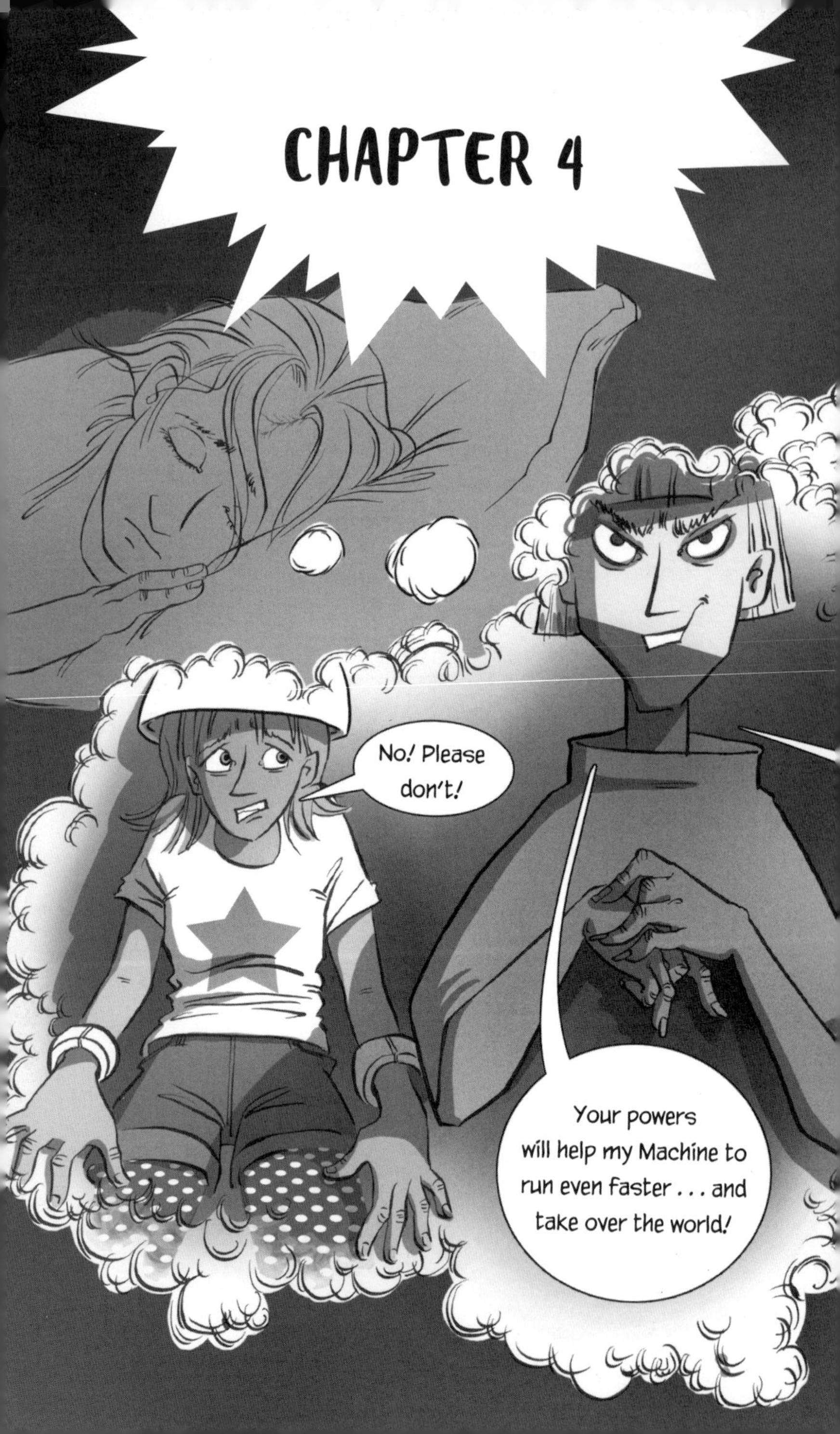
CHAPTER 4
No! Please don't!
Your powers will help my Machine to run even faster . . . and take over the world!

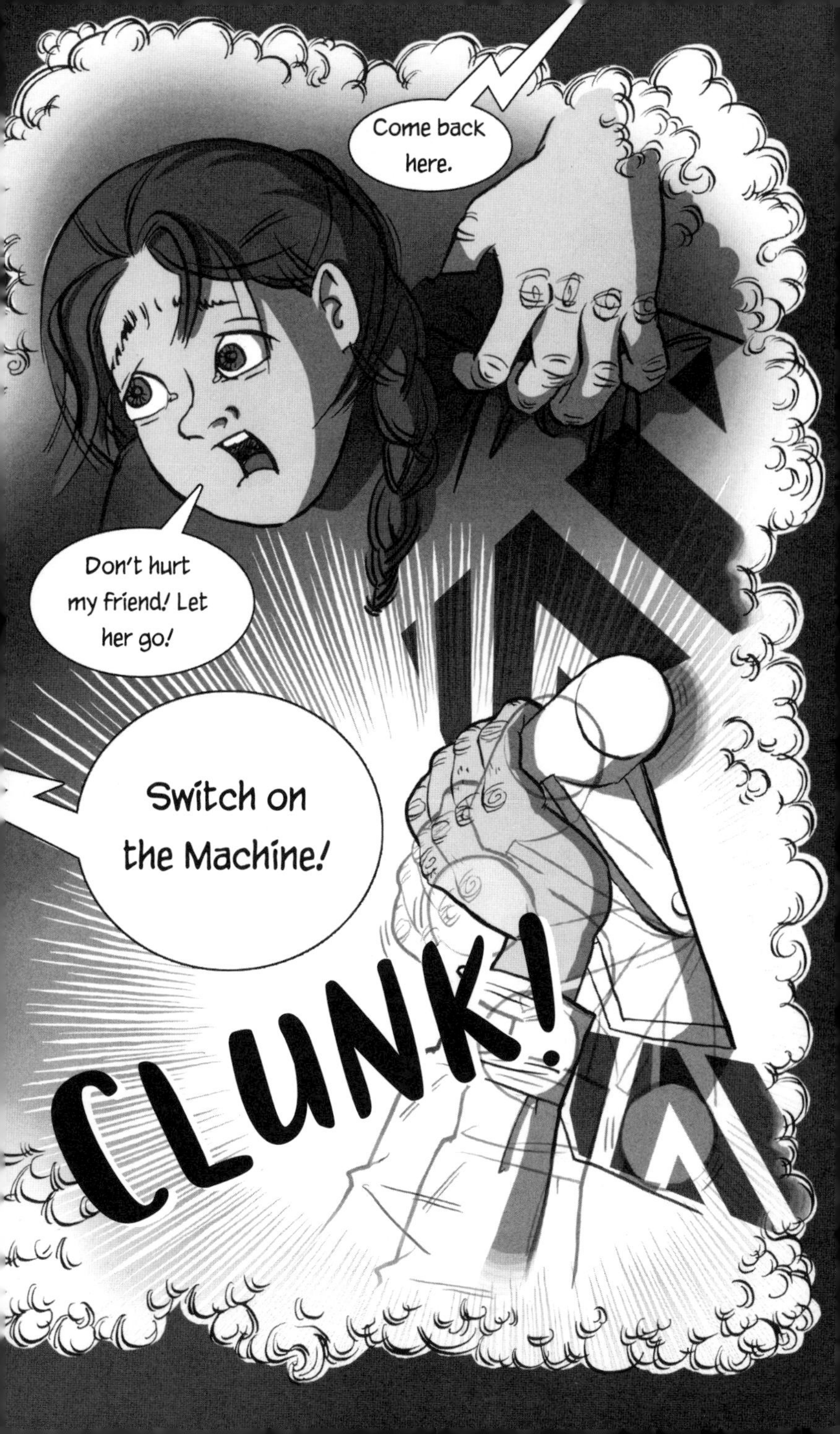
Come back here.
Don't hurt my friend! Let her go!
Switch on the Machine!
CLUNK!

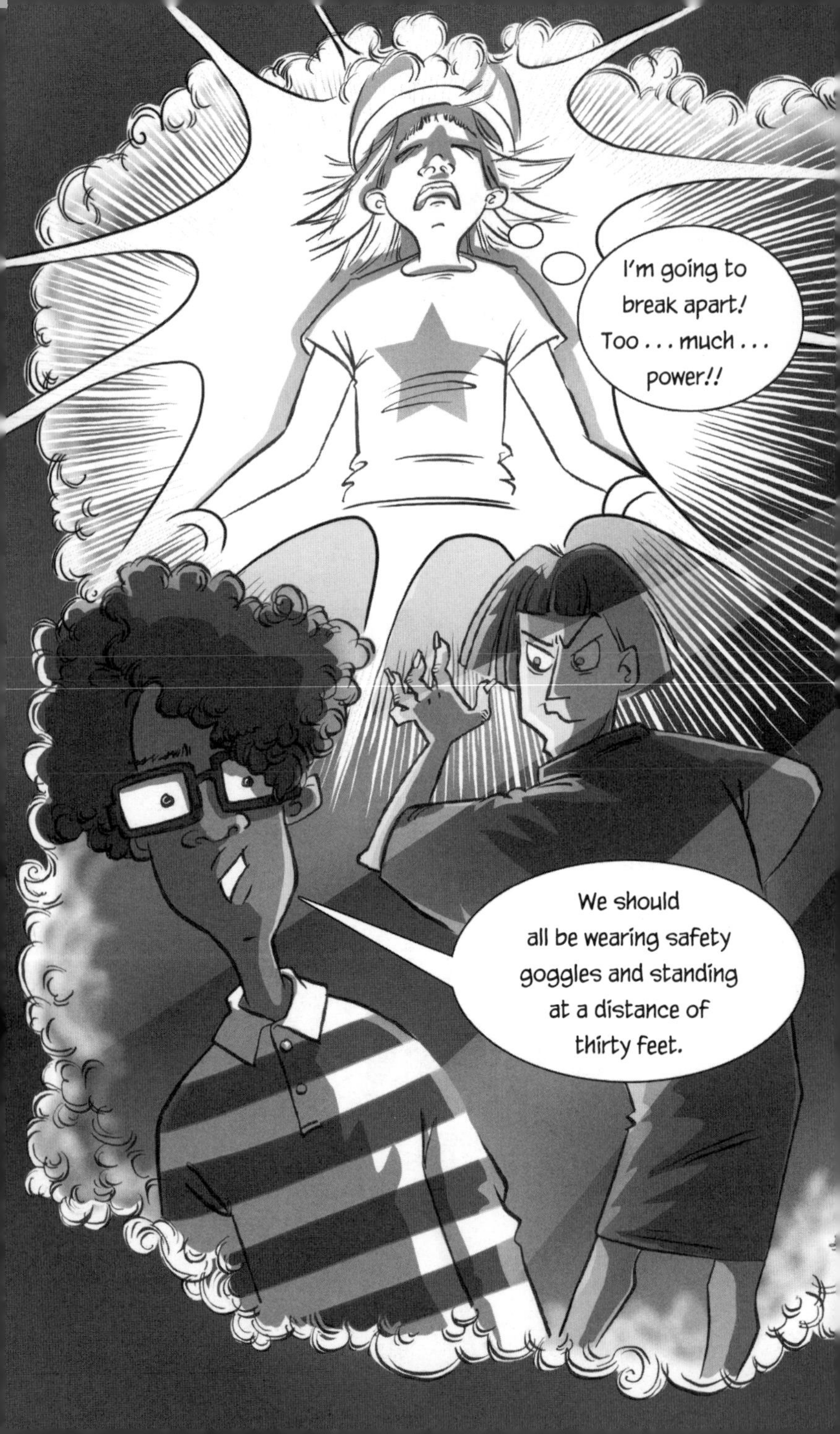
I'm going to break apart! Too . . . much . . . power!!
We should all be wearing safety goggles and standing at a distance of thirty feet.

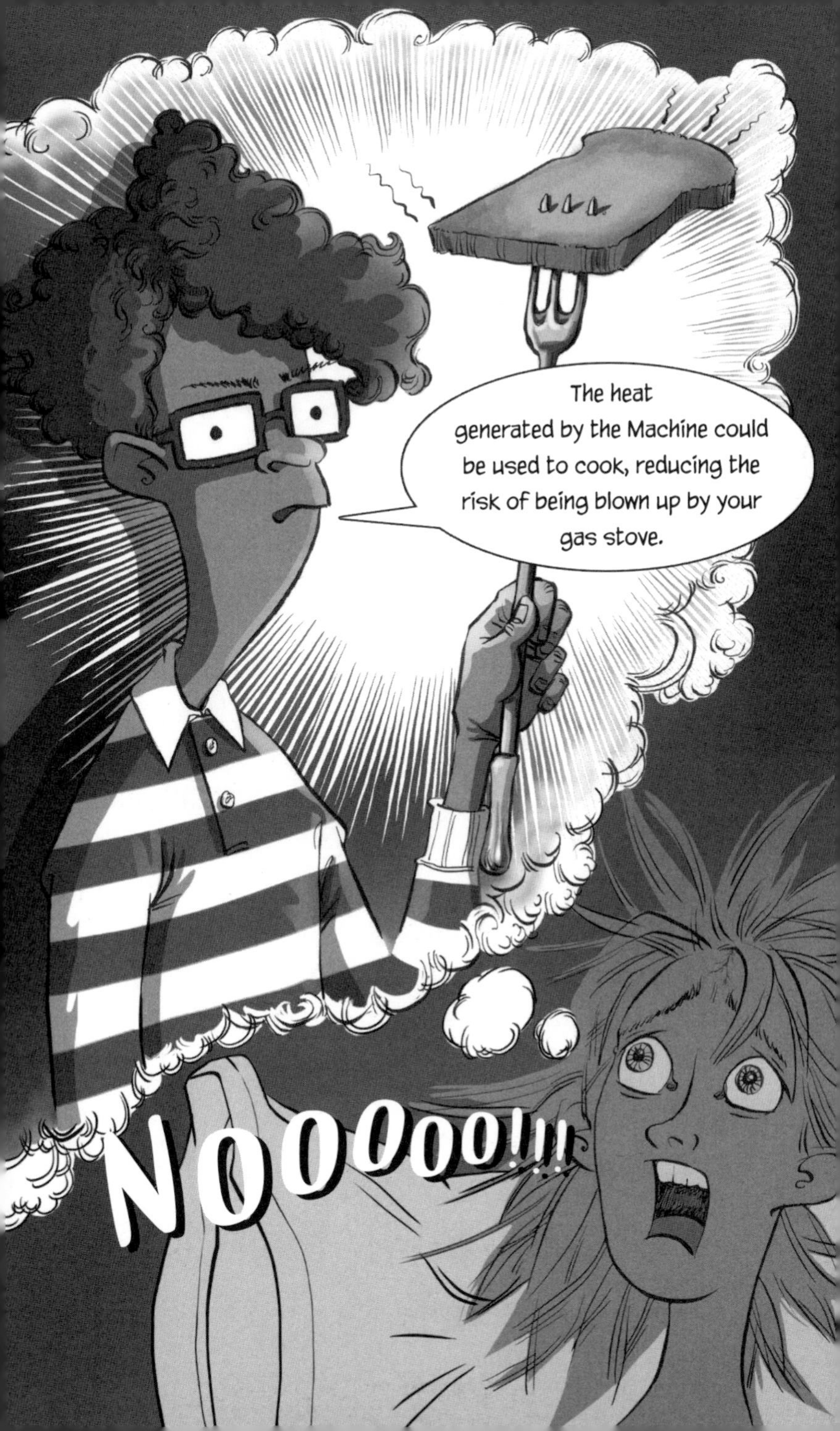
The heat generated by the Machine could be used to cook, reducing the risk of being blown up by your gas stove.
NOOOOOO!!!!

"**I AM NOT A TOASTER!**" I yelled, throwing off the covers and sitting bolt upright. Then I realized where I was. Early-morning light streamed in through the thin camper curtains.

Imogen was staring at me in fright from the other side of the bed. "Holly? What's the matter? Are you all right?"

"What's going on?" Mom appeared in the doorway, her hand clutching the side of her head. "Holly? Is everything OK?"

From the other end of the camper, I could hear Joe muttering, "Bad dreams."

"Oh, Holly," Mom said, coming to give me a hug. "I'm sorry. Were you dreaming about your accident again?"

"Yes," I said, hugging her back. I didn't like lying to Mom, but she didn't know the truth about me or about what really happened in **Macavity**'s underground HQ. She believed I'd gotten the scar on my head from a gas explosion in the building.

Imogen rubbed her face. "You scared me. I thought the kitchen was blowing up, like Cameron warned us."

Mom snorted. "I know how to operate a stove, thank you very much. Why don't the three of you go for a walk while I make breakfast? You could show Imogen the cove." She pulled open the curtain. "Look, the sun's out."

"It's not raining?" Suddenly, I couldn't bear to be inside for a minute longer. "Come on, let's go!"

Mom laughed. "Maybe you should get dressed first."

Joe grumbled but within a few minutes all three of us were outside and walking down to the beach. The campers were set up in eight rows, which we followed along. Then a wide expanse of grass stretched out between the campground and the sandy slope down to the beach. There was a brisk breeze blowing the trees enthusiastically, and out on the sea I could see little white caps on the waves. Instantly I felt better. I was **ELECTRIGIRL**! If Macavity *had* sent Cameron after me — well, he'd be no match for me!

"What were you really dreaming about?" asked Imogen.

I told her — including the part at the end about Cameron and the goggles and the toast. She giggled. "Holly, why on earth was *he* in the dream?"

Hesitantly I admitted, "Don't you think that maybe . . . I mean, I know it's crazy . . . but what if he's working for the **Professor**?"

Imogen and Joe both stopped and stared at me. "Holly, have you gone completely insane?"

"She could be here!" I insisted. "She said she would come after me — where's better than while we're on vacation? Off our guard?"

"Holly," said Joe patiently, "you're talking nonsense. Cameron is just a little different. He's not an evil sidekick."

"How do you know?" I challenged him.

Joe just raised his eyebrows at me.

I deflated. "I know, I know. It's crazy. I just . . . I see her everywhere. I keep wondering when she's going to come after me."

"Oh, Holly." Imogen gave me a hug. "We'll have warning. Steve will let us know if she's anywhere near us. You've got your pager with you, right?"

I patted my pocket.

"There you go, then. Stop worrying. You can't go around suspecting everyone of being evil, you know," Imogen said with a smile.

I nodded. "I suppose not. I'm so glad you came with us."

She grinned back. "Me too. If only to stop you going **BONKERS** and **BLOWING** us all up. And Cameron wouldn't like that *at all!*"

I laughed. "I've got to do something, though. I feel all tingly after that dream. Is anyone around?"

Joe looked back toward the rows of campers. "They're too close. Anyone could be watching. Wait till we're into the dunes."

The ground dropped away as we approached the beach, the sea sparkling like it was covered in turquoise sequins. There was no one else in sight, and as soon as the campground was hidden behind us, Joe said, "All right, here should be safe. But nothing too big."

"I promise," I said.

THEN I CLOSED MY EYES . . .

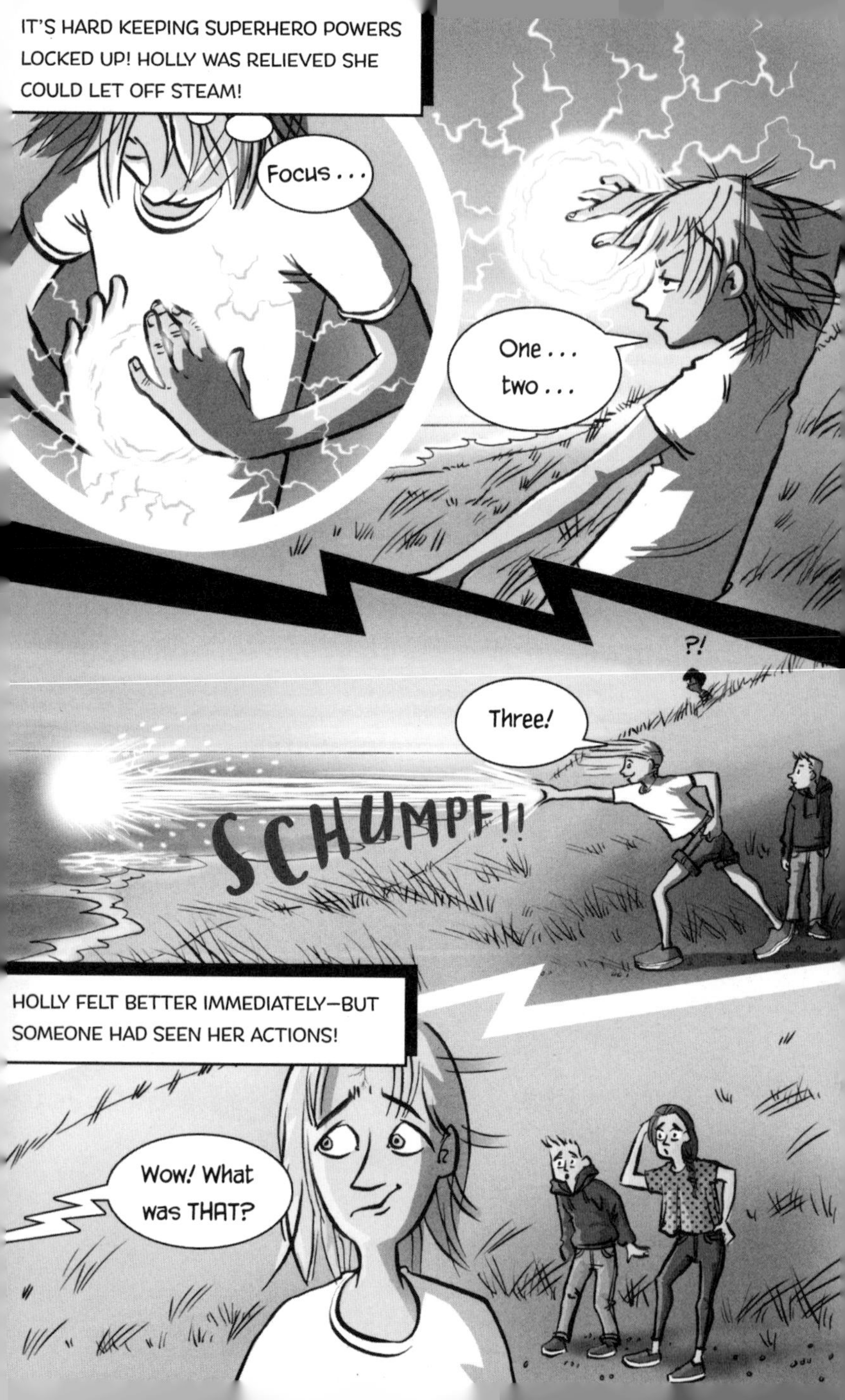
IT'S HARD KEEPING SUPERHERO POWERS LOCKED UP! HOLLY WAS RELIEVED SHE COULD LET OFF STEAM!
Focus . . .
One . . . two . . .
?!
Three!
SCHUMPF!!
HOLLY FELT BETTER IMMEDIATELY—BUT SOMEONE HAD SEEN HER ACTIONS!
Wow! What was THAT?

"Nothing too big?" my brother groaned as Cameron came clambering up the beach to meet us. "Now you've done it!"

Cameron's eyes were wide. "Did you SEE that?" he said. "Where did it come from?"

Typical! It WOULD be him!

"Er . . .," I said, pulling the neckline of my shirt up to hide any last traces of my burn pattern as it faded. "Er . . . see what?"

"That light!" said Cameron, turning to look out to sea. He peered into the distance for a moment. "It's gone now. It was — I don't know *what* it was."

"I didn't see anything," Joe jumped in, shooting me a look. "Just the sun on the sea. It's bright today."

Cameron shook his head. "It wasn't that. This was much brighter. Like a shooting star."

Ugh! "You must have imagined it," I said, irritated.

He looked offended. "I don't imagine things. I suppose it might be a discharge from the build-up of **ELECTRICITY** in the rocks. I read that can happen when you've got trace metals running through the granite — and the tin mine's not far away. I'd better mention it to Dad later in case he needs to go down and check the safety levels."

"In the tin mine?" asked Joe, distracted from glaring at me. "I thought that was all abandoned and locked up. It was last time we were here."

"It was opened six months ago," Cameron said. "My dad takes tour parties down there. It's a really interesting place."

"Is there still tin down there, then?" Joe's eyes lit up. It was just the kind of thing that got him excited. I did a pretend yawn, but he didn't notice.

Cameron turned to Joe. "Loads. And copper and iron. They chipped out as much as they could, but it was all by hand. I'll take you down there and show you, if you like. But you have to stick with me. Don't go wandering off down the tunnels on your own."

"Why not?" I retorted. "Will the Cornish pixies get us?"

Cameron's dark eyes fixed on me. "They might."

I laughed. "There's no such thing."

"Yes there is," he said simply. "I've seen them."

I was speechless. The boy was completely nuts! Joe took a step toward him. "You've *seen* them?"

he asked.

"I don't tell lies," Cameron said. "Ask my mom. Ask anyone."

Imogen, Joe, and I looked at each other. "Can *we* see them?" asked Joe.

Cameron hesitated. "I don't know if I can trust you," he said.

I was insulted! Him, trust *us?*

Imogen stepped forward. "Look," she said. "I think we got off on the wrong foot."

Cameron glanced down at her feet. "Which one is the wrong one?"

"No," said Imogen patiently, as I snorted. "I mean we didn't start off very friendly." She smiled and held out her hand. "I'm Imogen."

"Oh," said Cameron, and then to my astonishment his face broke into a smile. He shook her hand. "Hello. I'm Cameron."

"Go on." Imogen nudged Joe, who also shook hands and introduced himself.

Then Cameron turned to me, holding out his hand. Behind his back, I could see Imogen urgently mouthing, "*Be nice!*" at me.

"Oh, all *right!*" I said. "Hi, I'm Holly." I shook his hand. It felt dry and cool.

Cameron beamed at me. It was quite bizarre

to see him smiling. "It's very nice to meet you all. I don't have many friends in Polcarrow."

I wanted to say, "Really? Can't imagine why," but stopped myself.

"I thought pixies were just a myth," Imogen said. "Like fairies."

"Oh, no." Cameron was insistent. "They're real. I've seen them. In fact . . .," his voice dropped and he looked around to see if anyone was within earshot, "I'll show you, if you want. I've got one in a jar."

CHAPTER 5

"He *can't* be telling the truth," I muttered to Joe, as we followed Cameron down the path to the beach. We'd been back to the camper for breakfast, and Mom had sent us off again so that she could go to the store to buy food. I made sure my pager was in my shorts pocket, as always, and Joe was carrying his old cell phone, in case Mom needed to call. "Pixies aren't real. **THEY'RE JUST NOT**."

"Sherlock Holmes said that when you've eliminated the possible, whatever remains, even if it seems completely crazy, must be the truth," Joe muttered back.

Cameron glanced back at us, grinning. "Keep up!"

"I still don't trust him," I said.

Joe sighed. "Look, he's not **Macavity** in a mask, is he?" He ran on to catch up with the others while I panicked about what he'd just said. *What if Cameron was* **Macavity** *in a mask?*

No, he couldn't be. The **Professor** wore gray, all over — and even if she were dressed differently and wore a wig, her voice would still be the same. I'd know that lifeless monotone anywhere — the very memory of it sent chills down my spine.

Mind you, the thought *did* bring me comfort. Wherever **Macavity** was, she couldn't disguise herself from me. I'd always know her, as soon as she spoke. I ran to catch up with the others.

"Ooh!" squeaked Imogen as we reached the edge of the sand. "Shells!"

"Not now," I said, grinning. "We didn't bring a bucket, and we're going to see a pixie."

"But . . ." Imogen came reluctantly, looking longingly at the piles of shells at the high tide line.

"I'll show you where the best ones are later," offered Cameron. "Just as long as you don't go over the rocks. **IT'S NOT SAFE**."

Imogen and I grinned at each other. Cameron really was the king of health and safety!

It was still early, so the beach wasn't full of vacationers yet. A few families were trudging along, weighed down by bags and arguing about where to set up camp for the day. I took off my sandals and wriggled my toes in the sand. That felt better!

Cameron led us along the beach to the right, where the land rose sharply and gray rocks jutted out onto the sand. Here and there, shadows darkened the rocks. My heart beat faster. I wasn't a fan of darkness and enclosed spaces . . .

Cameron didn't hesitate. He ducked into a dark opening at the base of the cliff. Imogen and Joe followed. I took a breath. *Calm*, I told myself. *Focus. Just breathe.*

"You coming?" It was Joe's voice.

I took another deep breath and followed them in, moving slowly while my eyes adjusted to the sudden darkness. Cameron had a flashlight, but the thin beam played over the rocks ahead, leaving me to edge my feet forward on unseen ground. The walls were damp and close, and I couldn't help remembering the gray walls of **CyberSky** . . . the elevator that took me and Joe deep underground . . . the clouds of smoke that choked us on our escape, and how I nearly didn't make it out at all . . .

By the time we got to the back of the cave, I was a terrified mess, ready to **BOLT** at any moment. Worse, the beam from Cameron's flashlight suddenly disappeared — had the batteries died? "Hey, what happened to the light?" I heard Joe exclaim. In the dark, in a state of panic, the high levels of adrenalin made my fingers tingle with electricity.

Keep calm, I told myself. *Focus. Breathe. Remember your training.*

Then something suddenly rushed toward me in the darkness. "BOO!"

I screamed. "Get away! Get away!" I raised my hands, ready to strike.

"It's just me!" said Cameron. "Hey — it's me, see?" He switched on the flashlight and pointed it up at his face.

"You *idiot!*" I yelled at him. "I could have killed you!" I wasn't exaggerating either.

He looked taken aback. "Sorry. I thought it was funny."

"Well, it *wasn't*," I snarled.

"I can show you the pixie now," he said hurriedly. "To make up for it. Here." He turned his flashlight onto the wall. At first I couldn't see anything, but he reached out an arm, and I realized that there was a kind of shelf, a place where the rock hollowed itself out into a natural cupboard. There was a scraping noise, and Cameron pulled out a large glass jar. A sudden skittering noise from inside the jar made us all jump, and I felt Imogen's hand clutch my arm.

"What the . . .," whispered Joe. "What *is* it?"

Cameron held up the jar, and then pointed the flashlight so that its beam fell squarely onto what was inside.

I forgot to breathe.

Inside the jar was something small, about the length of my finger. It was hard to make out, but in shape it looked like a daddy long-legs: thin and spidery, with a pair of wings that fluttered in vain against the sides of the jar.

And it had eyes. Two tiny green eyes that glowed brightly in the light of the flashlight.

"I don't believe it," Joe whispered.

"A pixie," said Imogen softly. "A real pixie."

"But it can't be . . .," I said. I couldn't take my eyes off it. The tiny thing skittered and flapped inside its glass prison.

"It is," Cameron said proudly. "It's my pixie and I found it, and I'm keeping it safe. See? I told you they were real."

CHAPTER 6

"You shouldn't keep it in there," Imogen said. "It's trying to get out — can't you see?"

Joe was still peering at the jar, his nose only inches away. The pixie's wings flickered in the flashlight beam. "If only it would stay still so I could get a good look," he murmured. "We need to get it out into the light so I can see it better."

"No!" Cameron cradled the jar in his arms. "You can't! If anyone else knows, they'll want to **DISSECT** it!"

I stared at the frantic thing. I had some sympathy. I couldn't tell anyone my secret either, for fear of being experimented on by people who wanted my powers.

"It could be just a really big insect," Joe said, still squinting.

Cameron glared at him. "It's a pixie. Trust me. And there are more. Tons more. Not here, somewhere else. They're hiding from humans. Wouldn't *you*, if you were a pixie? I was lucky to trap one without waking the others."

"Can I hold it?" Imogen reached out her hand.

"No!" Cameron stepped back, jerking the jar out of her reach. But his actions were clumsy and as he swung back his arm, the jar bashed into the shelf of rock behind him.

There was the sound of shattering glass, and the flashlight beam wobbled wildly across the cave ceiling and then fell to the floor, plunging us all into darkness once more. My breath stopped in my throat and my hands clenched convulsively. I froze to the spot. Cameron let out a shout of horror. "Oh no! It's broken!"

Something flitted past my face in the darkness, and I closed my eyes, feeling my heart pound as the panic gripped me. I needed to find the exit! We had to get out! Before the building collapsed on top of us and we were trapped down here in the smoke with **Macavity**! My brain tried to tell me — you're in a cave, not *Cyber* **Sky** — but it was no good. My powers were springing to the surface!

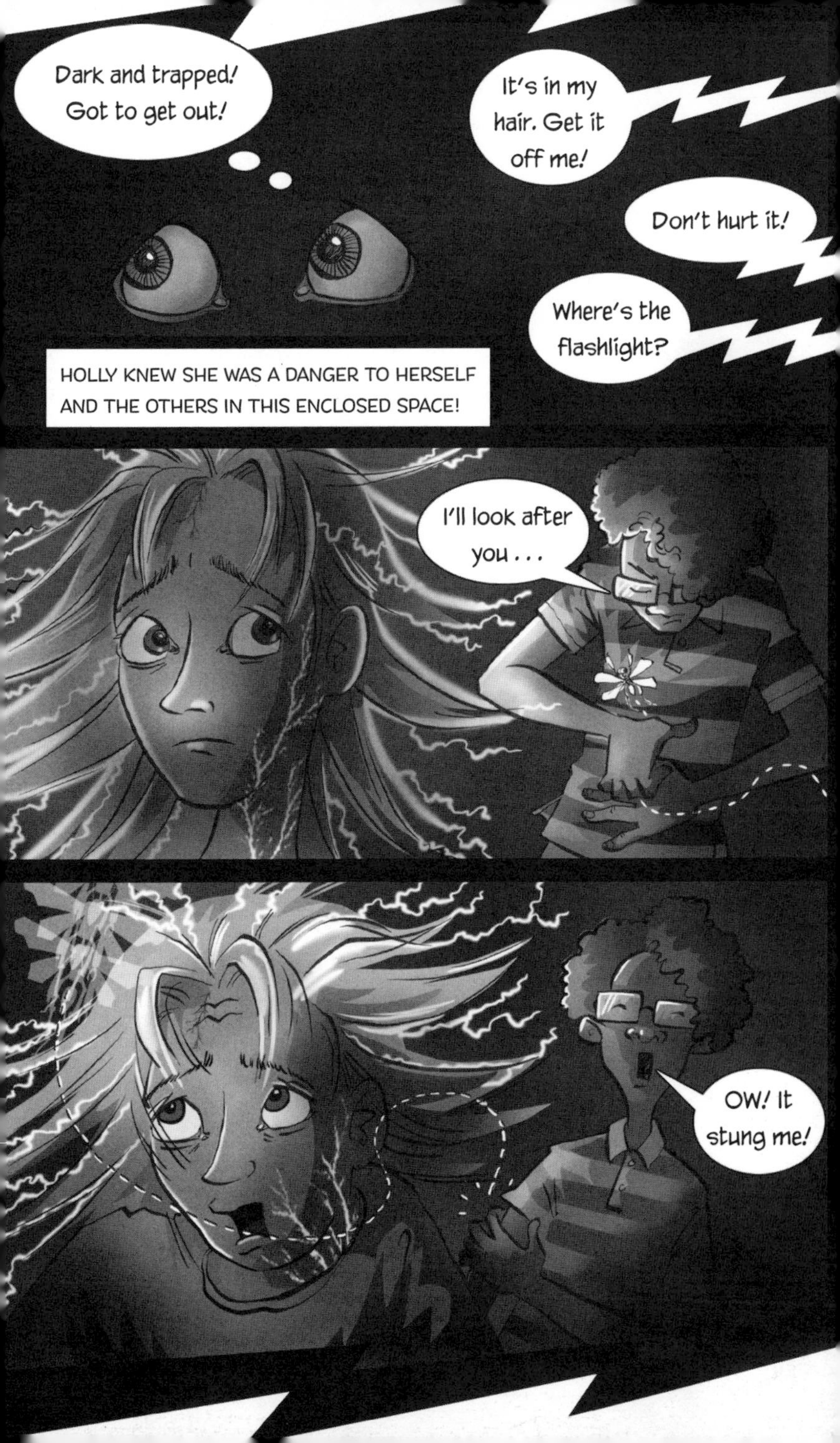
Dark and trapped! Got to get out!
It's in my hair. Get it off me!
Don't hurt it!
Where's the flashlight?
HOLLY KNEW SHE WAS A DANGER TO HERSELF AND THE OTHERS IN THIS ENCLOSED SPACE!
I'll look after you . . .
OW! It stung me!

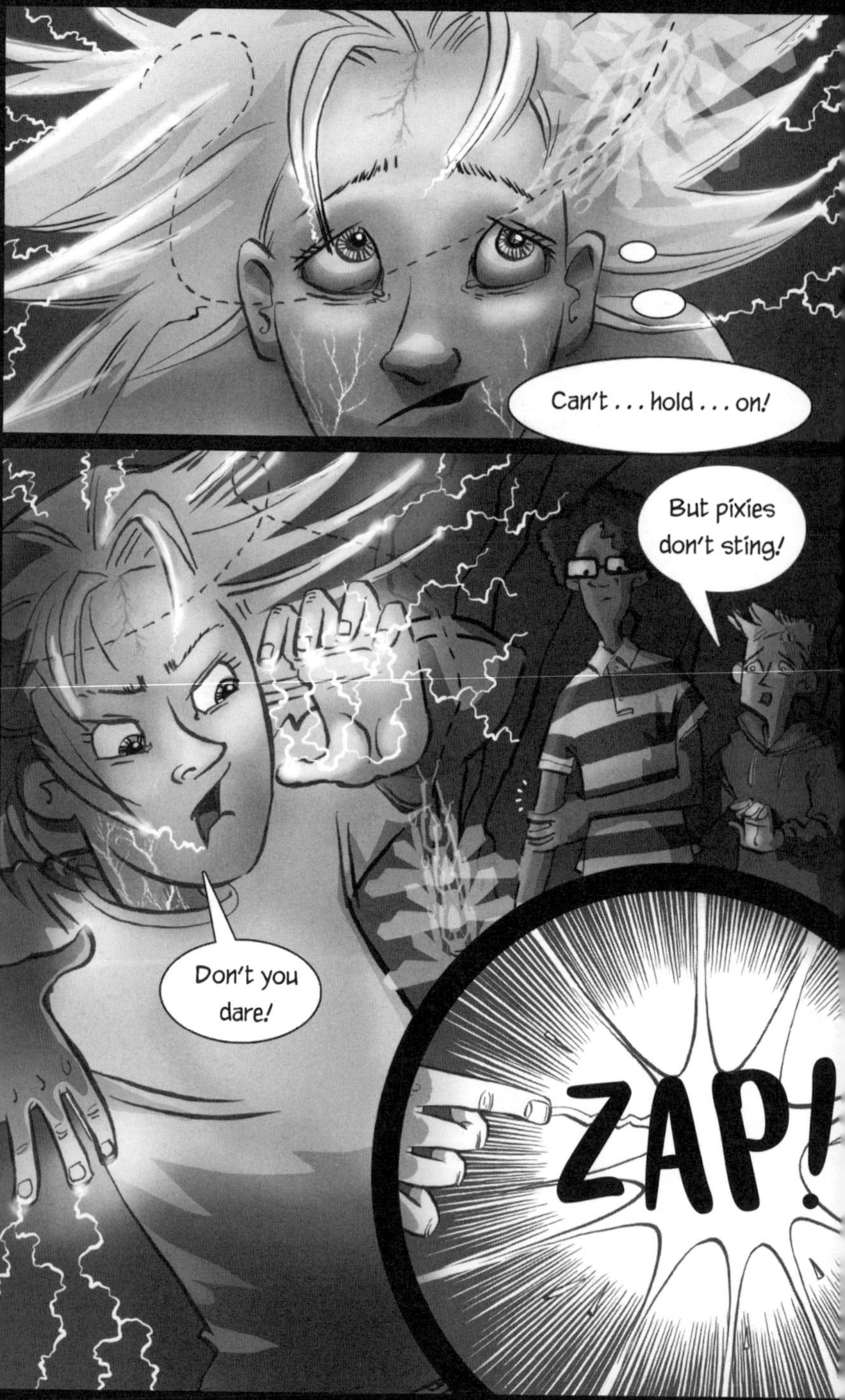
Can't . . . hold . . . on!
But pixies don't sting!
Don't you dare!
ZAP!

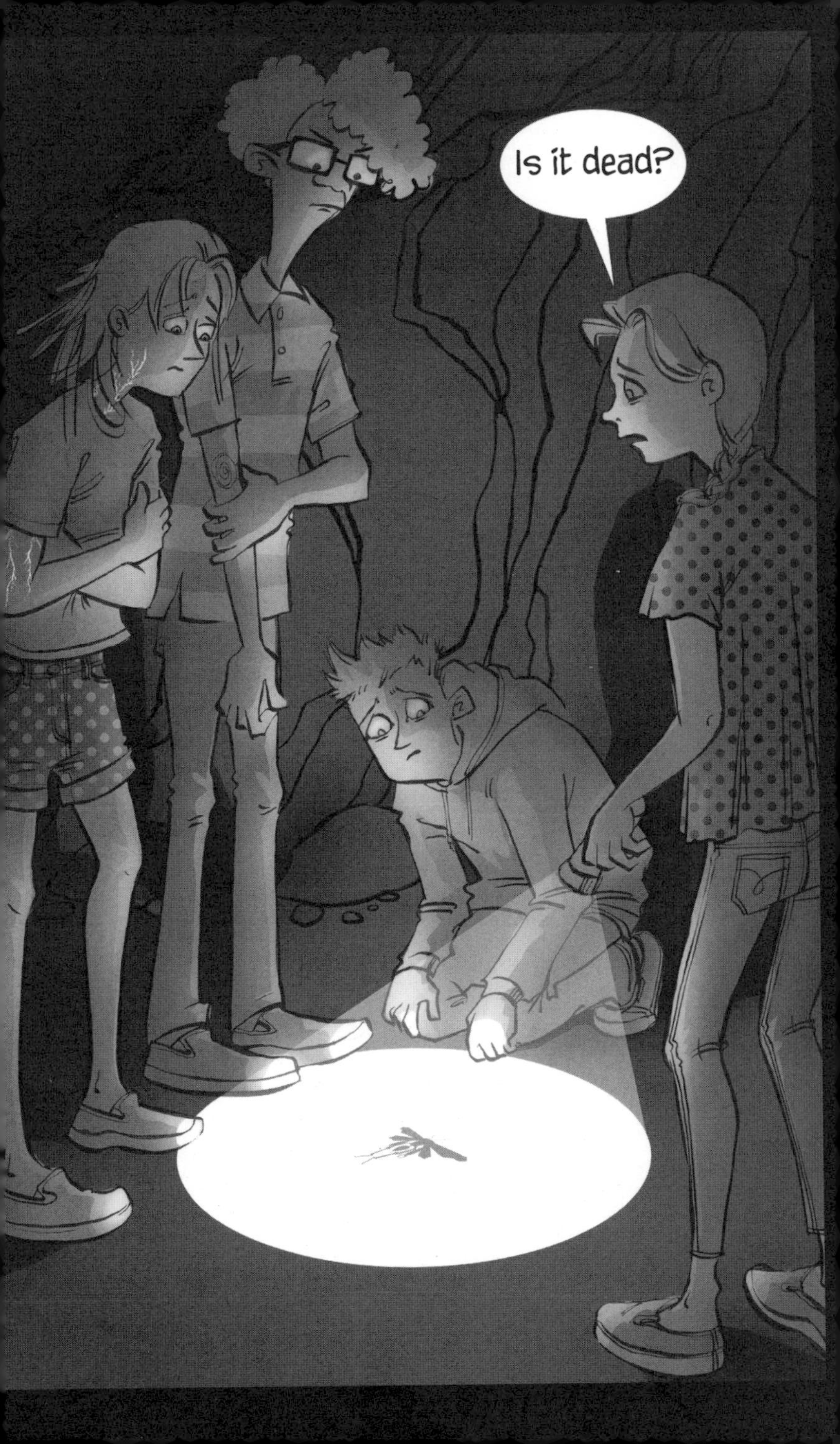
Is it dead?

Instantly, I felt my **POWERS** recede. The darkness was still frightening, but now my head felt a bit clearer. I didn't actually mean to zap the pixie like that — but it had a stinger! What kind of pixie has a stinger?

Cameron dived for the creature on the floor. "What did you DO?" he cried. "You killed it!"

"I'm sorry." I took a step forward, but he gathered the tiny thing up in his hands, tucking the flashlight under his arm.

"It's mine! Get away from me! You're dangerous!"

I blinked back sudden tears. No matter how much training I did, somehow I always made a mess of things! It wasn't long ago that I blew up my classroom.

Joe touched me on the arm. "We need to have a talk," he said quietly. "Mentor stuff."

I nodded and wiped my eyes. Although it was kind of annoying to be told what to do by my younger brother, he did know more about this kind of thing than I did.

There was no point keeping the pixie hidden in the cave now. We trooped back to the beach, Imogen reaching for my hand on the way to give it a squeeze. I felt grateful she was sympathetic. My hands were shaking, and I was very relieved to be outside again.

Cameron sat down on the sand, just outside the cave. There was a mark on his lower arm that looked like a bee sting. The pixie's wings and legs hung limply from his clasped hands. He dropped the flashlight and opened his hands very slowly. "It's not moving. I think it's dead." He sounded devastated.

"I'm so sorry," I said, feeling utterly terrible. "I didn't mean to, but it was heading right for me."

Joe crouched next to Cameron. "Can you put it down? So we can see it?"

Cameron reluctantly laid the creature down on the sand. In the sunlight it seemed strangely gray and spindly, arms and legs glinting slightly, and the wings revealed a kind of pattern that . . . looked kind of familiar.

Joe peered at it, his face set in concentration. "I don't understand . . .," he said. "This isn't . . . I mean . . . it isn't . . ."

Imogen said in a puzzled voice, "Is that . . . *metal*?"

I leaned over to see. "What? Where?"

"Everywhere. All over." Joe sat back. "The whole thing is made of tiny metal parts, even the wings.

THIS ISN'T AN INSECT.

IT'S A ROBOT."

CHAPTER 7

"A **ROBOT**? But . . ." I stared down at it. I'd never seen a robot like that before. It looked like a fairy — well, if fairies were about three inches tall and made of shiny gray metal. It had two arms and two legs, and a pair of really magnificent wings, with a criss-crossing pattern that made me frown. Why did it remind me of something?

"It's *awesome*!" Joe said excitedly. "I mean, it's like a drone. Those planes or helicopters you can operate by remote control . . . they're awesome — but *this*!" He shook his head. "I'd sell my sister for one of these."

"Thanks a lot!" I said, offended.

"So it . . . it wasn't *alive*?" asked Imogen. "It's not a real pixie?"

Joe glanced at Cameron, who seemed to be stunned. "No, sorry. It must run on batteries."

"It's not a pixie?" whispered Cameron. He was staring at the robot on the sand as though he couldn't believe what he was seeing.

"It's way cooler than a pixie," Joe said, trying to be reassuring. "I mean, this is a really amazing design. See this?" He pointed at a tiny metal arm, which ended in a sharp spike rather than a hand. "That's how it stung you. Pixies don't carry spikes, do they?"

Cameron rubbed the mark on his arm. "I didn't want it dead," he said. Then he turned to glare up at me. "You shouldn't have done that."

"I'm sorry," I said.

"What *was* that anyway?" He got to his feet. "There was all this light around you, and then something like **LIGHTNING** came out of your hand . . ."

I took a breath. What could I say? I glanced at Joe and Imogen, who stared back at me helplessly. "You can't tell anyone," I said to Cameron, and I heard my brother groan. "What?" I said. "He saw me! How do I explain it?"

"You have to tell him the truth," Imogen said. "It's only fair."

Joe threw up his hands. "So much for secrecy!"

I didn't want to tell Cameron. He was the *last*

person I wanted in on my secret, but I owed him an explanation — and what could I say apart from the truth? "I have this thing I can do," I said awkwardly. "A kind of — well, a kind of power. Like, um . . ." This was so embarrassing! It sounded so stupid and impossible out loud! "I can . . . make electricity."

He stared at me. "People lie to me sometimes," he said, "and I can't always tell when they do. Or if they're making fun of me."

"I'm not making fun of you," I said. "And I'm not lying. Honestly. I got struck by lightning — and now I can do stuff with electricity. That shooting star you saw this morning on the beach? That was me. So. Sorry about the robot."

His jaw dropped. "**BUT THAT'S IMPOSSIBLE**."

I grinned. "Hey, just a minute ago you believed in pixies. Why not a superhero?"

"But you're just a . . . girl." He blinked. "You look normal."

"That's because I am. Mostly."

Joe broke in. "Cameron, can I borrow your robot? I want to look at it under a microscope."

Cameron turned around. "No! It's mine! I found it." He rubbed a hand over his eyes and for a moment he seemed to stumble.

"Cameron, are you feeling all right?" asked Imogen, concerned.

"I feel weird," he said. He bent down to gather up the robot pixie. "I'm going home for a while."

"I could look after the robot for you, just for a little while. And I can bring it over later," Joe said pleadingly.

"**NO**!" Cameron suddenly blazed. "It's mine! Stay away!"

We all stepped back in shock, and Cameron started off back up the beach. To my surprise, he cut left way before the regular path and began to climb.

"He's going over the rocks!" Imogen said in alarm. "Why's he doing that?"

Joe stared. "He told us they were really dangerous."

"And he's always talking about safety," I added. "Should we go after him?"

"He doesn't want to have company right now," said Imogen. We watched as he climbed higher and higher and had soon disappeared from view.

Joe was frowning. "What's going on? His mom said he never does anything dangerous!"

"He's upset," said Imogen. "He doesn't have many friends, and look what happened when he showed us his treasure." She glanced at me.

"I didn't mean to!" I said hotly. "I *told* you! It was an accident! What was I supposed to do? It stung him and then it was coming straight for me!"

"It was precious to him," Imogen said.

"Oh yeah? He captured what he thought was a *fairy*, and he put it in a glass jar at the back of a *cave*!" I pointed out. "Did you see any air holes in that jar? Cuz I didn't! If it *had* been alive, he'd have killed it anyway!"

"*Holly . . .*"

"What?" I turned to my brother, wanting him to be on my side. "This isn't all my fault!"

Joe raised his eyebrows. "You lost control. You were already running high on energy when we went into the cave."

"I don't like confined spaces," I muttered.

"But you've got to stay in control," Joe said. "You've got to stop letting your imagination get the best of you."

"I don't have any imagination," I snapped. "People are always telling me that. And it's not imagination to think that someone's after you if someone actually is! She is! And don't tell me that I'm crazy to see her everywhere! Even that robot is gray, did you notice? Gray, like everything at **CyberSky**! OH!"

I felt my knees buckle under me. "Of *course*! *That's* what it was — *that's* where I've seen it!"

"What? Where?" Imogen was staring at me. "What are you talking about?"

"Its wings!" I said triumphantly. "The pixie's wings! They've got the same pattern on them as the **CyberSky** logo!"

There was a pause.

Then Imogen said, "I really think you're taking this too far, Holly. We're supposed to be on vacation."

My mouth dried. "You didn't see it?"

"I'm going back to the camper to get a bucket," she said. "And then I'm coming here to collect shells. I don't want to talk about **CyberSky**. I want a *vacation*." She turned and stomped off, heading for the path into the dunes further down the beach.

I turned to my brother imploringly. "Joe, you're my mentor. Didn't you see the pattern on its wings? Didn't it remind you of **CyberSky**?"

He sighed. "No, Holly. It didn't."

I couldn't believe it. How could they not have recognized it? "If you just look —"

"Well, I can't, can I?" snapped Joe. "Cameron's got it. So just drop it, all right? I'm going for a walk."

I stood on the beach as everyone walked away from me. Was I going mad? But surely . . . those wings . . . ! I could prove it to Joe, I knew I could! If he could just see the pixie . . .

Before I knew it, I was heading off up the beach toward the campground to find Cameron.

CHAPTER 8

I went straight to the office camper by the entrance to the park. Julie was in there doing some paperwork. She smiled at me. "Hello, Holly. I had a nice chat with your mom a bit earlier. Now, what can I do for you?"

"Um, I was looking for Cameron," I said.

"He's not here, honey. He might have gone up to the house. You could go and have a look there. Do you know which one it is?"

I shook my head.

"You go left out of the parking lot, and it's the first one you come to," she told me. "In a row of four houses. It's before you get to the shop. But maybe you'd better just mention it to your mom before you go? She was telling me you've been through quite an ordeal lately." Her eyes flicked to the burn pattern on my forehead. "Don't want her to worry."

"Oh, I'll only be a minute," I said, pulling my bangs forward. Before she could say anything else, I was out of the cabin and running down the driveway to the main road.

Their house was easy to spot. It was a normal-looking gray-brick house, with a black front door and big windows at the front and a chimney and . . .

I stopped dead in my tracks and gasped.

Cameron was on the roof. *On the roof.*

What the . . . what was he doing on the *roof?*

For a moment, I couldn't think, I was so stunned. Cameron was *obsessed* with safety. His mom had told us he never did anything dangerous and usually told other people off for doing dangerous things — and yet here he was, on his *roof!*

HAD HE GONE CRAZY? First crossing over the rocks, now this . . . it was almost like he'd suddenly **forgotten who he was**. I looked up, rooted to the spot in uncertainty. Cameron must have climbed out of one of the top windows. He was making his way along the ridge, one foot on either side, slipping and sliding on the shingles. When he reached the chimney, he stopped for a moment and reached out.

There was a big TV antenna on the roof. Cameron was holding the wire and was twisting it, trying to bend it into a new position.

Was he completely and utterly *insane*? One slip . . . one wrong move . . . and he'd be plunging to the ground!

What should I do? I didn't want to shout up to him, in case I startled him and made him fall. Should I run back to his mom and — what? Ask her to call the police? What would they do? Should I stay here, in case he fell off and I was the only witness to what had happened and needed to call an ambulance or something? Panic gripped me, slowing my brain to a standstill and turning my decision making to mush.

Cameron seemed to be having difficulty with the antenna. He pushed it and pulled it, and then stepped back to see if it would hold its new position.

AND THEN HE SLIPPED.

It was as though I saw it in slow motion. Seriously — like that bullet-time thing they do in films, where the person is suspended in midair while the camera goes around them. Or like cartoons, where the coyote runs off the edge of a cliff, realizes it's running on nothing, looks down, looks straight at the camera — and *then* plummets to the ground.

Cameron's right foot slipped on the shingle. He flung out an arm to grab hold of the antenna, but he was already tipping too far over and there was no way he could reach it. He slid down the roof, his arms whirling like a windmill, with no way of stopping.

WITHOUT EVEN PLANNING IT, HOLLY'S POWERS SWITCHED ON . . .

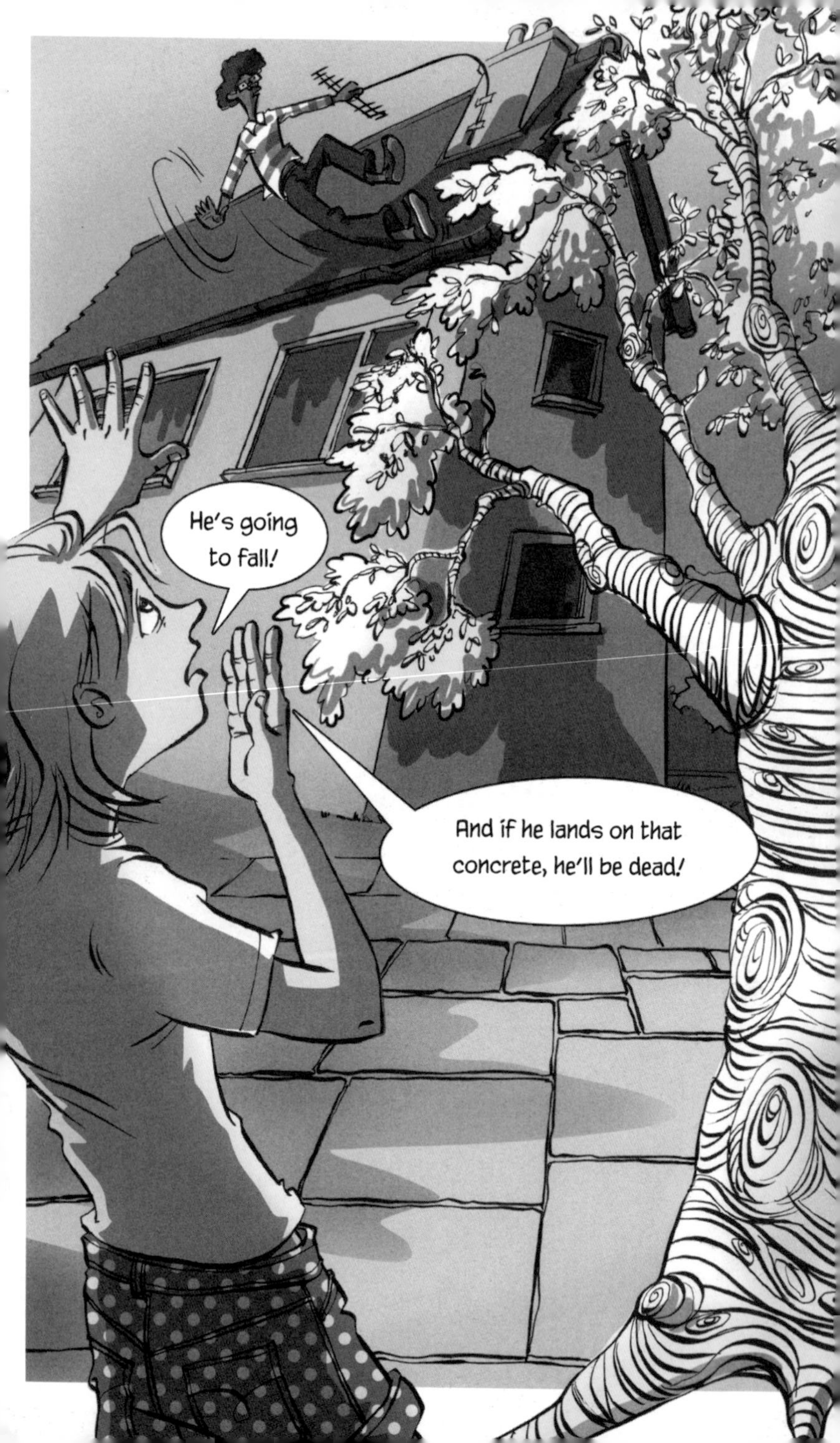
He's going to fall!
And if he lands on that concrete, he'll be dead!

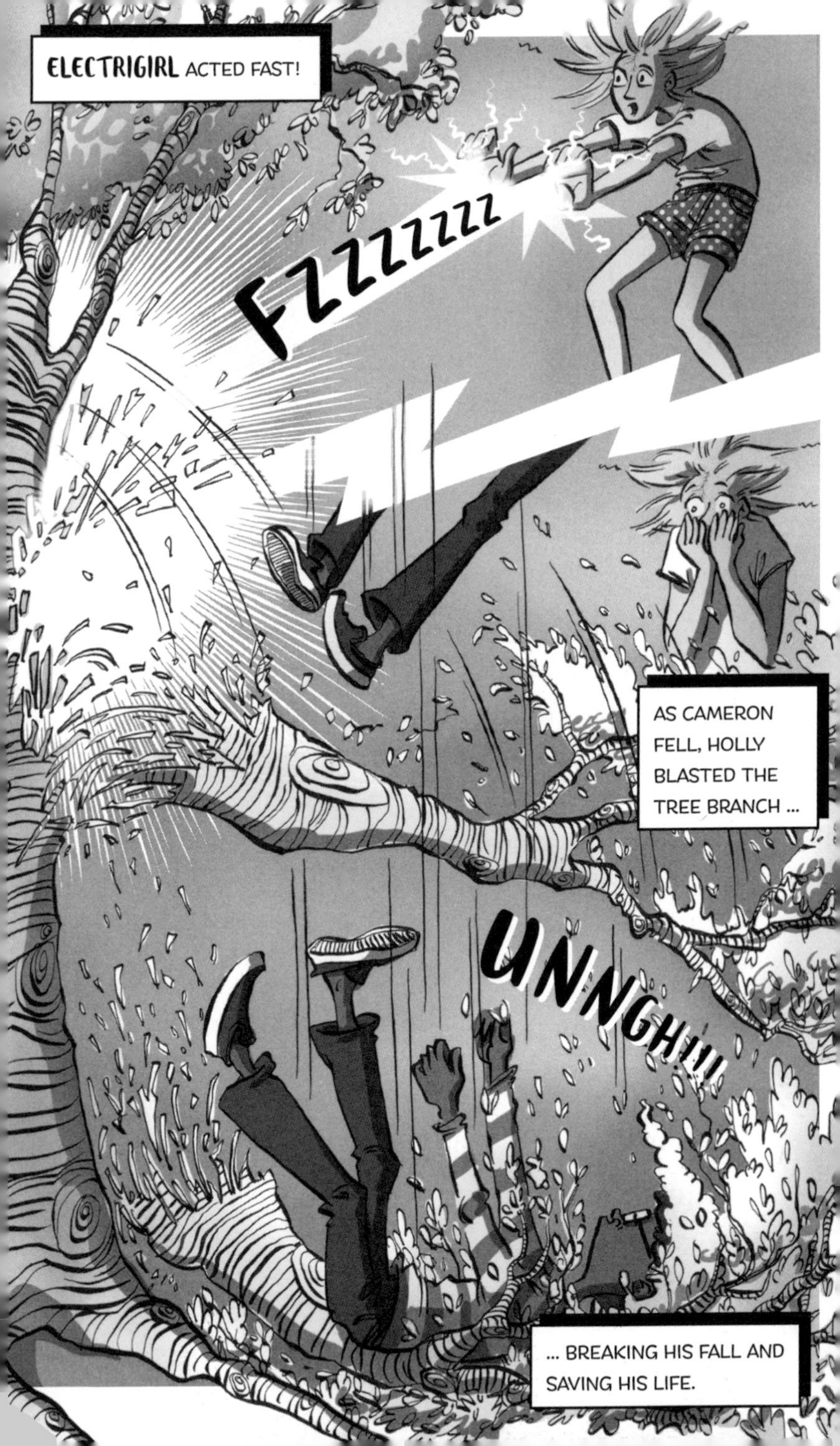
ELECTRIGIRL ACTED FAST!
FZZZZZZZ
AS CAMERON FELL, HOLLY BLASTED THE TREE BRANCH ...
UNNGH!!!
... BREAKING HIS FALL AND SAVING HIS LIFE.

I rushed over, trembling. "Are you all right?"

Cameron sat up from the middle of the pile of broken branches, spitting leaves, and staring around in astonishment. "What happened?"

"You fell off the roof," I said. "Are you hurt?"

He moved experimentally, making the remains of the tree rustle and creak. "I don't think so. I fell on the tree. This tree's about a hundred years old. I can't believe it fell just this minute! What are the chances of that happening?"

"Uh," I said. "Yeah. Do you need a hand?"

"I can manage." He crawled across the branches until he reached solid ground and stood up in front of me, brushing himself off. There were a few cuts and scrapes, but he seemed almost miraculously unhurt.

"I can't believe you didn't break anything," I said, staring.

"How did that tree fall down?" Cameron insisted. "The statistical chances must be billions to one!"

"Well," I said, reluctantly, "I might have had something to do with that. Lightning is kind of useful for making things fall down. I hope your parents don't mind."

His mouth dropped open. "You did that? Wow. That's fast work. Wish I'd seen it."

"You were too busy falling," I said. "What on earth were you doing up there on the roof?"

"The TV signal has been terrible for forever," he said. "Dad's been promising to get someone in to look at it. I thought I might as well go up and see if I could fix it myself."

"But that's really dangerous," I pointed out. "You shouldn't go climbing around on roofs. People have special equipment to do that."

"Yeah, I know," he said, "but don't you just want to do something dangerous every now and then? I mean, it's kind of **FUN**!"

I was speechless for a moment. "But . . . you hate danger! You're always talking about safety!"

He laughed. "I think maybe I've been kind of boring. Who wants to be safe all the time?" He glanced up at the roof. "I nearly had it. I'll go back up and fix it."

"You are *not* going up there again," I said firmly. "I'll run straight to tell your mom if you do."

"Oh, come *on*. Don't be such a killjoy."

I reached out to grab his arm as he turned to go. "Cameron, I mean it. I'll tell on you!"

"Ow." He pulled back his arm, rubbing it. "Don't, that hurts."

I saw the small mark left by the robot's stinger . . . and suddenly something went **DING!** in my head. The robot! What if it wasn't just a spike? What if . . . what if it was a *needle*, injecting something? Had Cameron been *infected?*

"Didn't you say you felt ill?" I asked abruptly.

"I'm all right now," he said.

I took a breath. "Please, Cameron. Please don't go up on the roof."

He looked at me from behind his glasses. "Are you asking me as a friend?"

"What?"

"A friend." He shuffled awkwardly. "Are you asking me as a friend?"

I remembered he didn't have many friends, and suddenly I felt sorry for him. "Yes," I said. "I'm asking as a friend. Please don't go up on the roof again."

He smiled at me. "All right."

I hesitated. "I don't suppose . . . look, could I borrow the — the pixie?"

"It's not a pixie," he said sadly.

"I know. Sorry. The robot. Could I — could I borrow it?" Given the suspicion that was forming in my mind, it was even more important that we take a closer look.

He sighed. "All right. Wait a minute."

Joe went into the house and reappeared, holding the tiny robot out to me. I took it, being very careful to avoid the silvery stinger. "Thanks," I said.

He nodded. "Don't — don't . . . I mean . . . Look after it, all right?"

"I will."

He gave a kind of sad shrug and went to close the door.

Impulsively I said, "See you later, Cameron. Maybe we can go out and do something later, all of us. Like friends."

The smile he gave me made me feel guilty and happy all at once.

CHAPTER 9

"He was doing *what?*" asked Imogen for, like, the fifth time. "And you did *what* to the tree?"

"I'm not going through it again," I said. "Look, we've got a bigger problem."

Joe nodded. "The robot."

"Am I crazy for thinking it's done something to Cameron?" I asked him.

It had taken me nearly an hour to track them both down, but once I'd shown them the pixie, Imogen and Joe were prepared to forget our argument and do some real investigating. "I need my kit," Joe said.

"Your what?"

"My kit. You know, my microscope, my notebook, my fingerprint stuff. It's in the camper."

I stared at him. "Are you telling me you brought all that with you on vacation?"

"What?" he exclaimed. "You never know when you might need it. And see? We do!"

Annoyingly, when we got to the camper, we found Cameron's dad, Mike, there. He'd come over to replace the bulb in the fridge. He and Mom were deep in conversation about the tin mine. Joe went in to grab his kit and brought it out to me and Imogen. It was impossible to find somewhere that wasn't in public view, so in the end we crouched down on the ground between our camper and the car, and Imogen was supposed to be on lookout if Mike came out.

The three of us couldn't take our eyes off the robot pixie. Joe was setting up his microscope and pondering my question. "You mean, Cameron's change in behavior is due to the sting he got?"

"Yes — don't you think it makes total sense? We *know* how obsessed he is with safety. And now he's clambering over rocks and climbing on roofs — I mean, how could someone change **THAT QUICKLY**?"

"You think this isn't a spike?" Joe said. "It's a needle? And it — what? Injected him with something?"

"Wasps do," Imogen said. "They sting you but it's an injection of venom, really. And mosquitoes do, when they bite you. They inject you with something else at the same time, which is what makes it all itchy."

I stared at her and she blushed. "What? I know stuff."

Joe lifted the robot onto the platform of his microscope and peered down the viewfinder. "I guess there'd have to be a little container of something attached to the needle, if that was the case . . . oh."

"There is, isn't there?" I guessed.

"Yes."

I shifted backward slightly, in case the robot pixie suddenly came to life again and stung us. "Is it empty?"

"I can't tell." Joe gazed down the viewfinder for another moment. "This thing is awesome. Super cool. It's got so many tiny parts. And how does it operate?"

"You said drones are operated by remote control," I said. "Do you think . . . do you think there was someone nearby controlling it?" I shuddered. Had someone been watching us there in the dark?

Joe shook his head, frustrated. "I have no idea. I can't imagine it. How would they know when Cameron would come back? You wouldn't hang around all the time waiting, would you? And I can't see an antenna. You'd need one for a radio signal. Maybe — maybe they're more like pigeons."

"Pigeons?" I repeated, baffled.

"Homing pigeons. Maybe they have a kind of base, and if they're taken away from the base, they automatically follow the signal to get back."

"Why did it attack us then?" I asked. "Why didn't it just fly off?"

"I dunno, but this spike is pretty serious. I mean, the thing has been *designed* to attack."

"Tiny attack drones," said Imogen, wide-eyed. "It's like something out of *Star Wars*. It can't be real."

"It's really cool **TECHNOLOGY**," Joe agreed.

I felt the familiar dread settle in my stomach. "**Technology** . . ." I began, but the sound of voices interrupted me, and I stopped as Mike appeared in the camper doorway.

"Let me know if you want to come on the tour tomorrow," he said to my mom, who was following a couple of steps behind. Then he caught sight of us. Joe just had time to shove the robot pixie under the car. "Hello! What are you doing sitting out here on the gravel?"

"Looking at shells under the microscope," Joe said promptly, holding up one of Imogen's treasures.

I was impressed. Trust my brother to have thought up an excuse **IN ADVANCE**!

Mom came down the steps toward us. "Mike's leading a tour party to the tin mine tomorrow. We should go."

"Oh," I said, "not for me, thanks."

Joe elbowed me in the ribs and said, "That would be great! Cameron was telling us all about it."

Mike laughed. "That boy! He's obsessed with the tin mine. He's got one of those brains that just soaks up information, you know?"

"Sounds like he'd get along well with Joe," Mom said, smiling.

"Cameron gets these fixations on things. Can't stop talking about magnetism — or wants to learn Japanese, or — or spends hours down at the library reading up about Cornish mythology."

Imogen, Joe, and I exchanged glances. Pixies, maybe?

Mike sighed. "The other kids don't understand. He's been bullied a bit at school because he's different, you know? But underneath he wants friends, like anyone. He just doesn't quite know how to get them in the right way. He upsets people by accident, but he doesn't mean to be unkind."

"It can be tough to feel different," said Mom softly.

I glanced up at her, struck by the tone in her voice. "It's a shame Dad isn't here," I said without thinking.

She gave me a sad smile. "Isn't it? He'd love it. Silly army with their silly rules about vacations."

"He'll be back soon though, right, Mom?" Joe said.

She nodded. "Soon."

"Well," said Mike, "I'll be off."

"You kids coming in?" asked Mom.

"In a minute," said Joe.

"All right. I'm going to the bathroom," she said, turning back inside.

"Too much information, Mom."

"Sorry!"

As soon as we were alone again, Joe pulled the robot out and put it back under the microscope. "I'm dying to know what company made this," he said. "I mean, it's not the kind of thing you can just order online."

"Why on earth would you *want* a creepy flying drone with a poisonous stinger?" I asked, repulsed.

Joe peered down the viewfinder. "It's bound to have a company logo on it somewhere."

"Did you look at its wings?" I asked. "That pattern — don't you think . . . ?"

Imogen said, "It does look a bit like that spiderweb effect in the **CyberSky** logo, I suppose. Now that I'm looking up close. But Holly, wings do have a kind of web pattern on them anyway. Veins and things."

"Yes . . .," said Joe, and he went very still.

"What?" I asked.

"I . . ." He swallowed. "I think you'd better have a look."

I don't know if it was something in his voice, but suddenly I had this awful sense of something really bad coming . . . and my powers sprang to the surface, my fingers **TINGLING** as I reached for the microscope . . .

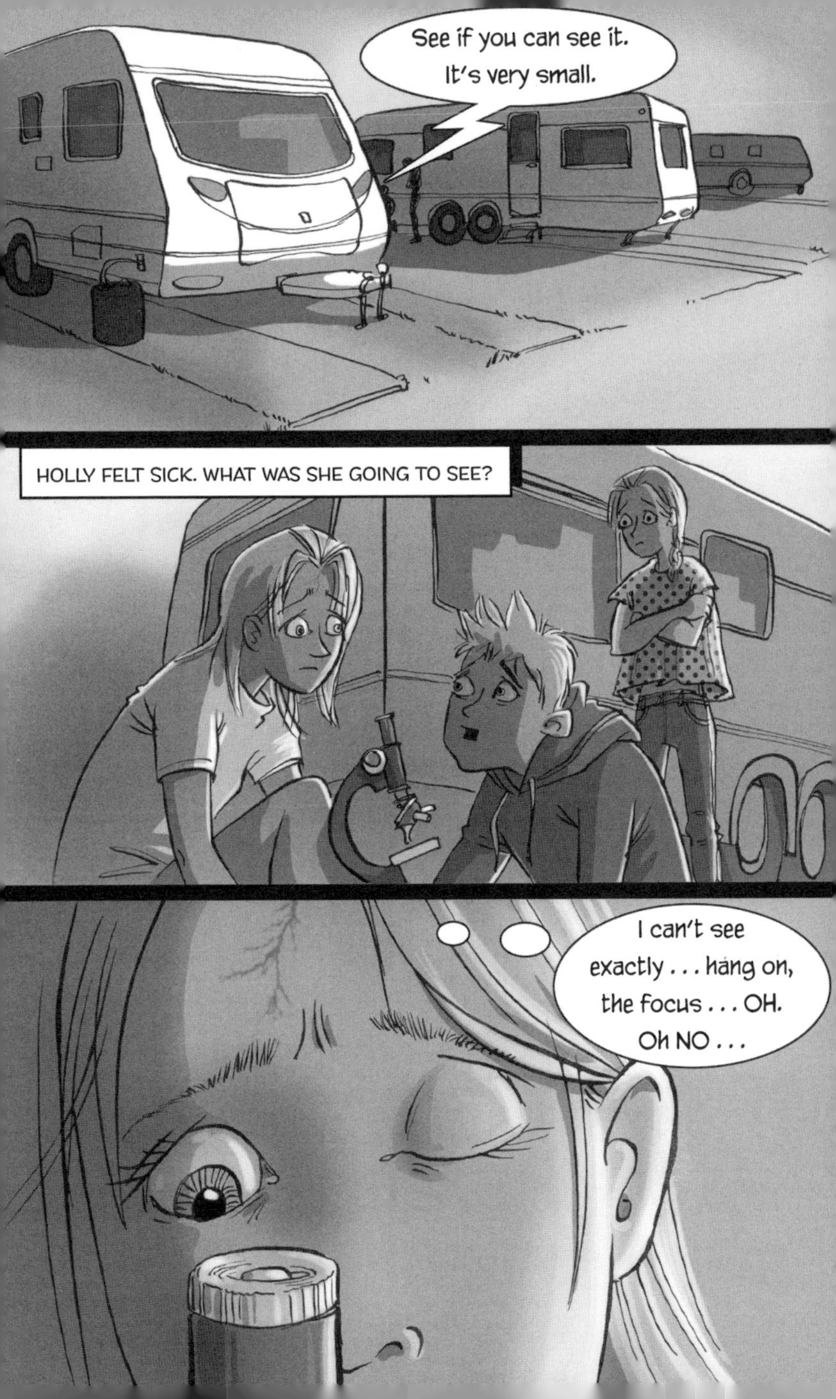
See if you can see it.
It's very small.
HOLLY FELT SICK. WHAT WAS SHE GOING TO SEE?
I can't see exactly . . . hang on, the focus . . . OH. Oh NO . . .

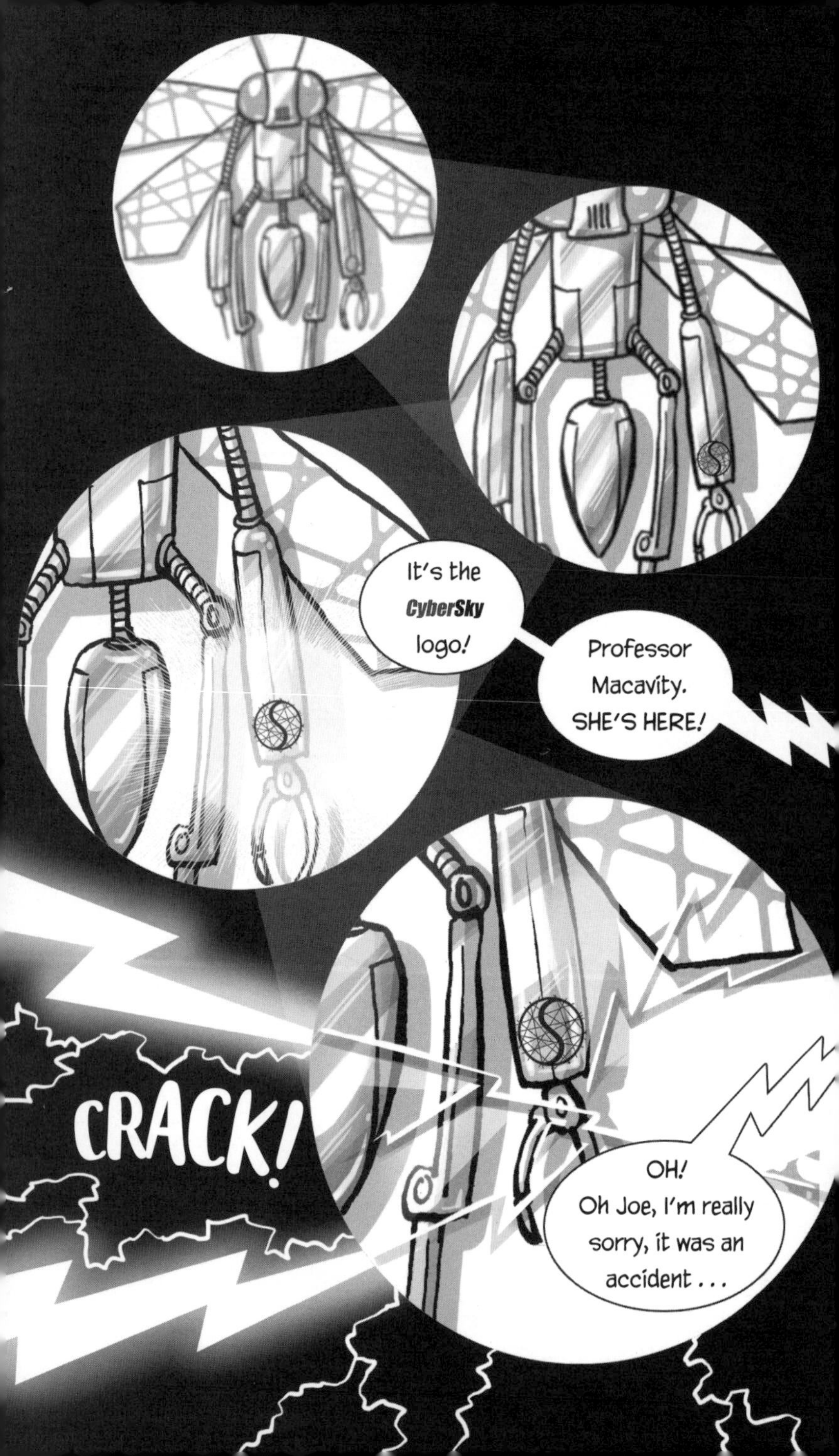
It's the CyberSky logo!
Professor Macavity. SHE'S HERE!
CRACK!
OH! Oh Joe, I'm really sorry, it was an accident . . .

CHAPTER 10

My powers disappeared instantly, like they'd been drained out of me.

Joe snatched the microscope from me. "Holly, can't you **EVER** stop breaking other people's stuff? What did you *do*?" He peered down the viewfinder. "You broke the lens. I can't believe it!"

"I'm stressed!" I pleaded. "I'm really sorry. I'll save up and buy you a new one."

"You'd better," he fumed.

Imogen interrupted. "Guys, guys. The **CyberSky** logo? It's actually part of the robot?"

"Yes," I said. "It's tiny, but it's there. On one of the middle pieces."

She stared at me. "But . . . then . . . Macavity . . ."

Then there was a long pause. My mouth was dry and my head ached. Even though I'd imagined seeing her everywhere; even though

I'd almost convinced myself that Cameron was working for her (I knew that was nuts *now*), I think, deep down, I hoped that maybe I was just plain wrong.

I immediately reached for the pager.

"Wait," said Joe, putting down his broken microscope. "I mean, obviously you have to call him, but hang on a minute." He looked at the robot. "This thing is really complicated. It must have taken months, if not years, of work."

Imogen said, "So, the cell phones — the ones that warped our brains — they weren't the only thing she was working on."

Joe nodded. "This is a different kind of project. And . . .," he gulped, "do you remember what Cameron said when he showed it to us?"

"What?" I asked.

"He said he was lucky to get this one away from the others."

I felt the blood drain from my face. "The *others*. There are *more*."

"More drones filled with poison," whispered Imogen. "*Oh no . . .*"

The pager buzzed in my hand, making me jump so hard I dropped it on the gravel.

"**FREAKY**," said Joe. "How did he know?"

"Uh . . ." My face felt hot. "I must have pressed the call button without realizing." I picked up the pager. The tiny screen showed one thing: a question mark. "He wants to know what's up."

The pager was very basic: to anyone who didn't know, it looked like a really old cell phone, with a keypad and a two-line screen. It only connected to one other pager — the one Steve had in his department.

"What should I say?" I asked. "There's only really room for a couple of words."

"We only need one," Joe said. "MACAVITY."

I typed, with shaking fingers, and pressed "send."

There was a pause. And then the pager buzzed again.

TREKENNA CASTLE 6 P.M.

I showed the others. "Well," said Joe, "looks like we've got a rendezvous."

CHAPTER 11

Mom took one look at us and declared we all needed hamburgers, fries, and ice cream, followed by a swim. "You look pale and miserable," she said, "and I can't think why. We're on vacation! Get your stuff and let's go have some fun!"

I had never felt less like having fun. But we couldn't tell Mom what was really going on, and there were six hours to fill before our meeting, so I stretched my face into a happy smile and set off with the others.

It's funny though how, sometimes, when you're pretending to have a good time, you really do end up enjoying yourself. We got hamburgers and fries and then went down to the beach. We swam in the slightly-too-cold water, built sand castles in the sun, collected more shells . . . well, I was having fun despite my worries. Imogen wailed when her toe got nipped by a crab. Joe claimed he saw a jellyfish, which made us ALL get out of the water super fast, but then it turned out to be a plastic bag, which sent Mom off on a rant about how we use too much plastic in our society. Joe, Imogen, and I looked at each other because Mom is always on some kind of mission to save the planet.

By the time it got to five o'clock and we were all salty and full of a second round of ice cream, I'd almost forgotten we had an appointment to keep. "How are we going to get rid of Mom so we can meet Steve?" Joe whispered to me as we watched the incoming tide break down the walls of our sand village. "We can't get back to the camper and tell her we're going out again!"

Help came from an unexpected source. When we got back, Cameron was waiting outside number seventeen. "Hi!" he said. "I haven't done any more climbing on the roof, I promise!"

Mom's jaw dropped as I slapped a hand to my head. Cameron had **SUCH** a problem with blurting things out! "On the roof?" Mom said in disbelief.

"Oh, I'm fine," Cameron said airily. "Holly saved —"

"It's great to see you again," I broke in desperately. Before we knew it, Cameron would have told Mom about my powers. "What are you doing here?"

"Oh — well, earlier you said we might all go out later. As friends. And now is later. And so I'm here."

Mom's face softened, and I could tell she was thinking about what Mike had said about Cameron being bullied. "That's so sweet," she said. "Why don't the four of you go for a walk together while I get tea ready? Be back in about half an hour?"

I could see Joe mentally calculating how long it would take us to get to Trekenna Castle and back again. "Um . . . maybe forty minutes," he said.

Mom gave him a puzzled glance. "Where are you planning on going?"

"Up to the town," Joe said promptly. "I want Cameron to show me where I can buy some batteries tomorrow."

"Oh, that's easy," said Cameron. "We don't need to go to town for that."

"Yes we do," said Joe firmly. "Come on!"

Cameron trailed out of the campground after us, still arguing that the shops were all closed and there was nothing to see in town at this time on a Sunday. When we got out onto the road, we all stopped. "We're not going into town," I told Cameron.

"Well, good," he said, "because I was thinking we could go climbing over the rocks. There's this cliff face that people never dare to climb, and I think it'd be cool to go up there!"

I rolled my eyes. "We're going to Trekenna Castle."

He looked baffled. "What? Why?"

Joe took my arm and muttered, "He can't come with us. What will Steve say?"

"He's our alibi," I muttered back. "And he's been stung. He's evidence."

Joe sighed. "I suppose so. All right." He turned to Cameron. "You can't tell anyone where we're going. And you can't tell anyone what happens."

Cameron's eyes widened. "Superhero stuff?"

"Yes," I said.

Imogen said reassuringly, "Don't worry, Cameron, we'll be perfectly safe."

His face fell. "Doesn't sound like much fun."

Trekenna Castle was about a fifteen-minute walk from the campground. The name made it sound really grand, but actually there was no castle there. There must have been one once, but now it was just a big clearing on a bit of a hill. It was a weird place to meet Steve, but I guessed he'd picked it because there were no houses nearby.

"Did you bring the pixie?" I asked Joe suddenly.

He looked scornful. "You don't imagine I'd have left it behind, do you? I've been carrying it in my swim bag all day. I stuck a bit of cork I found on the beach onto the stinger so it couldn't do any damage. It's in my pocket."

I could see, as we crossed a field and approached Trekenna Castle, that the wide open space was completely empty. Where was Steve? I guessed you could get an SUV up here and kept looking around to see if there was anything coming.

We reached the top of the mound and stopped. "He's late," Joe said, checking his watch.

"He's probably been doing something **TOP SECRET**," Imogen said.

"What's that noise?" asked Cameron.

A deep, low thrumming filled the air. "Helicopter," Joe said, looking up.

A tiny dot was approaching from the coast. "Coast guard," said Imogen.

Joe shook his head. "No way. Secret government agent. It just has to be." I could tell by the tone of his voice that he was practically bursting with excitement, and I have to say, I was kind of impressed too!

The sleek black helicopter reached us within seconds. We were all running off the mound, yelling to each other. My hair blew into my face and I felt like I might actually be blown off my feet as the helicopter descended to land lightly on the grass.

"WOW!" said Cameron. At least, I think that's what he said, but I could only see his mouth moving because the sound of the rotors was so loud.

Then the thrumming dropped, the rotors slowed, and I could see a man climbing out.

It was Steve — the man we'd first met walking his big dog, Thor, outside the *CyberSky* building in Bluehaven. The man we'd thought was crazy because he kept talking about aliens and then he turned out to be the real deal, running a secret department that investigated all kinds of unusual happenings.

He grinned at us as we ran over, his brown eyes crinkling at the corners. His mop of black hair was all blown over to one side by the wind, and it made me giggle. He didn't look anything like a secret agent, but I'd seen him in authority after the events at **CyberSky**, and there was a steely determination under the casual friendliness.

"Hi, kids. This had better be good, dragging me all the way down from Scotland." Then his eyebrows drew together in a frown, as Cameron ran up to join us. "Who's this?"

"Cameron," Cameron said helpfully. "I live here. Is that an Augusta Power?"

Steve raised one eyebrow. "It's had a few modifications, but yes."

"Can I fly it?" Before Steve could protest, Cameron had yanked open the cabin door and was climbing in next to the pilot.

"**NO**!" Steve reached in and grabbed Cameron's T-shirt, pulling him back out of the machine. "What do you think you're doing? This is not a toy!"

"Well, it is, really," Cameron said. "Just a toy for grown-ups."

Steve looked at him for a moment and then grinned. "That's true. But you can't fly it. It's worth more money than you'll earn in a lifetime. And I'd be fired on the spot."

"Better not stand on a spot then," Cameron told him earnestly.

Steve's eyes narrowed.

"Cameron's a bit . . . um . . . literal," Imogen jumped in hastily. "It's just the way he talks."

"What's all this about?" Steve asked. "I haven't got much time."

Joe pulled out the robot pixie. "It's about this, basically."

Steve took it from him and whistled. "This is a neat gadget. Why's it got a cork stuck on the end of its arm?"

"That's not an arm; it's a hypodermic needle," Joe told him. "We think it's carrying poison."

"I got stung," added Cameron helpfully. "It's my pixie — I found it."

"Pixie?" Steve looked baffled.

"Cameron thought it was a Cornish pixie," I explained. "And then it stung him, and I zapped it, and then we realized it was a robot."

"And then I looked at it under my microscope," Joe went on, "and it's . . . it's got the **CyberSky** logo on it."

In an instant everything about Steve seemed to sharpen, like he'd suddenly come into focus. "Are you sure?" he asked, and even his voice sounded different.

"Positive. It's really small, but it's there."

"What kind of poison?" Steve asked.

"We're not sure, but . . .," Joe glanced at Cameron, "it makes people behave differently."

"I'm fine!" said Cameron.

"You're dangerous," I told him.

"When we arrived," Imogen said, "Cameron went on about health and safety and not climbing over the rocks or anything. His mom said he's always been obsessed with rules and keeping safe."

Cameron shook his head. "The old me was really boring."

"And then he got stung and now he keeps trying to do dangerous things," I said, "like climbing on the roof of his house to fix the TV antenna."

"And . . .," Imogen said, "he said there are more of them. More robots."

"There are!" exclaimed Cameron. "Hundreds more! Like bats! I was really lucky to catch this one!" He beamed.

Steve paused for a moment, thinking. Then he said, "All right. I'll need to get this back to the lab. And I think" — he looked Cameron up and down — "we'll need a blood sample."

Cameron stuck out an arm enthusiastically. "Go for it! Can I watch?"

CHAPTER 12

I found it really hard to get to sleep that night. Watching Steve take off in his helicopter with the pixie and the blood sample made my heart sink. I don't know what I'd expected — he couldn't exactly hang around in Cornwall and come pixie-hunting, could he? And he did say he was doing something important in Scotland. But still . . . he was the only grown-up we could trust, and now that we knew **Professor Macavity** really was involved, it felt like we needed a grown-up around.

Steve had taken me aside before he left. "Talk to Joe," he said in a low voice. "I know it must be hard, having a younger brother as a mentor, but he has good ideas. And Imogen's a bright kid too. Use your support network."

"But we're on our own," I said, trying not to sound too disappointed.

Steve put a hand on my shoulder. "I'm only a bleep away. Well, a few hours by bleep. But I can get help to you faster if you need it. Come to think of it . . ." He glanced off toward the sea, and then grinned. "Tell you what: I'll assign someone down here to keep an eye on you."

"Who?" I asked.

"You'll see him when you need to," Steve said reassuringly. "Now listen. I want you guys to sit tight until I've got results back from the lab on the venom and the blood sample, all right? Don't go off looking for danger."

"What do we do about Cameron?" I asked.

Steve shook his head. "I have no idea! Try not to let him jump off any cliffs. And whatever you do, stay away from where he found the robots."

I nodded, but it was only after Steve had gone that I realized I didn't actually *know* where Cameron had found the pixie. And when I tried to ask him on the walk back to the campground, he ignored me completely. Instead he insisted on walking in the middle of the road and jumping to the side at the last minute whenever a car approached, missing him by inches and blaring its horn. Keeping him safe was going to be IMPOSSIBLE!

And who was this mysterious person that Steve was going to ask to look after us? Why had Steve grinned when he mentioned him?

Too many thoughts whirled around in my head as I lay wide awake . . .

"Wakey wakey!" Joe bounced onto the end of the bed, making it creak alarmingly. I blinked, groggily. Had I been asleep? What time was it?

My brother was looking ridiculously perky. "We need to do some training today," he said. "I've been planning some exercises for you."

"I'm tired," I complained. On the other side of the bed, Imogen mumbled something about how vacations were supposed to be restful.

"Oh, come on," Joe whispered. "Mom's got a migraine, so we have to go out anyway. It's a good time to get some training in. Because the chances are, we're going to come up against You-Know-Who before too long . . ."

"Voldemort?" I said sarcastically, pulling the covers over my head.

Joe tugged on it. "Holly. You know who I mean!"

I sat up, irritated. "Oh, so NOW you're all fired up about her? When I've been saying for ages that she's got some secret plan we don't know about, and how she's probably just around the corner, and you laughed at me and said I was imagining things?"

Joe had the decency to look a bit embarrassed. "Yeah, OK, so I was wrong about that. But this is the perfect opportunity. And you *wanted* to do more training, didn't you?"

I sighed. "Yes. Oh, all right. Just let me wake up a bit first."

I suggested going back to Trekenna Castle for training, but Joe disagreed. "Too exposed," he said. "We can be seen from a long way off. We need somewhere more sheltered."

"Cameron would know the best place," Imogen said.

"No way," I said, but Joe liked the idea.

"We can keep an eye on him at the same time," he said.

So in the end we called for Cameron, who (to my relief) was still alive and eager to watch some superhero training. Half an hour later, we were in a small cove on the beach, completely hidden from the clifftop above and only reachable by a winding path over the rocks.

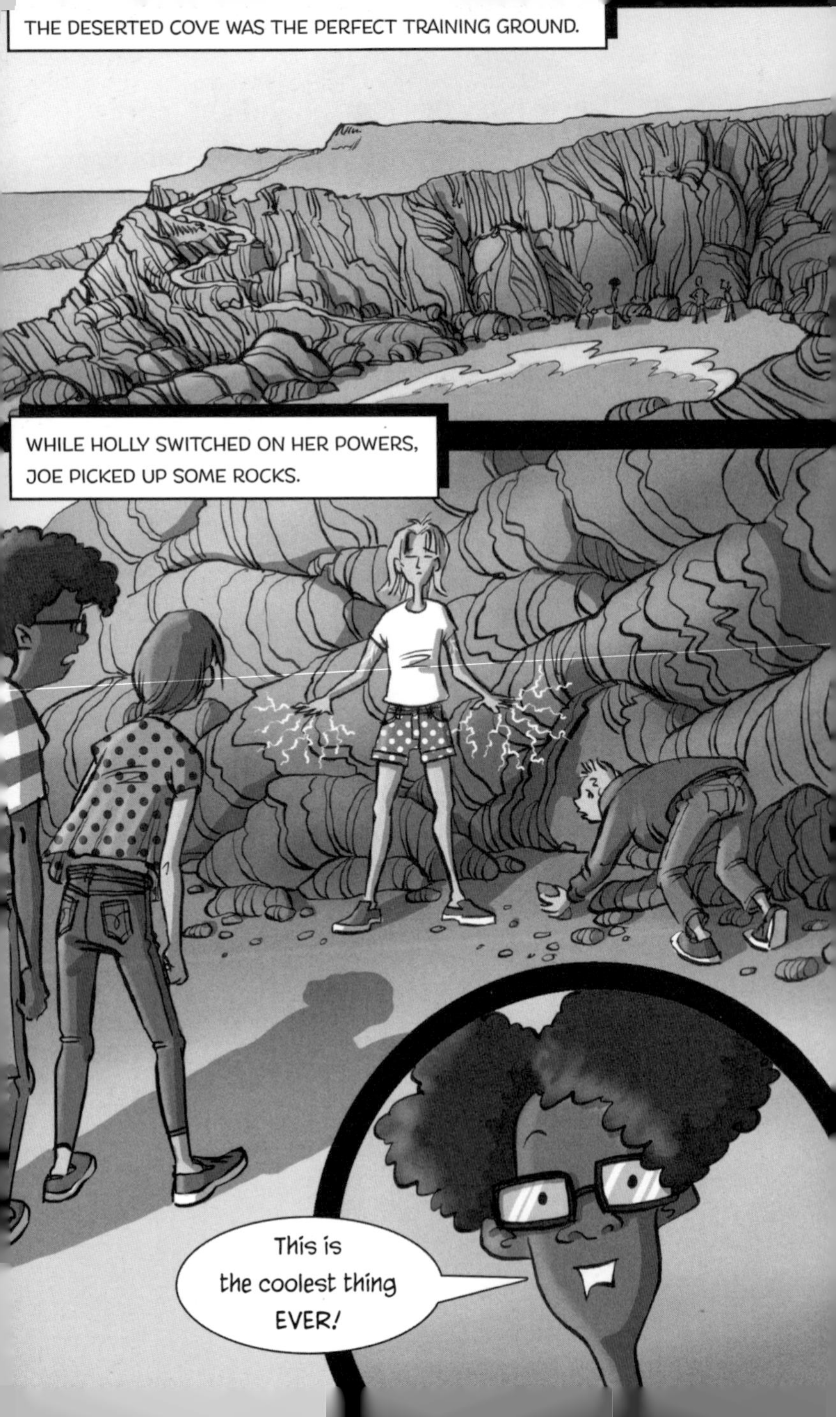
THE DESERTED COVE WAS THE PERFECT TRAINING GROUND.
WHILE HOLLY SWITCHED ON HER POWERS, JOE PICKED UP SOME ROCKS.
This is the coolest thing EVER!

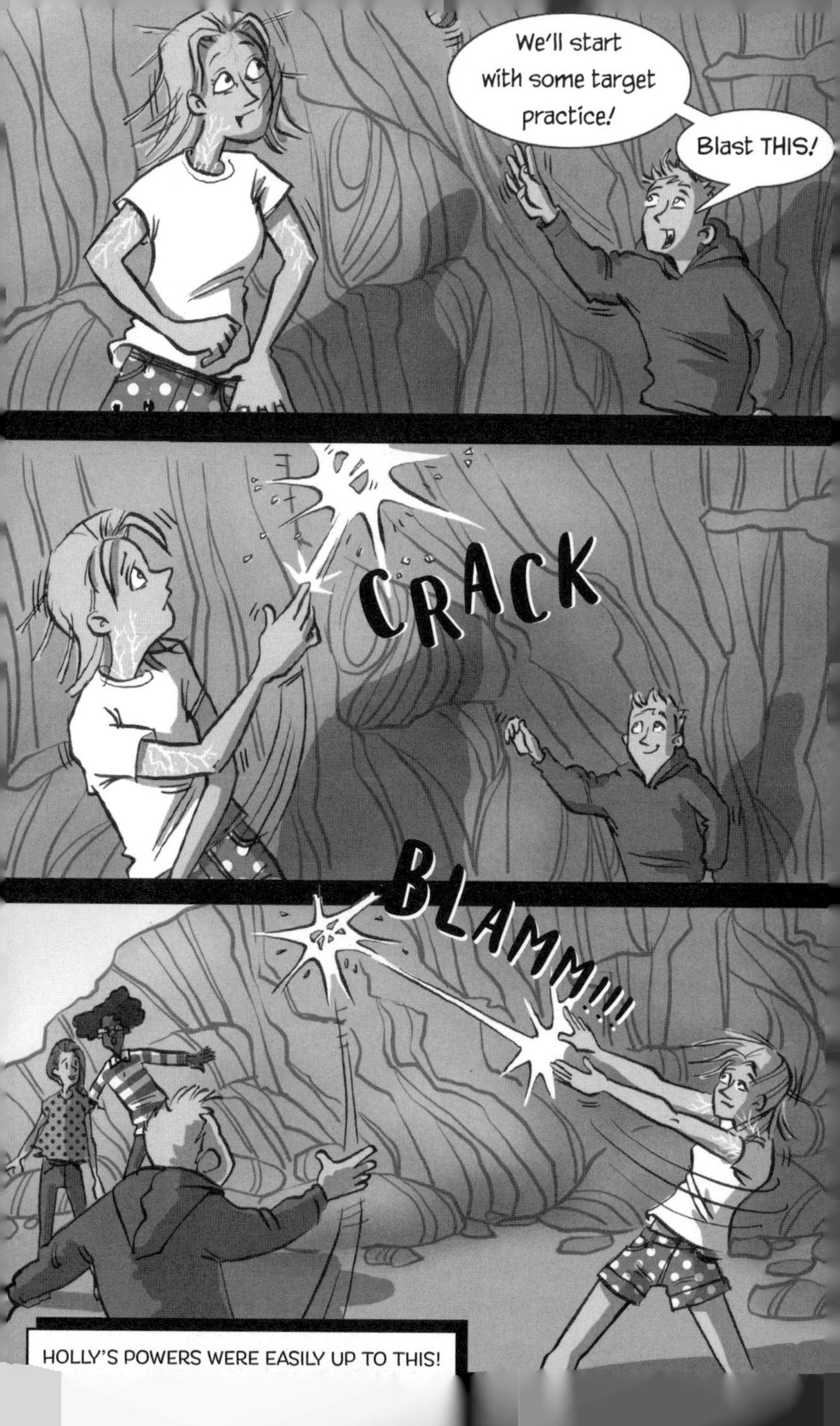
We'll start with some target practice!
Blast THIS!
CRACK
BLAMM!!!
HOLLY'S POWERS WERE EASILY UP TO THIS!

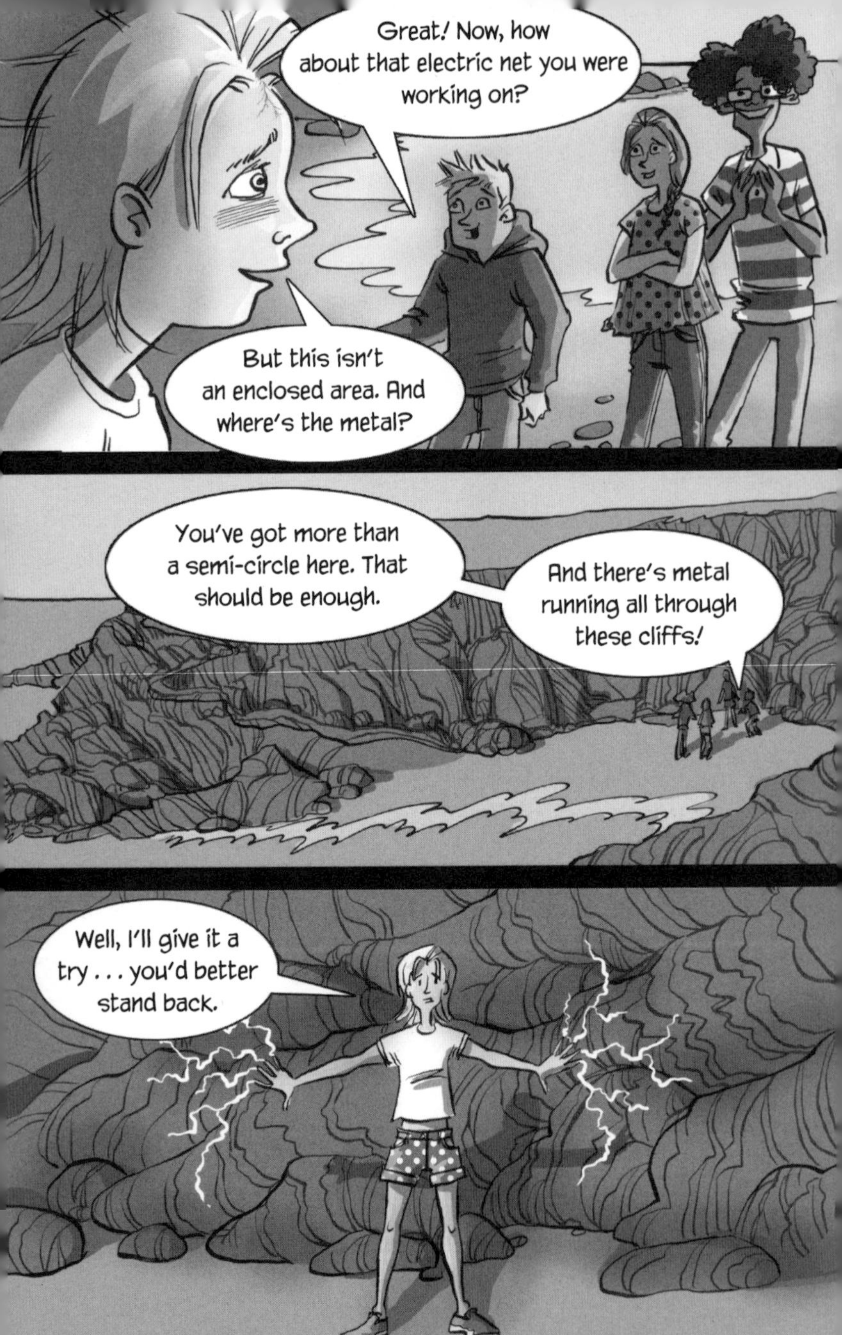
Great! Now, how about that electric net you were working on?
But this isn't an enclosed area. And where's the metal?
You've got more than a semi-circle here. That should be enough.
And there's metal running all through these cliffs!
Well, I'll give it a try . . . you'd better stand back.

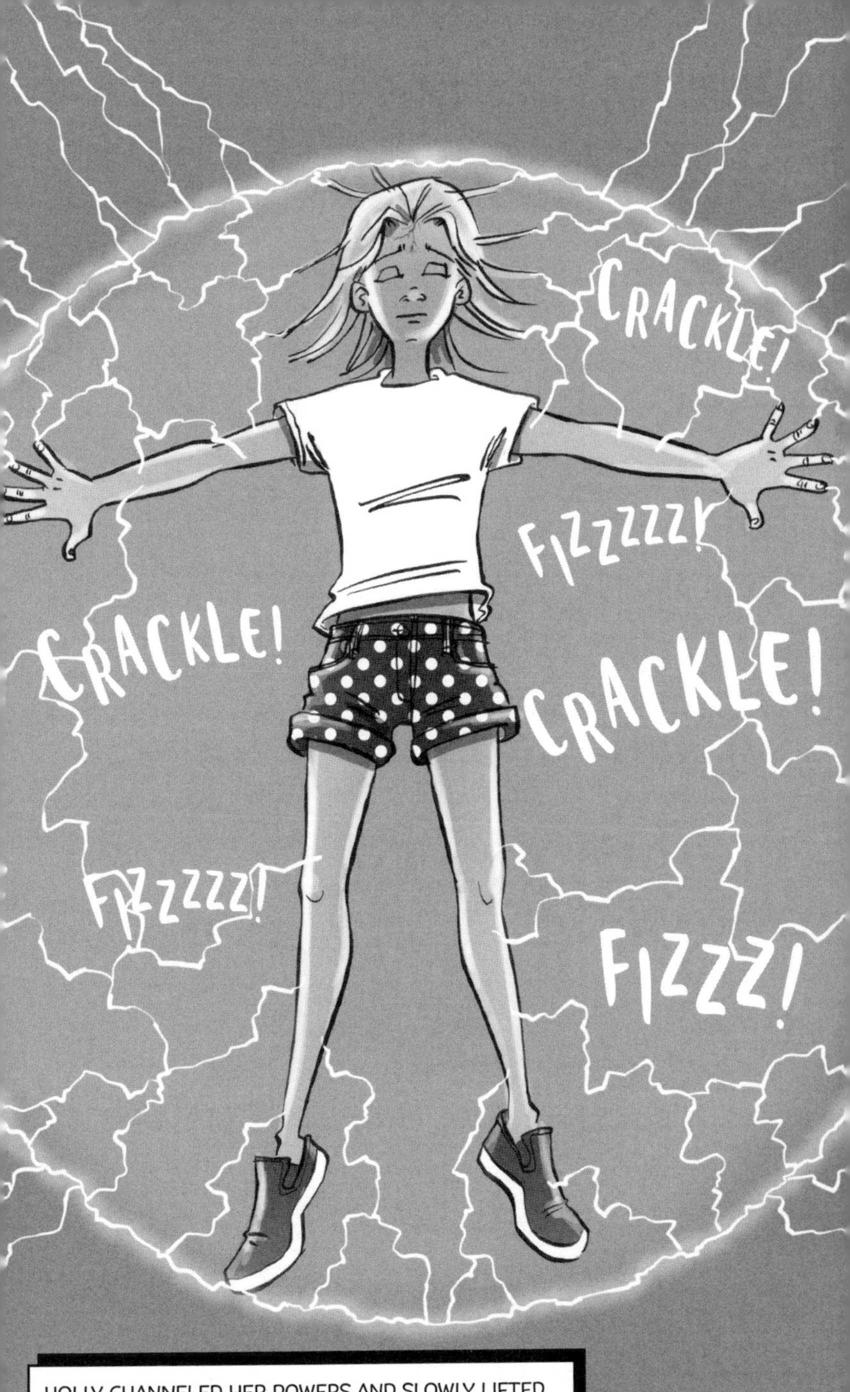
CRACKLE!
FIZZZZZZ!
CRACKLE!
CRACKLE!
FIZZZZZ!
FIZZZ!

HOLLY CHANNELED HER POWERS AND SLOWLY LIFTED OFF THE GROUND INSIDE A BALL OF ELECTRICITY!

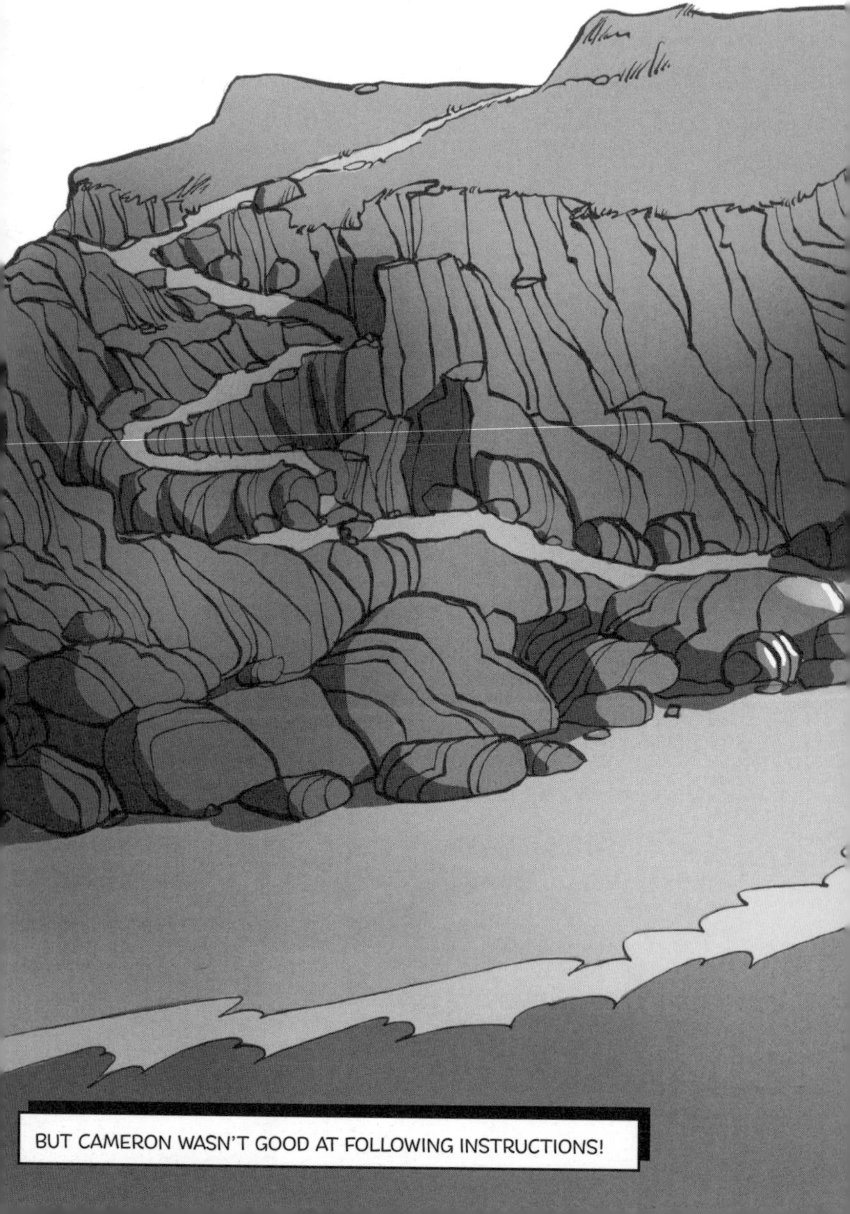
BUT CAMERON WASN'T GOOD AT FOLLOWING INSTRUCTIONS!

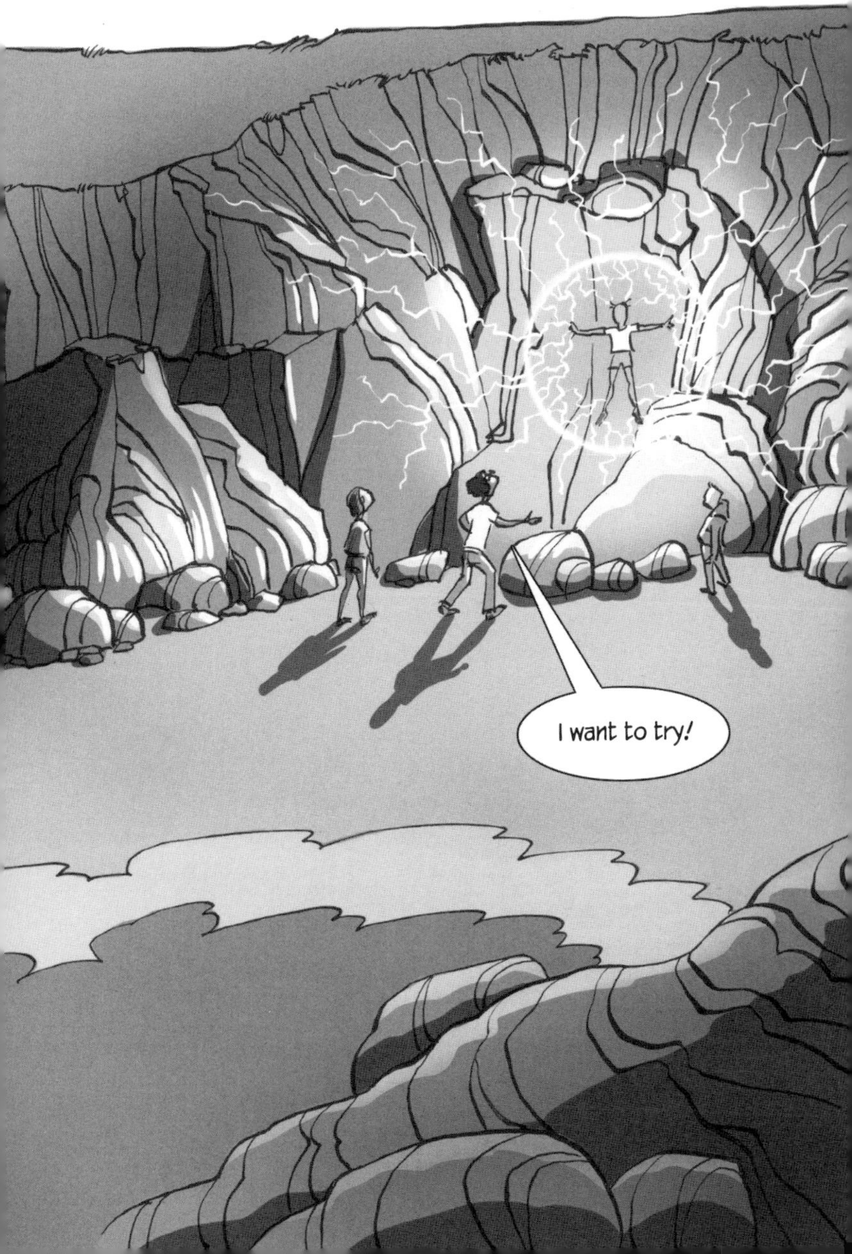
I want to try!

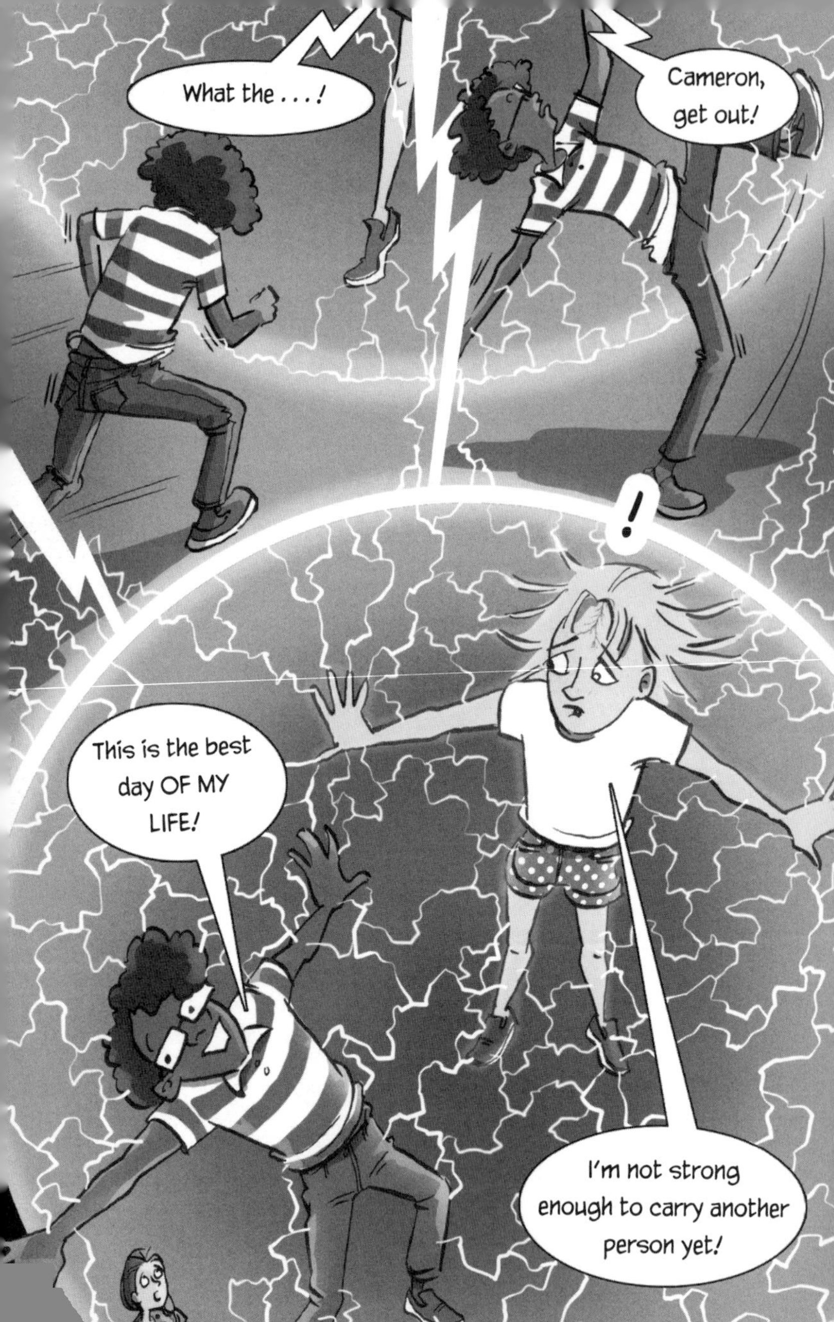
What the . . . !
Cameron, get out!
!
This is the best day OF MY LIFE!
I'm not strong enough to carry another person yet!

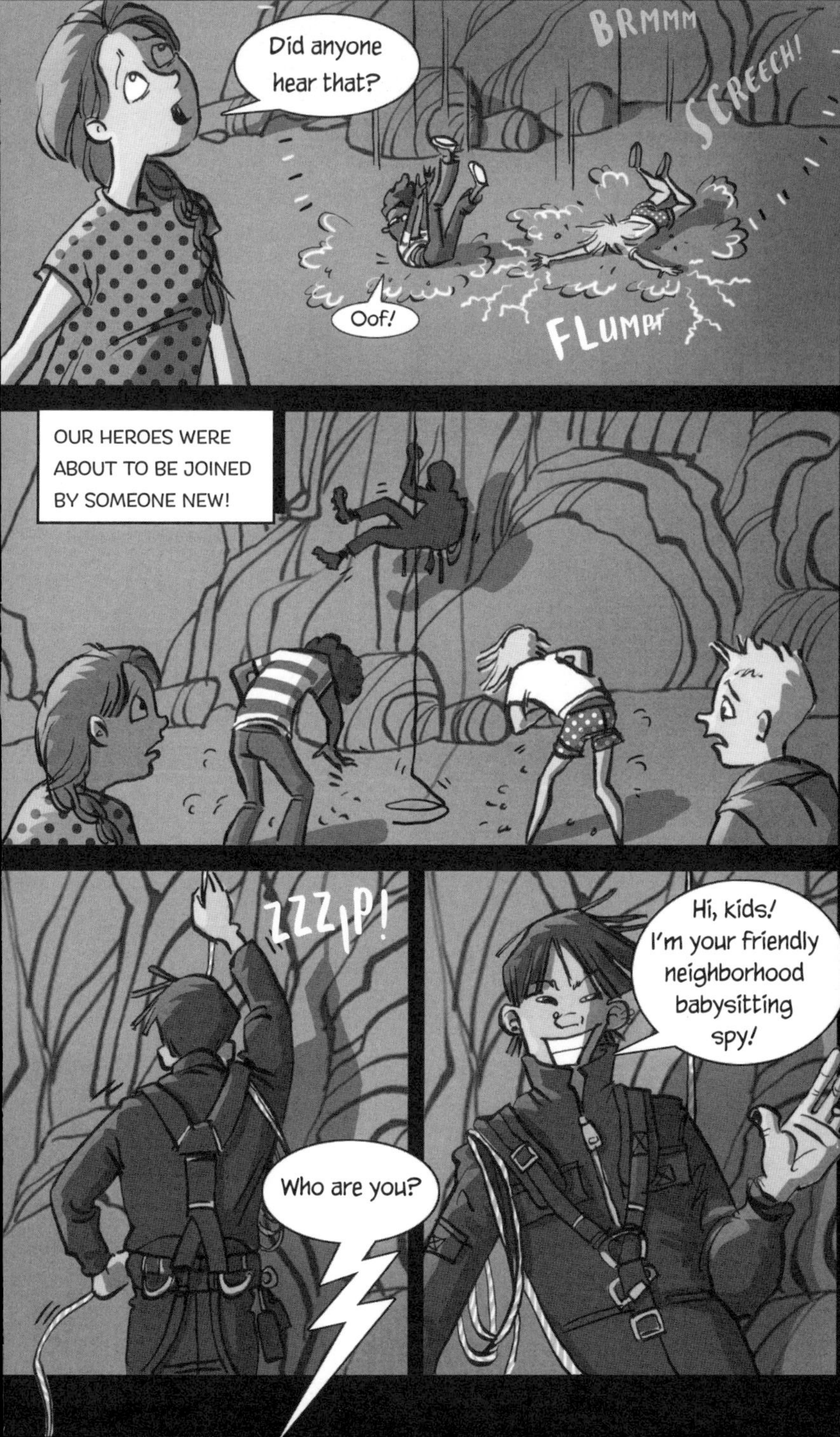
BRMMM
Did anyone hear that?
SCREECH!
Oof!
FLUMP!
OUR HEROES WERE ABOUT TO BE JOINED BY SOMEONE NEW!
ZZZIP!
Who are you?
Hi, kids! I'm your friendly neighborhood babysitting spy!

CHAPTER 13

"You're our . . . what?" I said blankly, but Joe jumped in.

"You're the guy Steve sent."

The young man grinned. "That's right. Secret agent, supersleuth, and now child liaison officer. I have to say, I wasn't expecting my career to go quite like this."

"How did you find us?" asked Imogen.

The man cast her a look. "Are you *seriously* asking me that?" His voice was teasing. "I can find anything. Anywhere. Except my own keys in the morning." He burst out laughing.

"What's your name?" I asked.

He stuck out a hand and I noticed he was wearing black nail polish. "Maverick. Mav for short."

"Maverick?" I asked, shaking his hand. "Is that your real name?"

"Of course not. It's my code name. But I'm not telling you my real name." He leaned forward and whispered, "It's safer that way."

"I'm Cameron," Cameron said, bounding forward like a puppy and shaking Mav's hand. "That was so cool, how you got down here so fast! Can I try that on your rope?"

"Sure," said Mav. "When you're eighteen."

Cameron's face fell and Mav laughed again. "You must be the kid with a danger addiction. The one who got stung?"

"That's right," I said. "And this is Imogen, my best friend, and Joe — my brother."

Mav nodded. "I've read your files. You guys have done some pretty awesome work already. I've got news for you on your robot fairy."

"Pixie," Cameron corrected him.

"Yeah, that. Well, you're right — it's definitely one of **Macavity**'s. We didn't know anything about it. No idea she was working on this at the same time as all the stuff that was going down in Bluehaven. We don't know why *here*, either. But she does like to try new technology out in remote places, it seems."

"Do you know where she is?" I asked, afraid of the answer.

Mav rubbed the back of his neck. "Between you and me, it's all a bit embarrassing. We were keeping tabs on her, but she's **SUPER SNEAKY**."

"You *lost* her?" Joe said.

"Yeah. Don't tell Steve I told you. He yelled a LOT at the surveillance peeps when he found out." Mav gave me a look. "Seems he thinks a lot of you."

I blushed. "What does he want us to do?"

"Nothing." Mav seemed a bit disappointed by this. "The lab people have analyzed the venom. They think it's a toxin derived from some plant or other. It makes people crave danger. They put their lives at risk. Climbing on roofs, for example." He glanced at Cameron. "It's pretty powerful. Hard to resist. Your blood cells have binding agents attached that are repressing neural signals."

"Huh?" said Cameron.

"You have weird blood."

"Oh."

"Does it wear off?" asked Joe.

"They don't think so. Could be permanent. Which means we need an antidote. They're working on it." He smiled at Cameron. "We'll get you back to normal."

"I don't want to be back to normal," Cameron sulked. "I was boring."

"Well, whatever. But you're supposed to enjoy your vacation, OK? I'm on the lookout for **Macavity,** and you kids are supposed to have a fun time. When we've got more news for you, I'll come and find you again, but for now, just stay out of trouble. There's no evidence that this project has anything to do with you, **ELECTRIGIRL**. So leave the sleuthing to me and get on with vacation stuff. Sand castles, swimming . . . um." He looked blank for a moment. "That sort of thing."

"Oh," I said, not sure whether to be relieved or disappointed.

"Keep up the training though," Maverick said. "Especially that net thing. That's beautiful work."

"Oh. Thanks."

He thought for a moment. "Listen, I'm going to give you my cell number. Call me only for emergencies, OK? I don't want to know if you've run out of ice cream."

Joe took the little business card and grinned at him. "We'll get our own. You want some too?"

Mav laughed. "Coffee flavor, thanks. I need all the caffeine I can get." He clipped the rope back onto his harness, pressed a button on his belt, and shot off the ground up to the top of the cliff, letting out a whoop as he went.

We stared.

"Whoa," said Cameron quietly. "When I grow up, I want to be HIM."

CHAPTER 14

"I'm sorry your mom isn't well," Mike said. "Julie gets migraines sometimes. I will get her to stop by later with the herbal tea she takes for it."

"Thanks," I said.

He smiled at us. "It's great that the three of you are joining us though. This mine is a slice of history, as they say."

Joe, Imogen, and I had joined Mike and Cameron and a small group of people at the tin mine, which was about a twenty-minute walk from the campground. I hadn't wanted to come. In fact I'd rather have gone climbing on a roof than go down the mine. But after Maverick had gone, we'd headed back to the camper only to discover Mom was still lying down in the dark. "Sorry, kids," she said weakly. "I'm being so boring."

"It's not your fault," I told her.

"I don't want you running around unsupervised," Mom whispered. "I promised Imogen's mom. She called while you were out. Your gran's doing OK in the hospital, Imogen."

Imogen looked relieved. "Thanks."

"Why don't you go down that old tin mine?" Mom suggested. "Mike will keep an eye on you. You could tell him how sorry I am that I can't come today."

"Oh . . .," I said, my mind swirling in a panic. "Oh, that's fine, we'll find something else to do." Not the mine! Not underground!

But Mom had given me a stern glare — made even sterner by the pain lines across her forehead. "Please, Holly. Do as you're asked. I need to know that you're being properly supervised."

What could I say?

Cameron had bounced with delight when we told him the plan. "It's cool!" he said. "You'll LOVE it!"

"No," I said. "I won't."

"No, honestly, you will."

"Honestly," I said. "I really won't. I don't do dark, enclosed spaces. Especially underground."

"It's not dark," he said triumphantly. "There are lights. Ha!"

I exchanged glances with Imogen. She reached for my hand and squeezed it. "We'll be OK," she whispered to me. "Just keep calm."

Cameron had led the way, talking nonstop to Joe about granite and veins and something called a stope, while I tried to control my **BUZZING** brain.

And now here we were. There was one huge building still standing, and two walls of a second. A tall thin chimney rose up behind it, pointing straight into the blue sky. A family of a mom, dad, and twin boys was peering at a guide book, and another man had come on his own with what looked like a really expensive camera. To the left of the buildings, an elevator shaft poked up out of the ground, the metal cage open and waiting.

Cameron was hopping from foot to foot like an excited grasshopper.

"All right," said Mike, "before we go down, I'll go through a few safety rules."

I took a breath and let it out slowly. *You can do this*, I told myself. *These tunnels have been fine for years. They won't collapse. You won't get stuck.*

We were given hard hats to wear. Joe grinned in delight and immediately started making faces. Even Imogen smiled. I just couldn't. The hat reminded me of the metal helmet I'd worn in the basement of the **CyberSky** HQ, when **Professor Macavity** had strapped me into her awful Machine and I'd been drained of all my powers. My hands trembled as I put it on, and I felt angry with myself. *Get a grip, Holly!*

We all got into the metal cage, and then Mike pressed a switch and we began to descend. I closed my eyes, concentrating on my breathing. The last thing I needed was for my powers to switch on! Goodness knows what would happen with all this metal in the rock . . .

Mike was talking about how the miners would find a vein of tin or copper on the surface and then dig straight down to follow it. Cameron kept interrupting, adding in bits his dad had forgotten. Mike didn't seem to mind. I suppose he was used to it.

"It goes a long way down, doesn't it?" whispered Imogen to me.

"Yes," I said, biting my lip.

"How are you doing?"

"Not all that well," I admitted.

The elevator clanked at the base of the shaft.

"All right," said Mike. "Follow me, but remember that these tunnels are very narrow. Make sure you follow me, and don't go down any side passages because they're not all safe. As you go, look at the walls of the tunnel and you'll see the vein of tin running through it. That's what the miners dug out with hammers and explosives, and when we get back to the surface, I'll show you how the tin was extracted from the rock. Ready? Off we go."

The tunnel was narrow and not very tall, and I hated it. Hated every second; hated concentrating on putting one foot in front of the other. It wasn't too dark because there were electric lamps every few feet, but I kept bumping into the wall because my legs felt wobbly. Worse still, my fingers went **TINGLY** when they came into contact with the tin in the walls, as though there were some kind of primeval electrical energy running through the hills . . . and then something happened

SORT OF BY ACCIDENT . . .

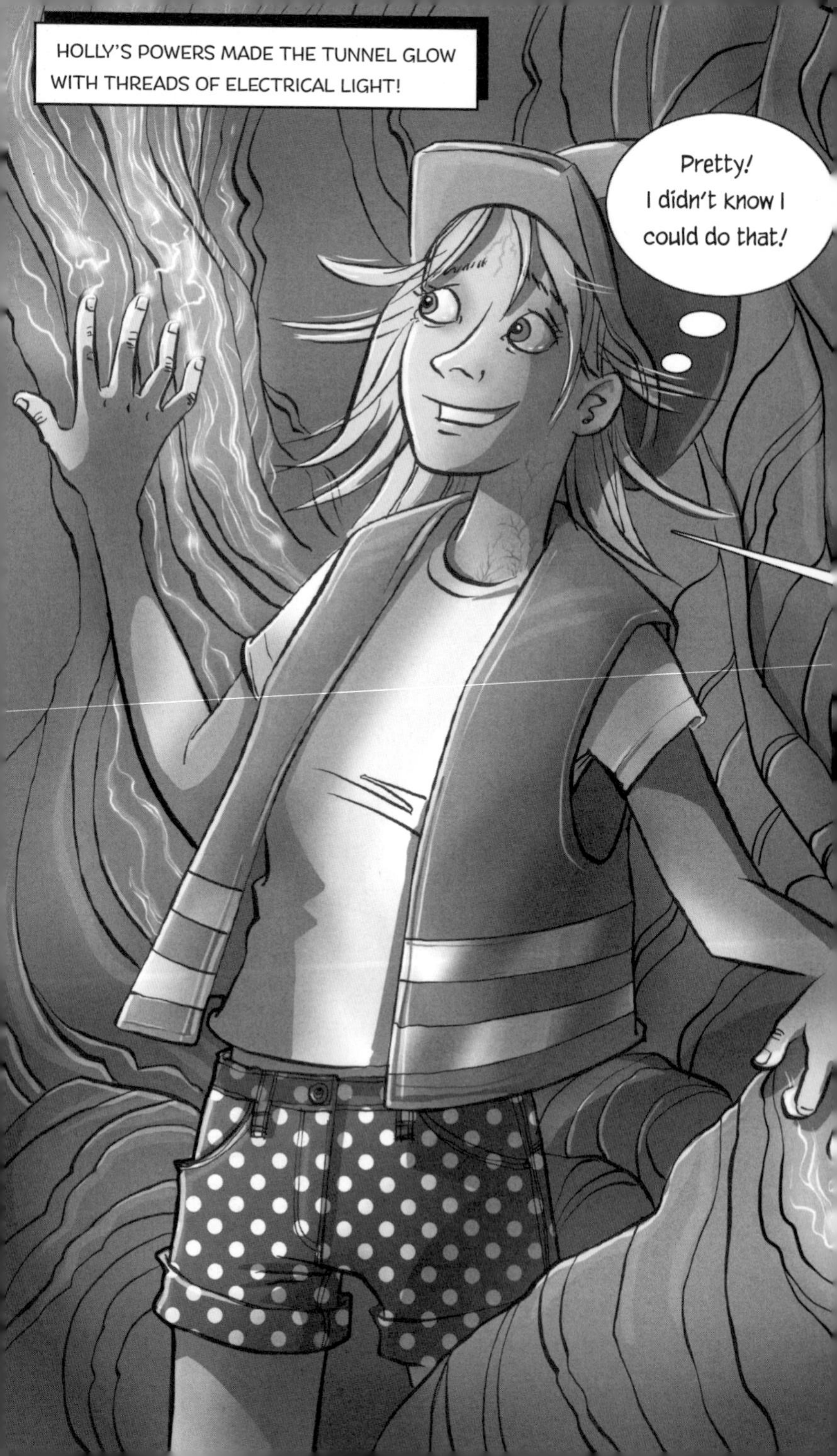
HOLLY'S POWERS MADE THE TUNNEL GLOW WITH THREADS OF ELECTRICAL LIGHT!
Pretty! I didn't know I could do that!

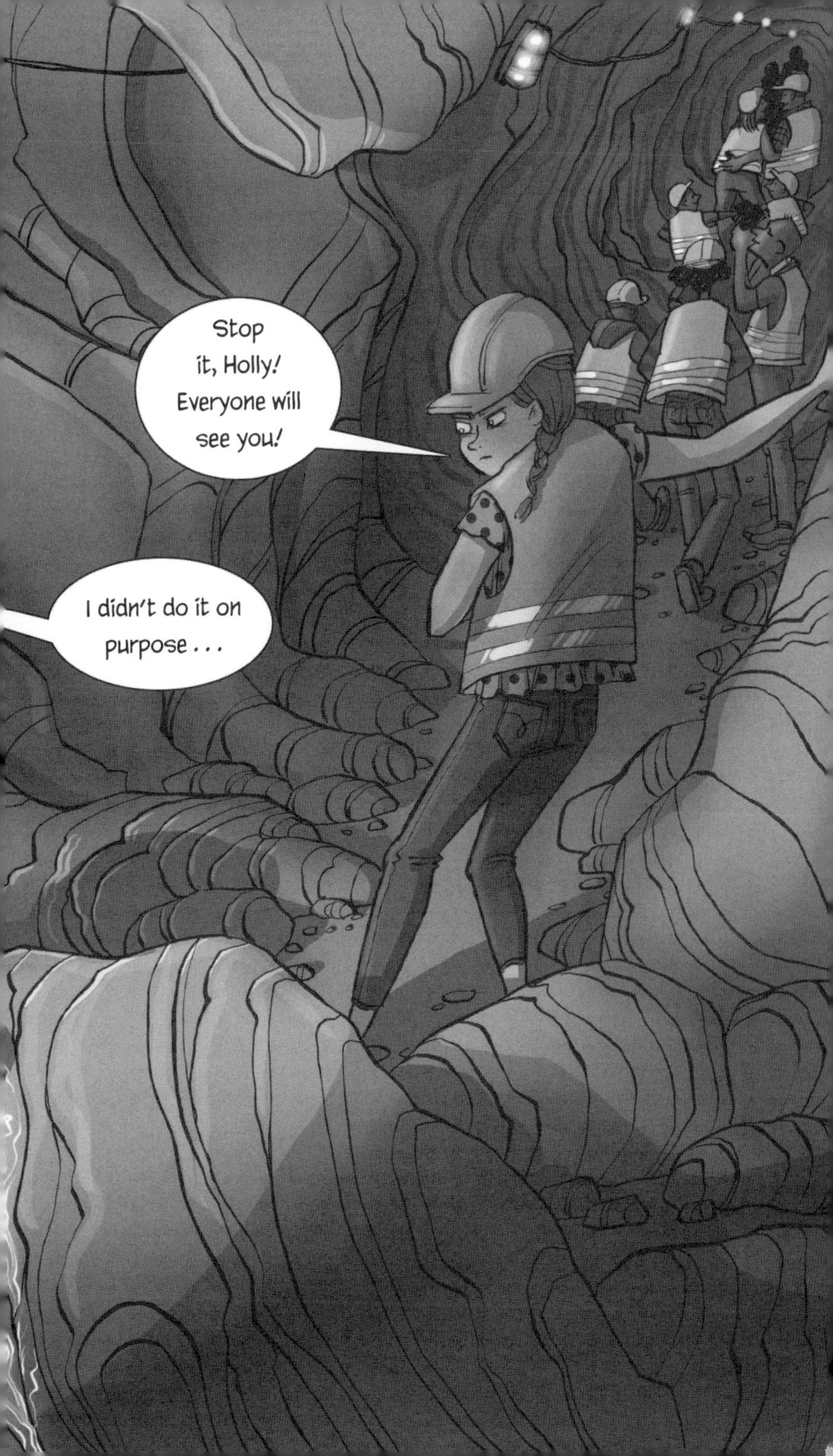
Stop it, Holly! Everyone will see you!
I didn't do it on purpose . . .

Sulking, I switched off my powers and felt fear grip me again. How long before we reached the next mine shaft and had a bit more room?

Not long, thankfully. Within another minute, I was clambering out of the tunnel and into a much wider area. Mike was standing in the middle of the group, pointing upward. "Ah, good!" he said, smiling. "Haven't lost anyone. If you look up, you can see another shaft — this one is much shallower than the one we came down."

I felt slightly dizzy looking up. A narrow rectangle of light showed at the top of a chimney of darkness. A metal ladder was fixed to the side of the chimney. "People actually climbed up and down that?" Imogen whispered.

Mike heard her. "Yes — and carrying all kinds of equipment too. This is one of the smaller mines, older than some of the rest. The miners who worked down here did so with hammers and pickaxes, and any stone they hacked out of the walls, they had to lift to the surface somehow. It was hard work. And if you look at the walls, you can see holes about an inch across. They used man-powered drills: two men taking turns to hit a metal peg held by a third man, who twisted it at the same time. Then when the hole was deep enough, they packed it with gunpowder and lit a fuse."

"Bet they didn't live long," said the man with the camera cheerfully.

The twin boys giggled.

"You're right," Mike said. "The life expectancy was around forty. Anyone who worked down here was at risk of all kinds of things. Tunnel collapse, injuries from flying rock chips, eyesight problems, hearing problems — not to mention the arsenic and other nasties in the dust they breathed in."

"Arsenic?' echoed one of the boys. "Cool!" His mother nudged him and told him not to be disrespectful.

"You'll see there's another passageway leading off this shaft," Mike said, pointing. "So there's the one we came up, the one we're going to go down next, and that one. That's a very narrow one, set on a diagonal because the miners were following the angle of the vein of tin. It opens out a bit further on, but it's a very tight squeeze, so we won't be going down there today."

I glanced across at the narrow slit of the opening and felt thankful to be spared an even narrower tunnel. And then I realized Cameron was looking right at me with a kind of burning intensity . . .

I frowned. "What is it?" I mouthed at him.

He beamed with the widest smile I'd ever seen him give. His teeth shone white in the lamplight. And then he lifted his arms, just a little, and flapped his hands up and down.

My breath stopped in my throat as I felt a sudden heavy realization sink into me.

THE PIXIES WERE DOWN THAT TUNNEL!

CHAPTER 16

I went cold all over. Maverick had told us specifically to stay out of trouble. We weren't supposed to be looking for the rest of the robots. We were supposed to stay safe. We KNEW Cameron was a **DANGER-NUT**, and yet we'd blindly agreed to come down here with him! No wonder he'd been hopping like a cricket up top! He couldn't wait to get us into the mine!

"What is it?" Imogen whispered urgently. "You look like you've seen a ghost. Are you sick?"

I quickly whispered in her ear. She went pale. "Are you sure?" Then she glanced across at Cameron. "You're right. He *wanted* us to come down here and put ourselves in danger!"

Joe was at my shoulder. "He gets a thrill out of dangerous situations. We should have guessed."

"What do we do now?"

Mike was answering questions from the others and hadn't seemed to notice the three of us holding back. Cameron stepped toward us.

"Are you crazy?" I cried.

His eyes were gleaming. "Come on, I'll show them to you! Follow me!"

"No —" I said, but Cameron had already disappeared into the dark opening!

"We have to go after him," Joe said urgently. "Before he wakes up all the other pixies. I'll go, I've got a flashlight. You two should get the rest of the people out of here."

He took a step into the dark, narrow opening. My heart pounded. "It should be me," I said without thinking, and almost swallowed my own tongue. I didn't want to go in there — what was I saying? "I'm the one with powers."

"Yeah," said Joe, "and look how dangerous they could be down here! You could cause a rockfall."

"What if he wakes up the pixies?" I countered. "How are you going to protect yourself?"

Joe hesitated.

"Look, I know I'm not exactly safe," I went

on in a low tone, "but Cameron is dangerous and he's walking into a nest of deadly stinging robots. What are you going to do, show them your Batman comics?'

He glared at me. "Fine." He stepped out of the tunnel. "Just try not to die, all right?"

"It's not high on my list," I snapped back.

"Don't fight," Imogen said with tears in her eyes. "He just doesn't want you to get hurt."

"Well, he's got a funny way of showing it," I said, unwilling to let go of my temper. If I could stay mad, I wouldn't be frightened. "Go and get the others out." I turned my back on them and stepped into the tunnel. That flipping Cameron! I'd drag him out of here if I had to . . .

The tunnel was barely wide enough for me to squeeze along, and I kept banging my knees on the walls and tripping over my own feet. That kept me irritated too, but the farther along I went, the darker and quieter it seemed, and the tighter the walls.

MY FINGERS TINGLED,

and I put out my hands to steady myself on either side . . .

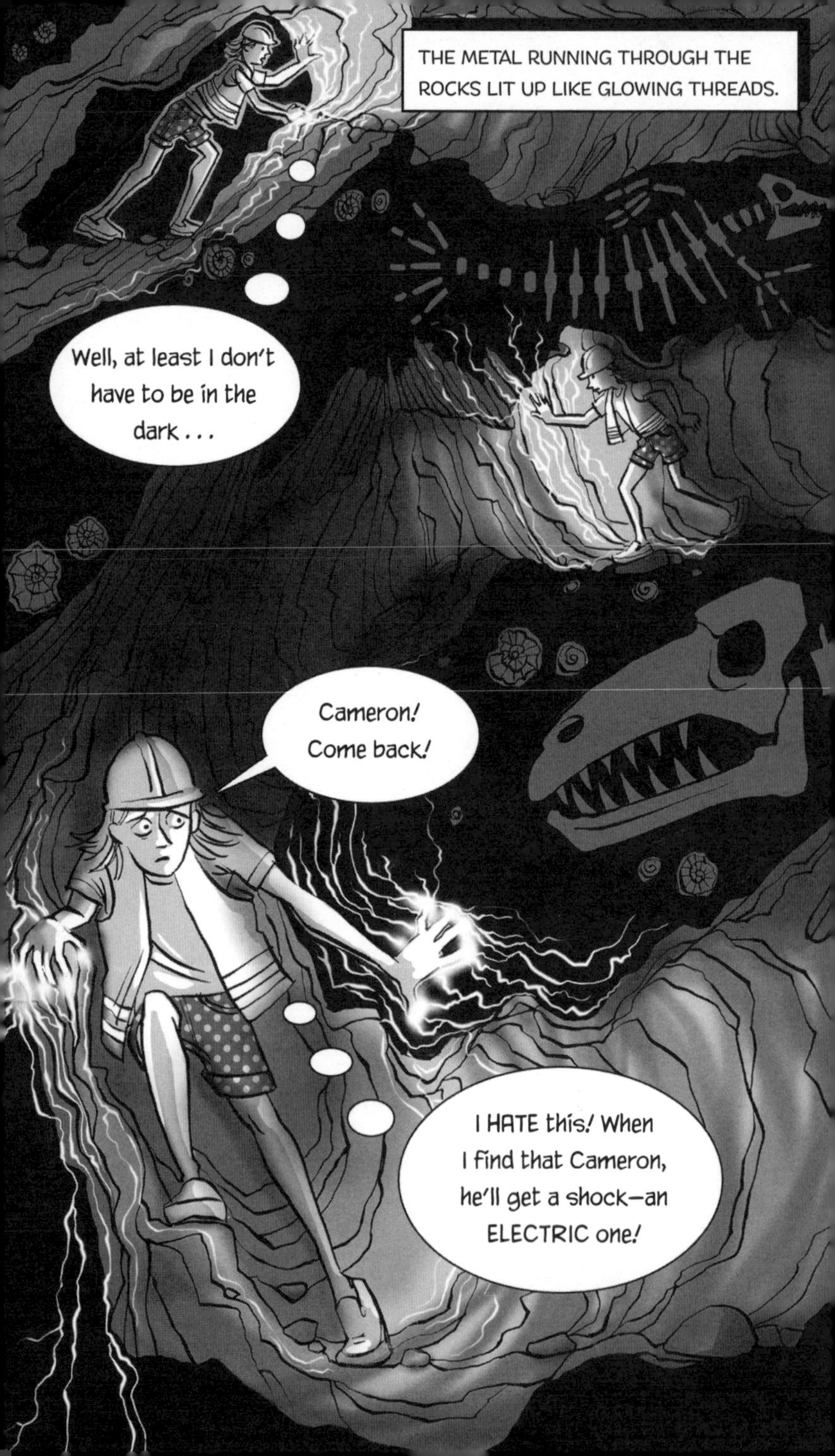
THE METAL RUNNING THROUGH THE ROCKS LIT UP LIKE GLOWING THREADS.
Well, at least I don't have to be in the dark . . .
Cameron! Come back!
I HATE this! When I find that Cameron, he'll get a shock—an ELECTRIC one!

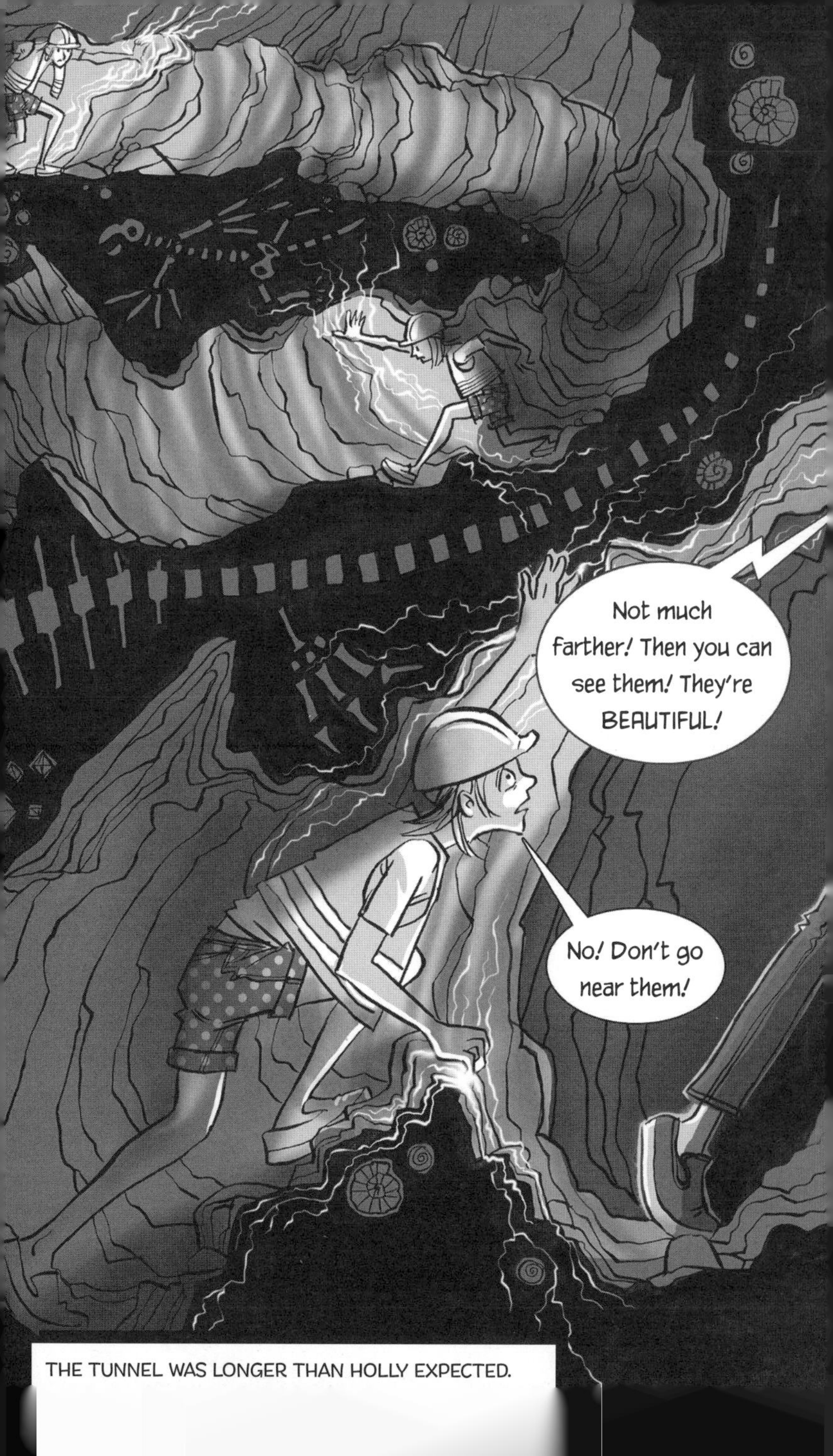
Not much farther! Then you can see them! They're BEAUTIFUL!
No! Don't go near them!
THE TUNNEL WAS LONGER THAN HOLLY EXPECTED.

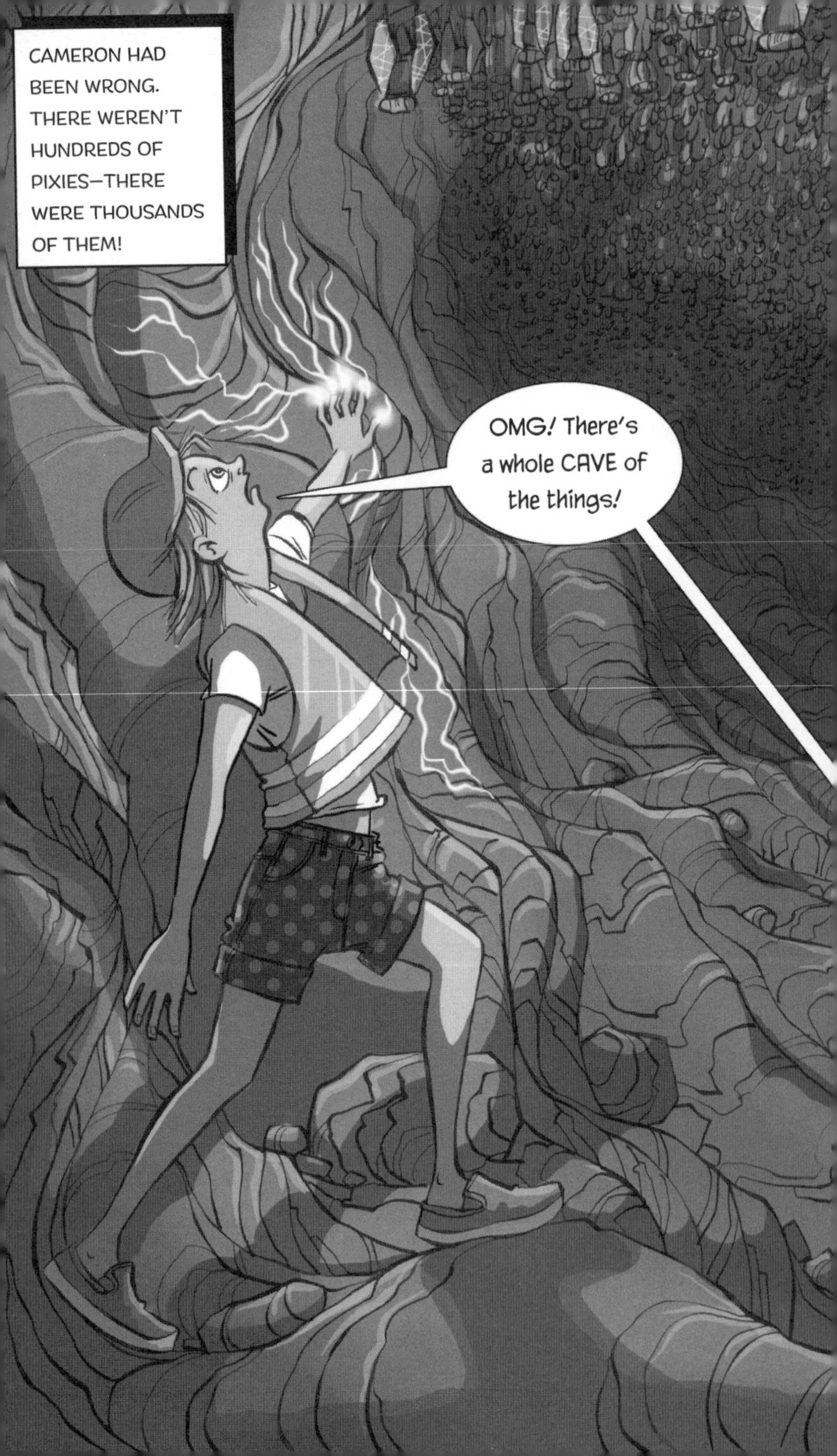
CAMERON HAD BEEN WRONG. THERE WEREN'T HUNDREDS OF PIXIES—THERE WERE THOUSANDS OF THEM!
OMG! There's a whole CAVE of the things!

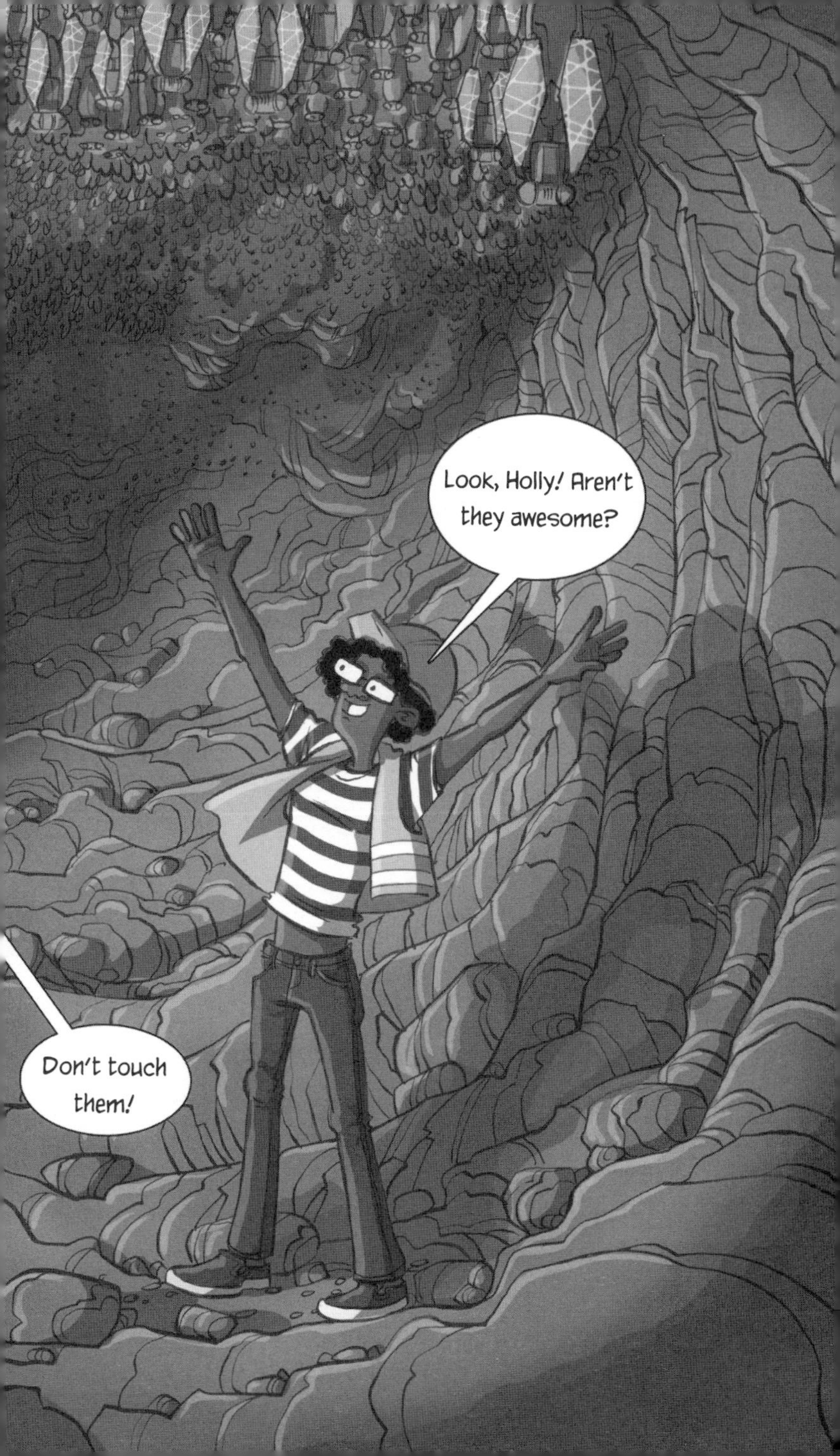
Look, Holly! Aren't they awesome?
Don't touch them!

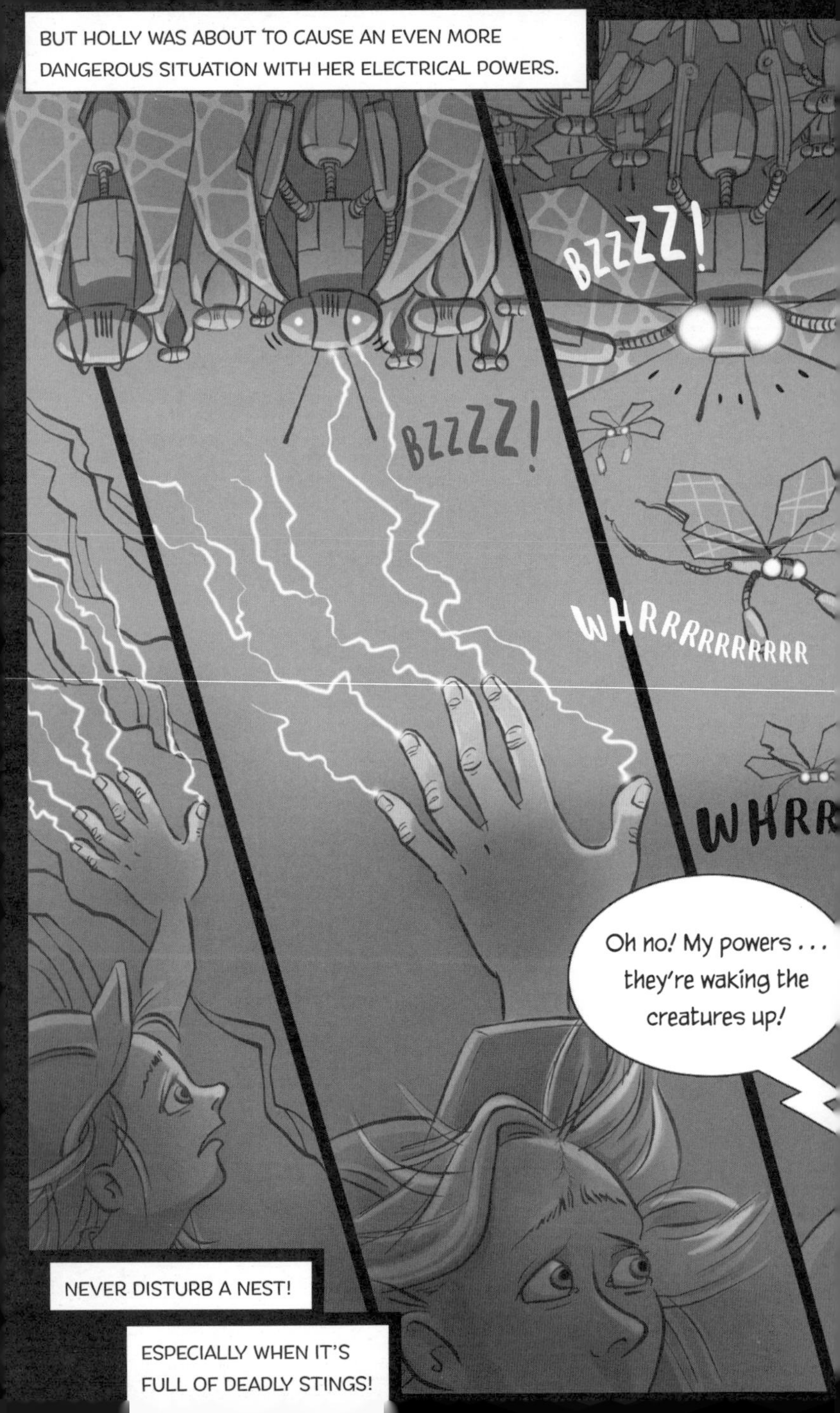
BUT HOLLY WAS ABOUT TO CAUSE AN EVEN MORE DANGEROUS SITUATION WITH HER ELECTRICAL POWERS.
BZZZZ!
BZZZZ!
WHRRRRRRRRRR
WHRR
Oh no! My powers . . . they're waking the creatures up!
NEVER DISTURB A NEST!
ESPECIALLY WHEN IT'S FULL OF DEADLY STINGS!

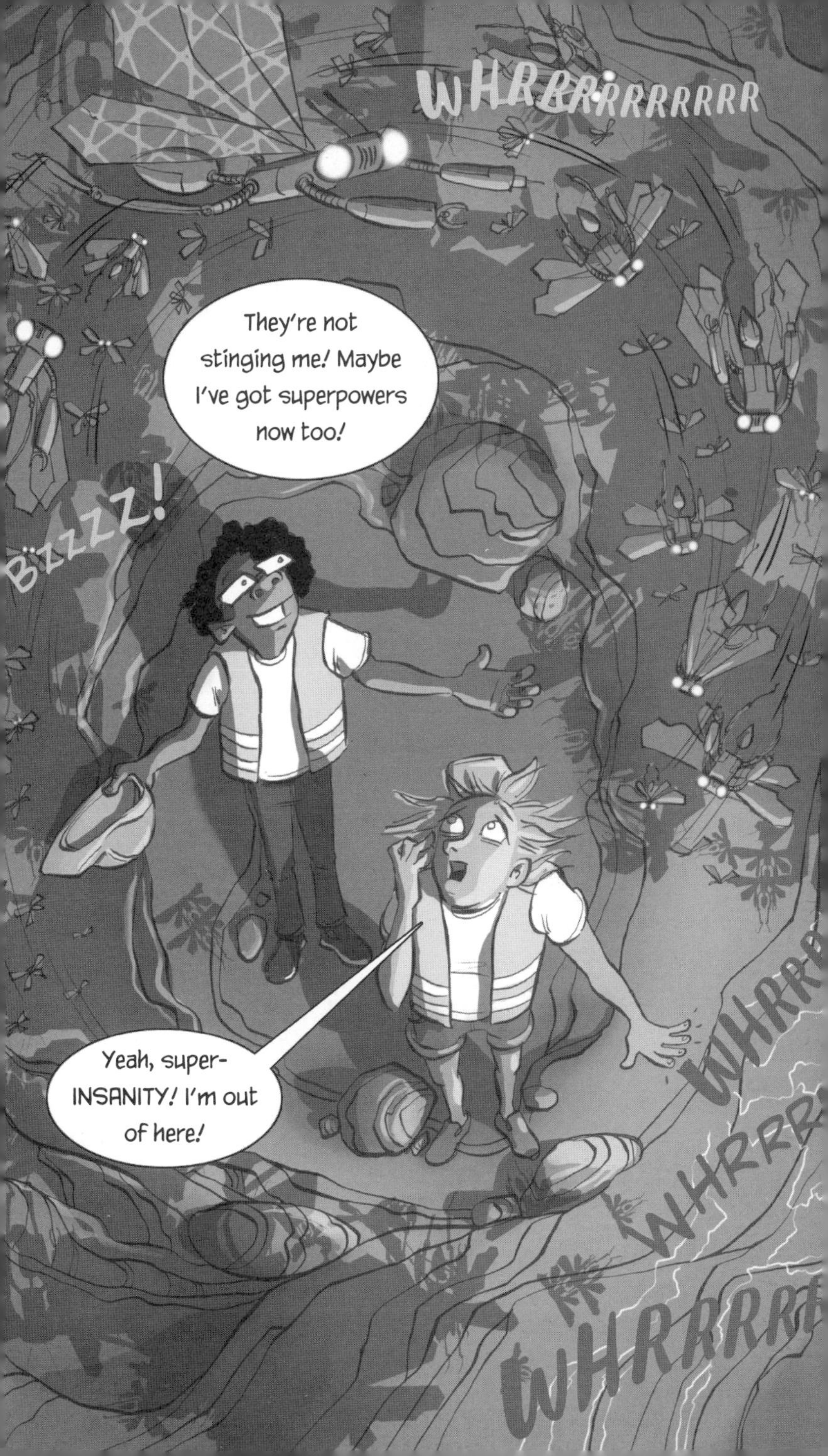
WHRRRRRRRRRRR
They're not stinging me! Maybe I've got superpowers now too!
BZZZZZ!
Yeah, super-INSANITY! I'm out of here!
WHRR
WHRRR
WHRRRRR

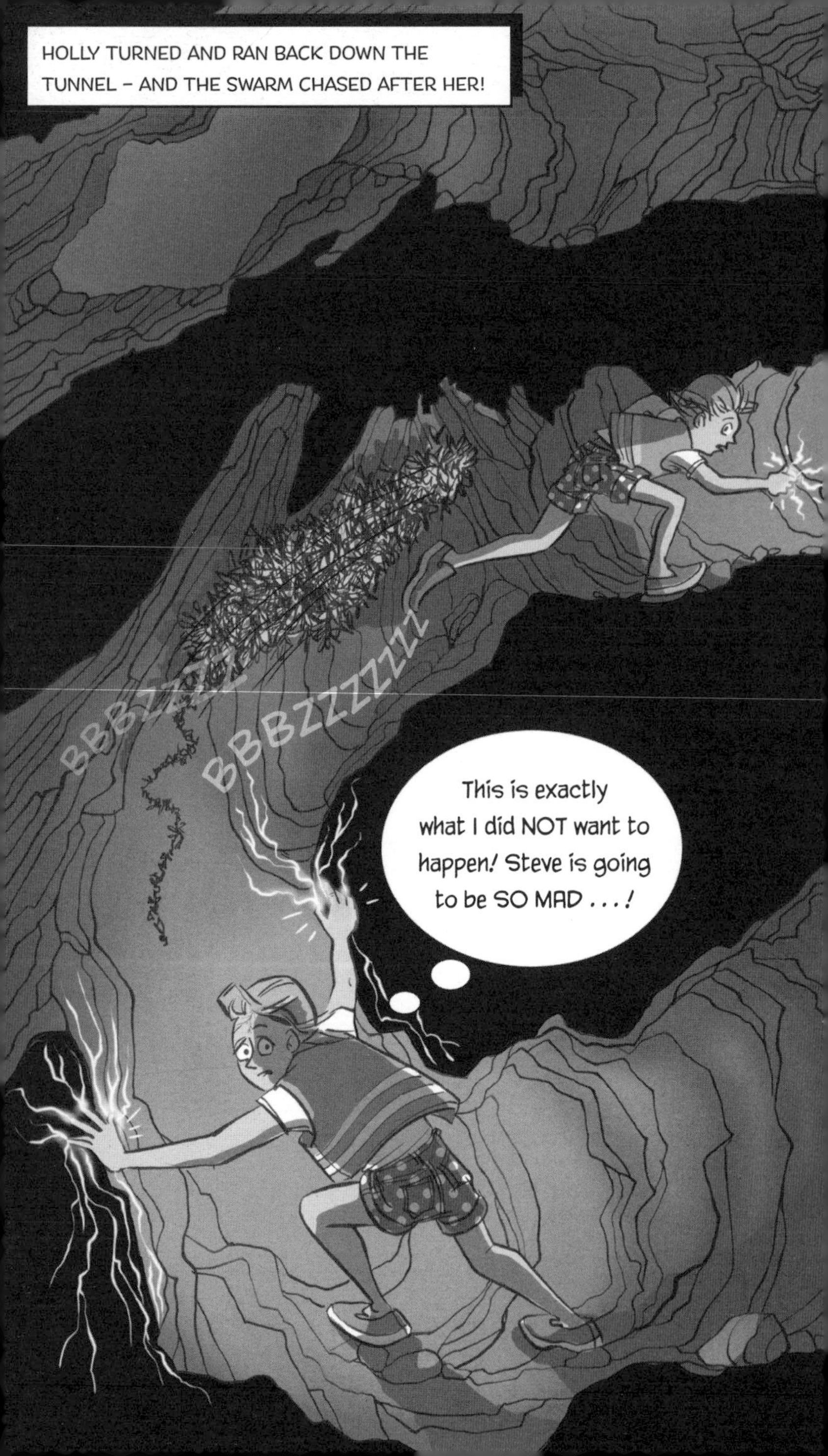
HOLLY TURNED AND RAN BACK DOWN THE TUNNEL – AND THE SWARM CHASED AFTER HER!
BBBZZZZZ
BBBZZZZZZ
This is exactly what I did NOT want to happen! Steve is going to be SO MAD . . . !

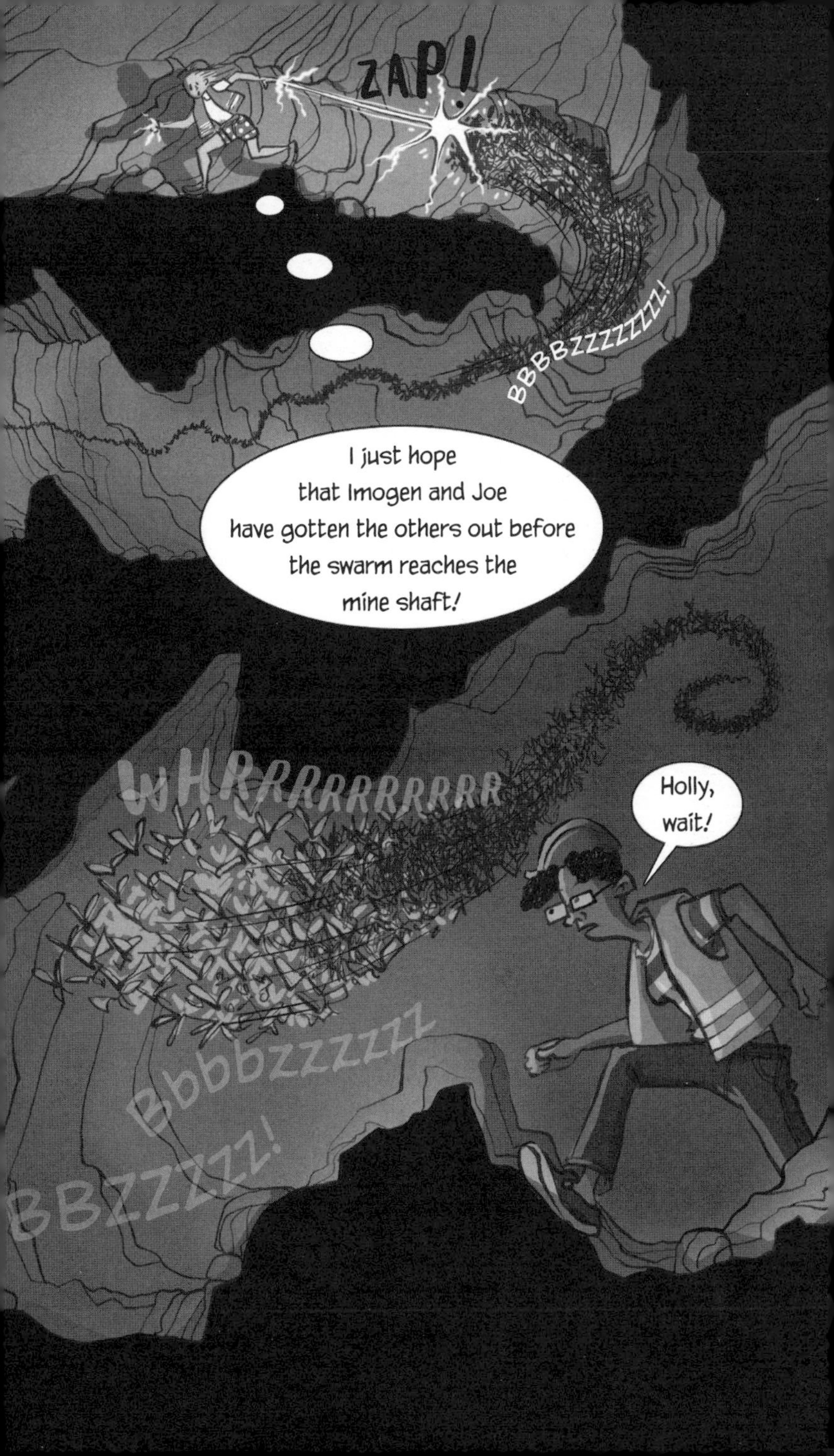
ZAP!
BBBBZZZZZZZ!
I just hope that Imogen and Joe have gotten the others out before the swarm reaches the mine shaft!
WHRRRRRRRRRRR
Holly, wait!
Bbbbzzzzzz
BBZZZZZ!

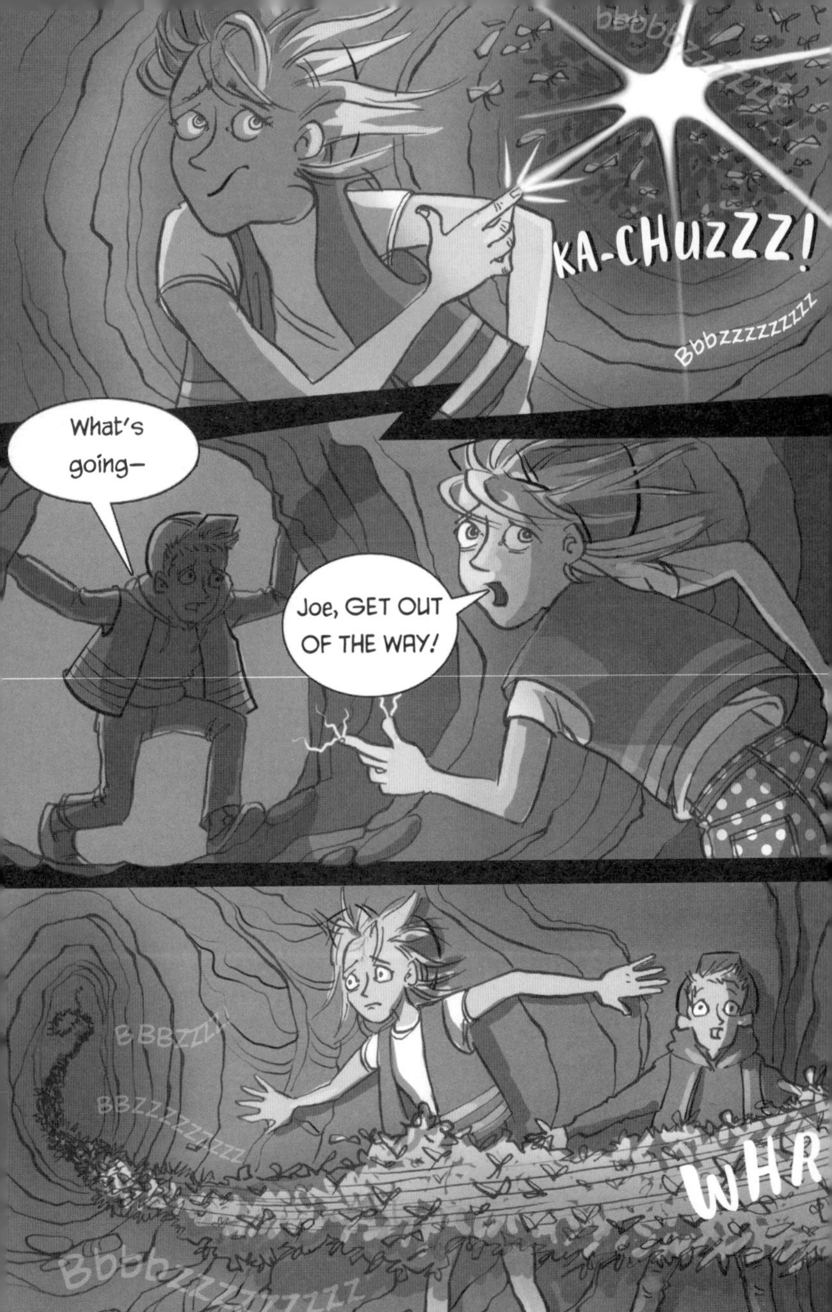
KA-CHUZZZ!
Bbbzzzzzzzzz
What's going—
Joe, GET OUT OF THE WAY!
BBBZZZ!
BBZZZZZZZZZ
WHR
Bbbbzzzzzzzzz

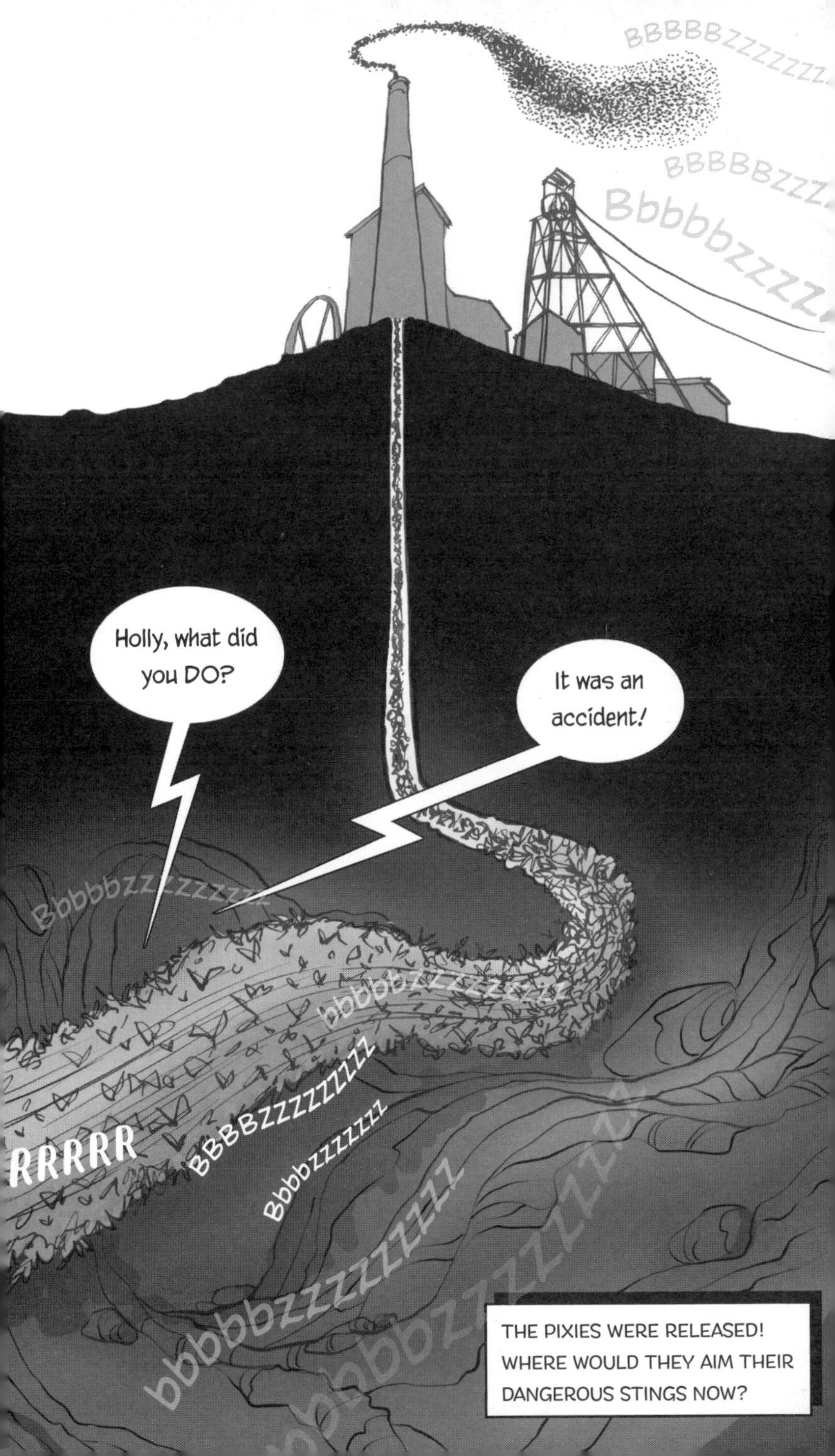
BBBBBZZZZZZZ
BBBBBBZZZZ
Bbbbbbzzzzz
Holly, what did you DO?
It was an accident!
Bbbbbzzzzzzzz
bbbbbzzzzzzzz
BBBBZZZZZZZZZ
RRRRR
Bbbbzzzzzz
bbbbbzzzzzzzz
bbbbbzzzzzzzz
THE PIXIES WERE RELEASED! WHERE WOULD THEY AIM THEIR DANGEROUS STINGS NOW?

CHAPTER 17

I stared up at the clear sky.

"Was that all of them?" Joe asked in a voice that wasn't quite steady.

"I don't know."

"What's happened to Cameron?"

"I don't care." My face felt hot and tight. "We have to find the pixies and destroy them."

"Why did they wake up?" Joe asked. "Did Cameron do it?"

I bit my lip. "Not exactly." How could I tell him it was my fault — that their eyes had opened when my electricity touched them?

To my relief, Joe didn't ask any more. "We can't leave him down here."

I looked at him, frustrated. He glared back.

"Oh, all *right*," I grumbled.

Joe went to the opening of the narrow tunnel and called, "Cameron! Cameron, you OK?"

There was a distant shout and then the sound of footsteps getting closer. Cameron emerged, covered in dust and beaming from ear to ear. "Wasn't that **AMAZING**?" he exclaimed.

I clenched my fists to stop myself from punching him. "Amazing?" I repeated. "We've just let loose a swarm of dangerous robots!"

"Don't worry," Cameron said cheerfully, "there's still a bunch back there in the cave."

My jaw hit the floor. Well, you know, not for real. But I was speechless.

"Where did everyone go?" asked Cameron, looking around.

"Imogen pretended to faint," Joe explained. "So your dad had to cut the tour short. I told him you'd taken Holly down that tunnel and he was really mad, but then Imogen did another faint and he had to take everyone back up to the surface."

Cameron was disappointed. "I wanted to show him the pixies."

"Cameron," I said, through gritted teeth, "the pixies are *dangerous*. Can you imagine what would happen if lots of people got stung? Everyone wanting to take risks? Putting themselves in danger all the time?"

"Oh, lighten up, Holly," said Cameron. "Taking risks is fun! You're just jealous because superheroes have to be all goody-goody."

Joe held me back. "We've got to go," he said. "We have to find that swarm. Can you blast them, Holly?"

I hesitated. "There were a lot of them, Joe. But I can give it a try."

"Let's go." Joe cast a glance at Cameron. "We've got important things to do now. Don't go climbing any more roofs, or Holly might not be there to save you."

"I won't need saving," Cameron said confidently. "I know what I'm doing."

I was so relieved to be out in the fresh air again. I didn't think I'd ever like being underground!

Mike and the other members of the tour party were clustered around Imogen, who was sitting on the ground looking a bit embarrassed. "Holly!" she said.

"Hi!" I said. "Are you all right? I hear you fainted."

"I was just saying I should take her to the hospital to get her checked out," Mike said.

I felt bad for fibbing to him. "Oh, I'm sure she'll be OK. Imogen faints a lot, don't you?"

"Um . . . yeah. Yeah. Low blood pressure."

"Oh." Mike stood up. "Well, if you're sure. I do think you should go back to the camper and rest though."

"I'll take them," Cameron offered. I fumed. It was his fault we were in this mess! If he hadn't gone down that tunnel . . . ! *And if you hadn't followed him*, a little voice in my mind said. I shook my head. There was no point in blaming anyone now. What mattered was what we did next.

We handed back our helmets and headed quickly out of the gates. I filled Imogen in as we went. "They're loose?" she said in alarm. "How many of them?"

"A LOT," I said grimly. "We have to find them."

"Should we call Maverick?"

I hesitated. We'd had strict instructions to stay out of trouble — I cringed at the thought of Steve knowing what had happened. "Not yet," I said. "Let's see if we can fix it." Joe opened his mouth to disagree. "We haven't got time," I said quickly, and he shut it again.

"All right," said Imogen. "Where should we look?"

"They're programmed to attack people," Joe said. "So they'd go where there are lots of people."

"Lots of people . . ." I looked up at the sky. There wasn't a cloud to be seen and it was a beautifully hot day. "The beach!"

"Come on!" yelled Cameron, setting off. "I know a short cut over the rocks!"

CHAPTER 18

Even before we reached the beach, I could tell we were going in the right direction. Screams and shouts were almost drowned out by a loud **BUZZING**. The four of us raced toward the dunes and stopped when we got to the edge of the sand . . .

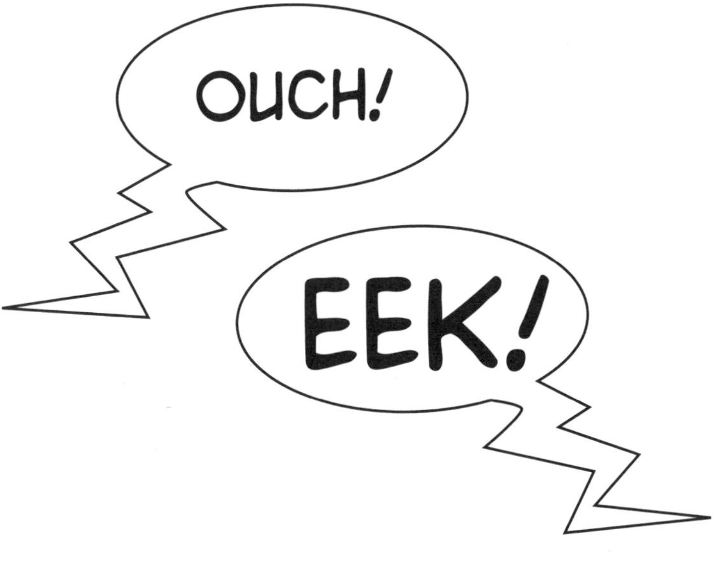
OUCH!
EEK!

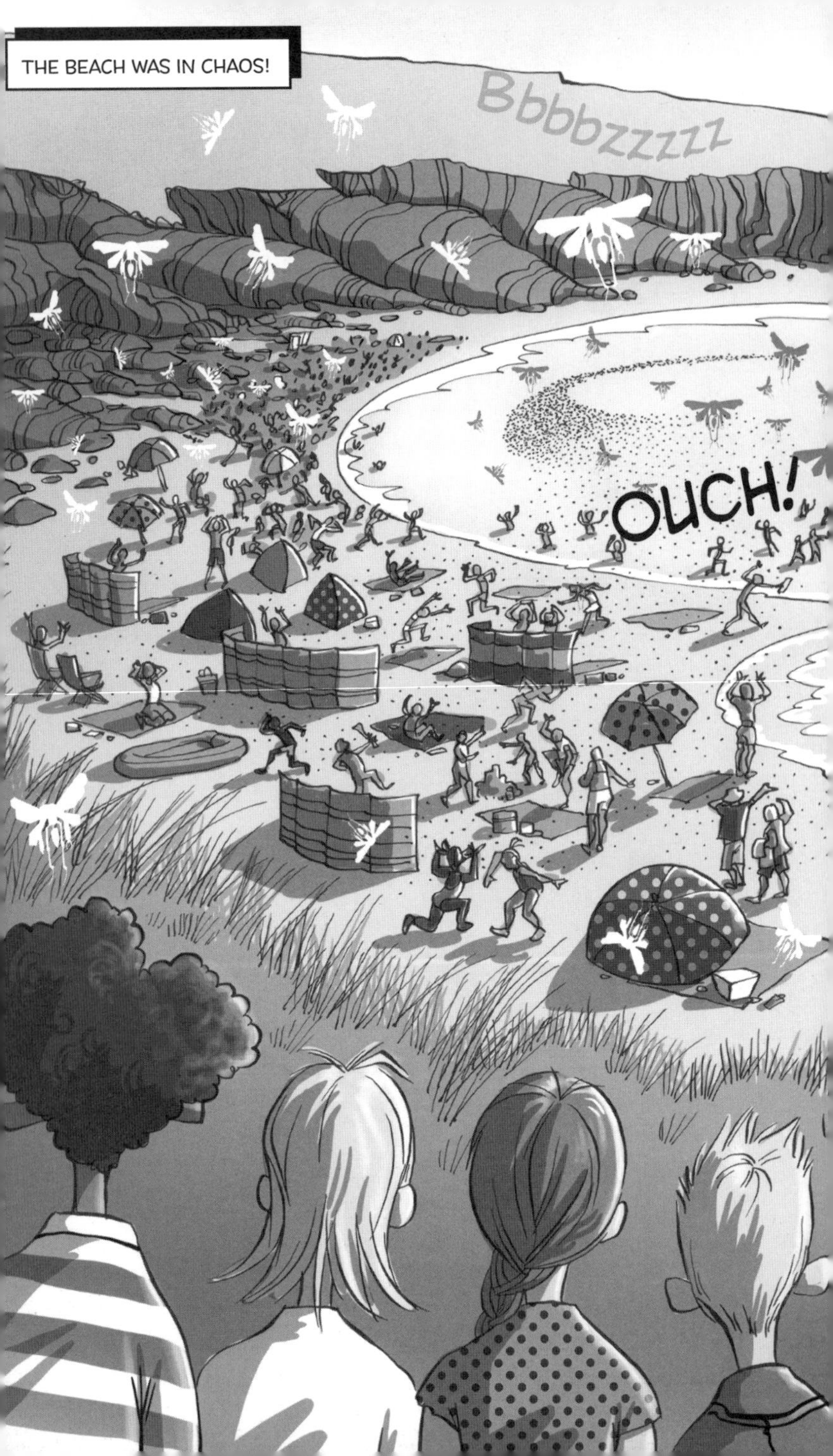
THE BEACH WAS IN CHAOS!
Bbbbzzzzz
OUCH!

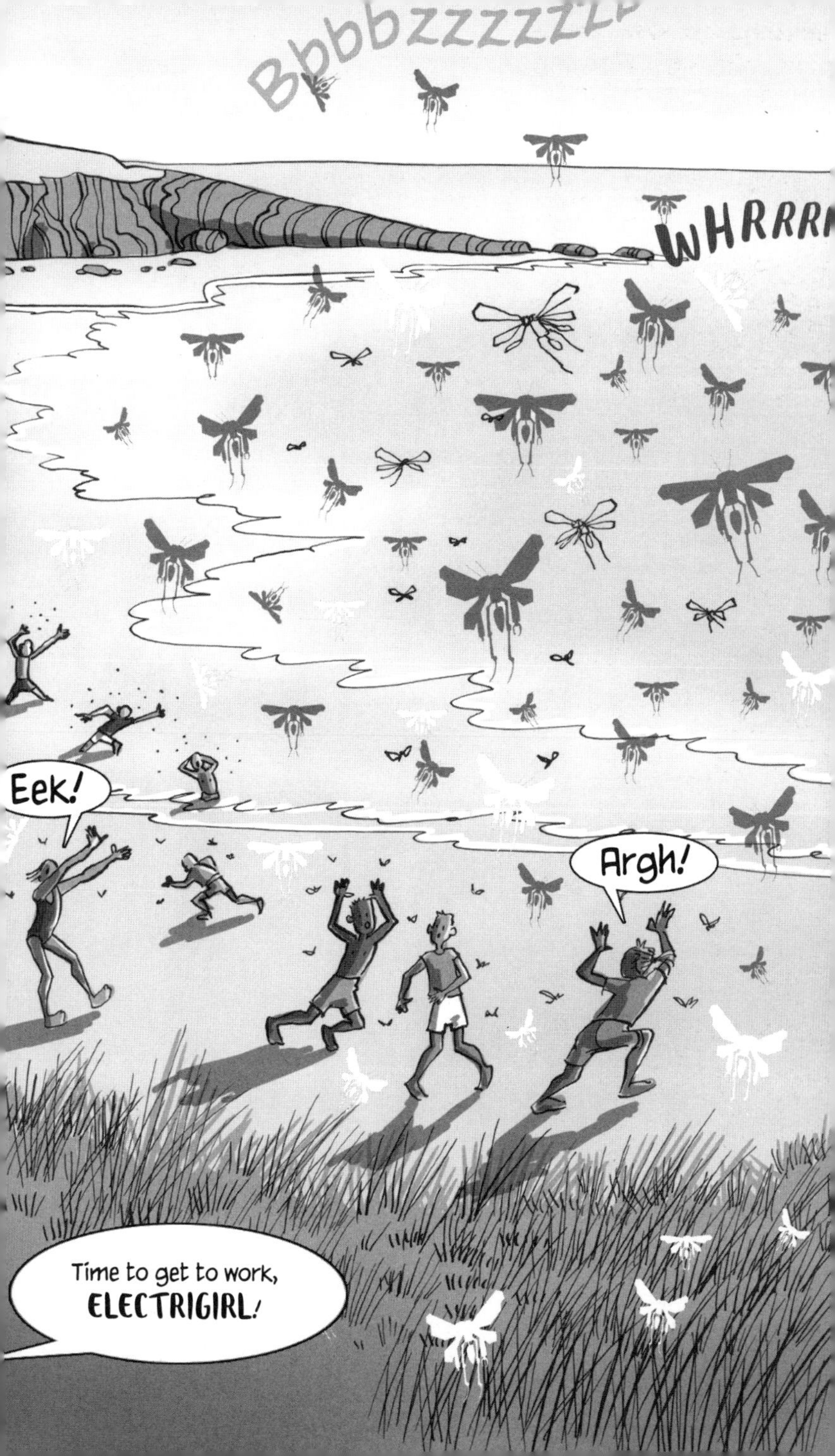
Bbbbzzzzzz
WHRRR
Eek!
Argh!
Time to get to work, ELECTRIGIRL!

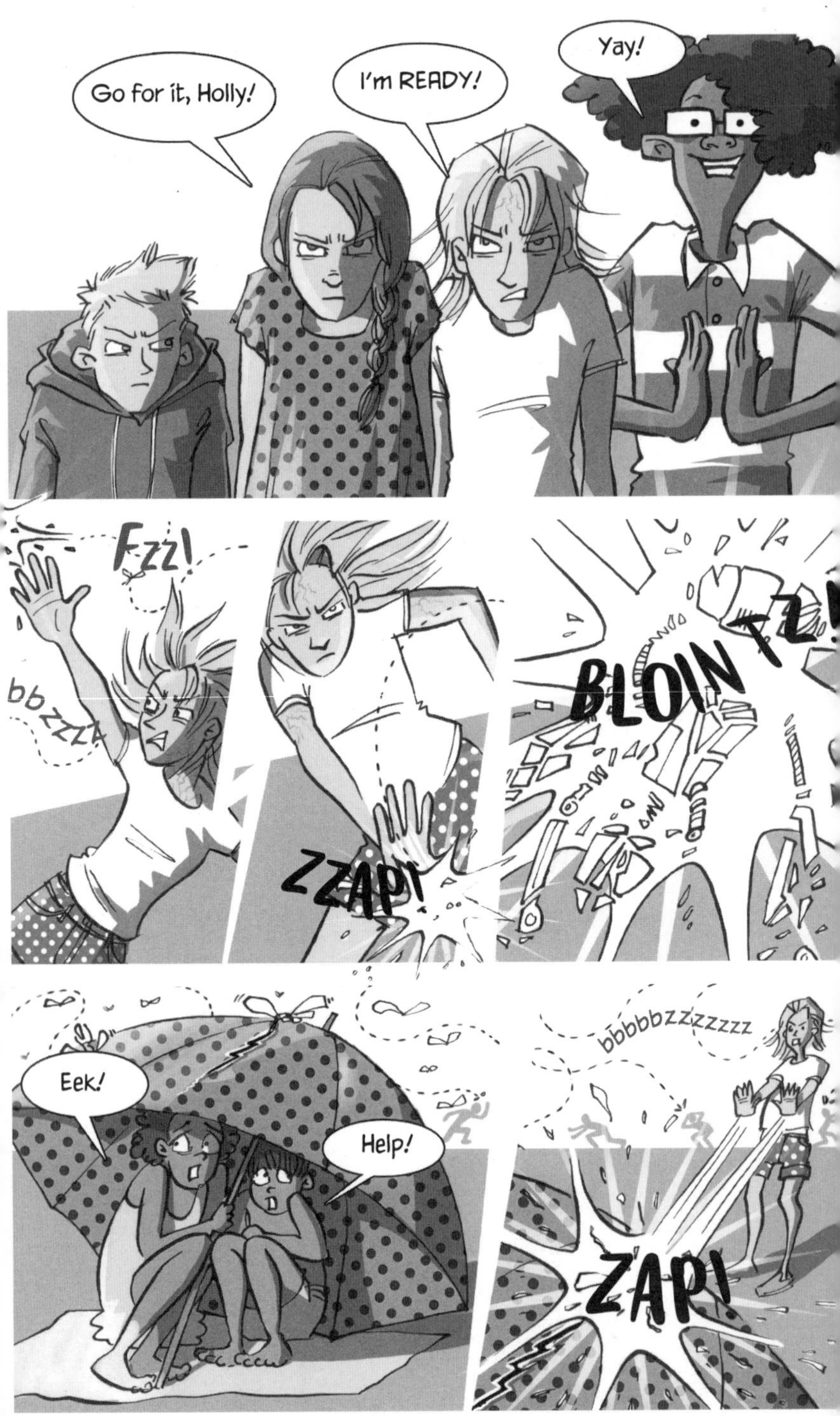
Go for it, Holly!
I'm READY!
Yay!
Fzz!
bbzzzz
ZZAP!
BLOIN
FZ
Eek!
Help!
bbbbbzzzzzzz
ZAP!

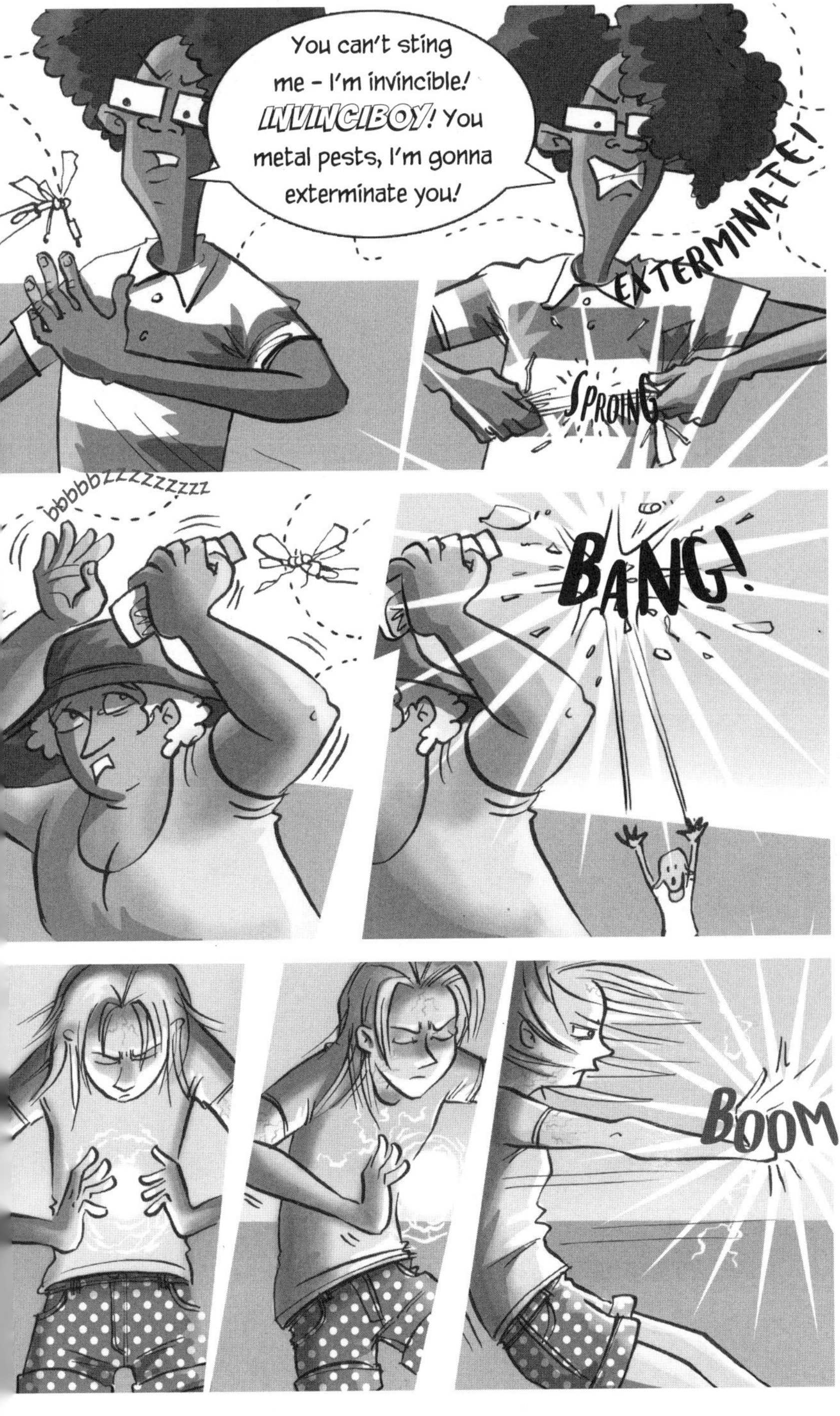
You can't sting me - I'm invincible! INVINCIBOY! You metal pests, I'm gonna exterminate you!
EXTERMINATE!
SPROING
bbbbbzzzzzzzzz
BANG!
BOOM

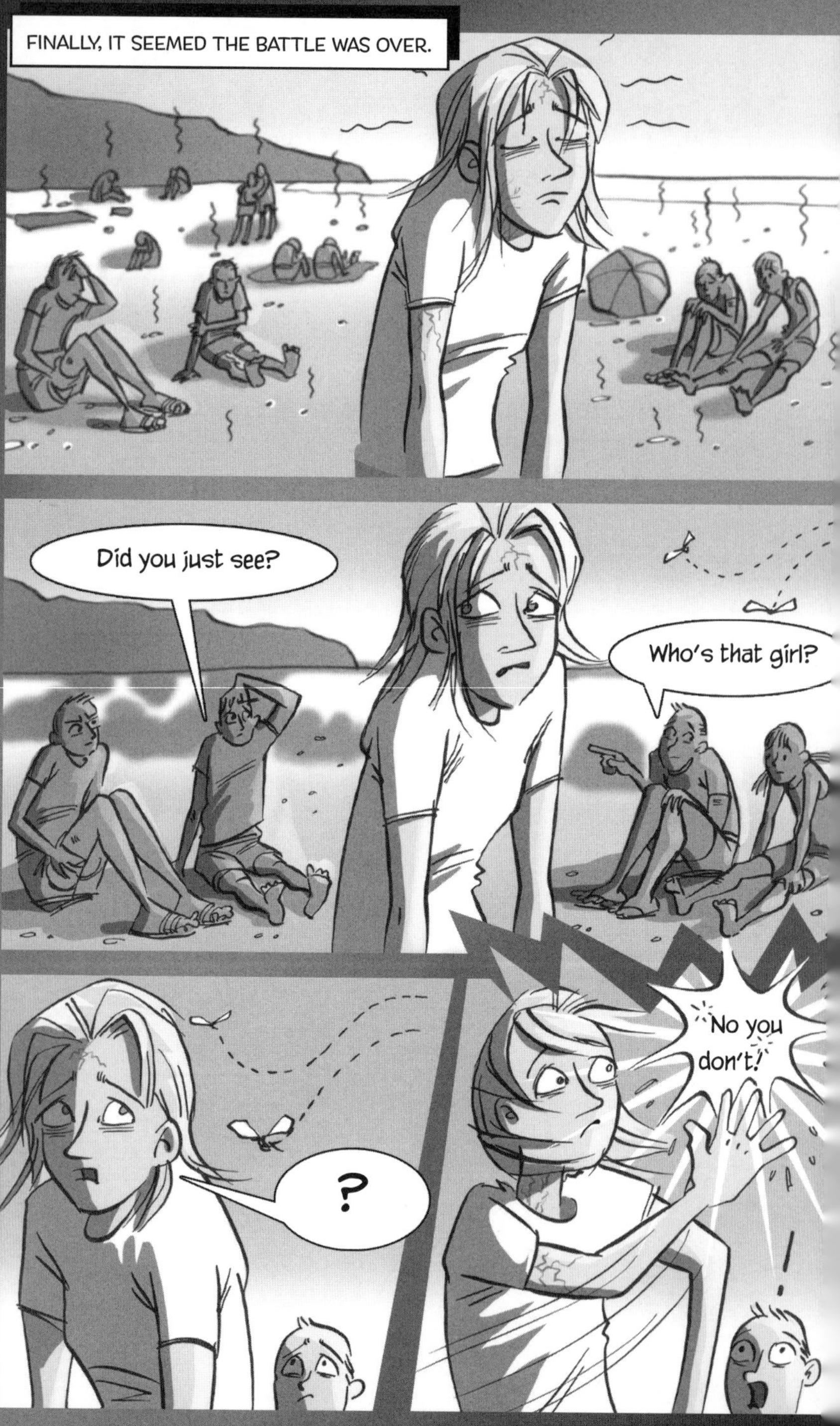
FINALLY, IT SEEMED THE BATTLE WAS OVER.
Did you just see?
Who's that girl?
?
No you don't!
!

As my powers faded again, I became uncomfortably aware of the number of people staring at me. "Oh . . ."

A child came running up. "That was totally *awesome!*" she shouted, her face alight. I noticed a puncture mark on her arm. "Are you a superhero? A real one?"

I didn't know what to say! "Um . . . well . . . sort of . . .," I mumbled. Maybe it was time to seriously consider some kind of disguise for moments like this!

A faint humming reached my ears and I frowned. It sounded like —

A motorbike screeched to a halt at the top of the nearest dune, showering sand over the three people standing closest. Maverick, clad in his black gear, pulled off his helmet to reveal a brightly colored bandana tied around his head. "All right, folks, party's over!" he shouted.

I turned to my brother, raising my eyebrows. He looked guilty. "All right, so I called him! I thought we might need some help."

"Gather round!" Maverick called. "I'm from Homeland Security, and we've had a technology breach. If you could come this way, I'll explain what's going to happen next."

People shuffled forward, rubbing arms and legs and staring, puzzled, at Maverick.

I was puzzled too. What was he going to tell them?

Mav grinned at us and gave a weird kind of wink. I frowned. It looked like he'd blinked both eyes at us instead of just one, like when a child tries to do it. Definitely at odds with his super-cool persona. "Now," he called to the crowd, reaching for something in one of his many jacket pockets, "I understand you'll have a lot of questions, but this projection should help to answer them!" He threw something small into the air. About five hundred pairs of eyes followed it.

Joe grabbed my arm hard. I turned. "**OW**! That —"

There was a blinding flash from above. Joe had his eyes tightly screwed shut. I whirled around again, pulling free. "What was *that*?"

Maverick was coming down the dune toward us. The people, gathered in an untidy bunch, looked around, rubbing their eyes and reaching out to hug each other.

Imogen reached for my hand. "You're my *best* friend, Holly. You know that, don't you?"

"Uh . . ." I said, somewhat surprised.

Cameron took my other hand. "You're my best friend, too. And Imogen. And Joe. Isn't life *amazing*?"

"*Maverick*," I said, "what did you DO?"

He grinned at me as I tried to let go of Cameron's hand. "It's a kind of neural tranquillizer. It uses light receptors in the eyes to trigger synaptic responses in the emotional cortex."

"*What*?"

"It makes people feel happy and spaced out when they look at it," he said.

Joe was chuckling. "*Cool*. I love it."

"How did you know not to look?" I asked.

"Mav signaled to us," he said. "Didn't you see it?"

"That was a signal?" I said. "I thought he was trying to wink!"

My brother rolled his eyes. "Good thing I'm around. We can't have **ELECTRIGIRL** spacing out in times of need."

"Speaking of which," said Mav, surveying the beach, "it looks like you've been busy."

The sand was still littered with the metal bodies of the pixie robots, but the vacationers didn't show the slightest interest in them, heading slowly back to their towels and bags, laughing and hugging each other along the way.

"Clean up time," Mav said. From another pocket he produced a tiny bag. He blew into it and suddenly the whole thing expanded to about seven feet across. "Synthetic net," he explained to me. "It's a polymer — "

"Whatever," I said, shaking free of Imogen and Cameron, who instantly took each other's hands and sat down on the sand to gaze at the sea.

Joe, Mav, and I worked quickly, picking up the pixies as carefully as we could and dropping them into his bag. When the beach was finally clear, Mav straightened up and tied the bag tightly. "Just in case any of them suddenly come back to life," he said, grinning. "The bad ones always come back to life just when you least expect it. I've learned that from watching horror films."

"How are you going to carry them off?" Joe asked, looking at the motorbike, which didn't seem big enough to support the enormous bag of pixies.

"Oh, I'll call for a pickup," Mav said. "Steve'll be delighted we've got so many more specimens to work on. Though it's a shame they spiked so many people while they were out."

"Oh, yeah . . .," I said. "Sorry."

He looked at me more kindly. "Want to tell me what happened?"

Joe and I explained. I even awkwardly confessed what had triggered the wake-up, but Mav seemed less interested in that than their numbers. "**WHOA**! You mean this isn't all of them?"

I shook my head. "Nowhere near."

"This is big, man." Mav sounded almost admiring. "I mean, you've got to hand it to the woman. Nutty as a fruitcake she may be, but **SHE'S GOT AMBITION**!"

CHAPTER 19

It was an hour later, and the four of us and Mav were sitting outside a sea-front cafe in Polcarrow. Within ten minutes of Mav calling for backup, a black pickup truck had roared up the dunes. A beautiful Chinese woman with sleek black hair and sunglasses hopped out, hefted the bag of pixies into the trunk, and drove off, with a nod to Mav, who looked faintly disappointed that she hadn't stopped to chat. "That's Lin," he said with a sigh. "She speaks seven languages and is a black belt in karate. She once knocked me out flat in training. Good times." Joe and I exchanged a glance. Lin sounded **AWESOME**! I made a mental note to ask for karate lessons when we got home.

And now we were just finishing our ice cream and fizzy drinks Mav had insisted on buying for us. I'd thought he was being kind, but then

I noticed that his ice cream was about twice the size of everyone else's — and it was all coffee flavored. With a cup of coffee on the side.

"Isn't it bad for you?" I asked.

Mav waved his spoon at me. "Vital. I can't function without caffeine. Seriously. I have to have an espresso just to get me out of bed in the morning."

Imogen and Cameron had stopped holding hands and being goofy and now just looked mildly embarrassed. "Now that the neural thingy has worn off," I said, "won't the people on the beach remember me blasting all the pixies?"

"Nah," Mav said. "It messes with your short-term memory a bit. Anything that happened on the beach will seem like a dream, if they remember it at all." He took another spoonful of ice cream. "It's a clever gadget, but it's only temporary. Wipes out a few minutes, that's all."

"Did you blast all the pixies then?" Imogen asked, puzzled.

"Well," I said, "yeah — I did, mostly. Don't you remember?"

"Yes. No. Not sure." She grinned at me. "Good job."

"No word from Steve yet?" Joe asked.

Mav patted his pocket. "I'll tell you as soon as I get anything. Though I don't think he's going to be thrilled about this."

"No . . ." I looked down guiltily.

"Well, I think it's brilliant," Imogen said. "I mean, last time, I was strapped into an evil machine and had my mind warped, and I didn't even know what was going on until it was nearly over. This time, I'm in at the start, and we've got a real chance of bringing down **Macavity**!"

I stared at her. "What do you mean? What chance? We don't even know where she is!"

"We'll find her," Imogen said confidently. "And when we do . . . **BAM**!" She smacked her spoon on the table.

"What, you're going to hit her with a spoon?" I said sarcastically.

Imogen shot me a look. "No, we're going to bring her DOWN. Permanently."

A strange suspicion crossed my mind. "Imogen, are you OK? You sound . . . different."

"What do you mean? I'm fine."

"She's right," Cameron said. "This **Professor** isn't going to mess with us. Not now that we're invincible!"

I groaned. "*Please* tell me you haven't been stung, Imogen."

She shifted on her seat. "Holly, I'm fine. It hardly even hurt."

"Show me," I demanded.

She gave an exasperated sigh and stood up. On her right knee, a red mark showed up against her pale skin. "I feel fine," she insisted.

I glanced at Mav. "Not surprising," he said to me. "Given the number of pixies swarming around. You were lucky not to be stung, too."

"Those pixies!" Joe shook his head. "They need to be destroyed. Holly, you should go down into the mine and just blow them all up. Then they can't do any more damage."

I felt sick and dizzy. "Oh no, Joe, not you too . . ."

"Hey," Joe said, "who wants to try walking along that railing over there?" He pointed to a thin rail that ran along the edge of the walkway by the sea.

"Me!" Imogen and Cameron shouted at the same time.

Then all three of them got up and ran across the road, without even bothering to look for traffic. There was a squealing of brakes and some very rude language from a driver, but fortunately no screams of pain.

I put my head in my hands. "I can't look. They've all been infected. What am I going to do?"

The James Bond theme suddenly started playing from Mav's jacket. He reached in and pulled out a slim black phone. "Yup?" he said.

Across the road, Imogen and Joe were fighting to be the first onto the railing, whereas Cameron had run along to the next break in the wall and was practicing jumping across the gap. He fell heavily, scraping his leg, but in the next minute had bounded to his feet and was trying again. I covered my eyes.

"Yeah, I know," Mav was saying, "there's loads of them. But at least you've got more venom to help synthesize the antidote . . . I dunno how many people were on the beach. Maybe four hundred? Most of them got stung, I'd guess, before Holly zapped the robots . . . Yeah, that's right, more of them down in the mine . . . Are you *sure*?"

I looked up, aware that the tone in Maverick's voice had changed. "No," he said, "it's not that I don't think she can do it, but . . . yeah, I'll tell her. What? . . . Oh. Um, I used the visual tranquilizer." He held the phone away from his ear, wincing as the voice on the other end suddenly became loud enough for me to hear that it was very, very angry. In a small pause, Mav interjected, "But it's not *permanent*. I *meant* to sign it out . . . Yeah. Bye." He hung up and shrugged ruefully at me. "They don't like me borrowing stuff from the lab without asking. I wasn't authorized to use the tranq, and now I've got to fill out a report. I hate writing."

"What do you have to tell me?" I asked. "What don't you think I can do?"

For the first time since we'd met, Maverick looked uncomfortable. "Look, you could just say you're not going to do it. Though obviously that might cause a bit of bad feelings —"

"What am I supposed to do?" I demanded.

Mav sighed. "They want you to go into the mines and destroy the rest of the robots. First thing tomorrow morning."

CHAPTER 20

Mom was up and about the next morning, her migraine much improved. She felt my forehead anxiously. "Are you OK? You're pale."

"I didn't sleep very well," I admitted.

"Try eating something," she advised. I did try, eating some toast, but every mouthful I took felt like cardboard.

"I saw a poster for the fair over in Trewissick," Mom said. "This afternoon — we should go. It's got some big rides."

"Oh, *yes*," Imogen and Joe chorused enthusiastically.

Mom smiled. "I didn't know you were into rides, Imogen."

Imogen nodded. "I wasn't, but now I am. The bigger the better!"

Mom glanced at me. "Hopefully you'll feel better later, Holly. Why don't the three of you find something quiet to do this morning?"

Imogen shot me a look and then said, "That's a good idea. We could stay here and read. I've got my sketchbook."

Mom nodded. "Excellent idea. I've got plans but I'll only be out for a couple of hours. We could take the car over to Trewissick for lunch and then go on to the fair. What do you think?"

"Sounds great," said Joe.

While Mom brushed her teeth, Imogen leaned over to me. "That worked out well, didn't it?" she asked cheerfully in a low voice. "It gives you time to go down in the mine this morning and . . . *you know* . . ." She mimed, **BOOM**!

I bit my lip. "Yeah. Boom. Right."

"Don't worry, I'll come with you," she added brightly.

"*No!*" I said, horrified. With no sense of danger, Imogen would be a liability in the mine.

Her face fell. "I was just offering. Because I know you don't like it down there."

"Thanks," I said. "That's really kind of you, but I'll be OK. Maverick will be there."

"He is *so* cool," Imogen sighed, and her face went all kind of dreamy. "Do you think he'd let me ride on his motorbike?"

"No," I said shortly. "He's in enough trouble over the tranquillizer as it is."

"The what?"

"The thing he used on the beach. Oh, you won't remember."

"Do you think he gets into trouble a lot?" Imogen asked.

I hesitated. Was that why Steve had assigned him to us? To get Mav off his back? "I don't know."

"Wonder what the most dangerous thing is that he's done," mused Imogen, a light in her eyes. "I'll ask him."

"You're not coming," I told her. "You have to stay here. It's not safe."

She sulked. "You're such a spoilsport."

How I wished I had the antidote right there and then to turn Imogen back into the friend I knew!

"You can help me," Joe told her. "I'm designing a **BOMB**."

I was horrified. "A *bomb*? Joe, are you totally insane?"

He looked offended. "It's not insane. We need to protect ourselves against **Macavity**. This would be lightweight and portable. Like a grenade. But I'm not very good at drawing."

"I can draw!" exclaimed Imogen.

He nodded. "If you can do the diagrams, I can make the prototype. It's really easy to get a hold of explosive materials if you know how."

I couldn't believe what I was hearing. "Joe, you could get into SO much trouble. You can go to jail for making a bomb!" I put my head in my hands. "How can I go out now? I'll come back to find you've blown yourselves up experimenting!"

"Honestly, sis, I'm not an idiot," Joe said crossly. "I'm supposed to be your *mentor*."

"Not while you're infected with the venom," I told him sharply. "I can't trust a word you say. You've gone bonkers — both of you."

Imogen took my hand and squeezed it. "Holly, I'm still me. I know we've been stung, but honestly, it doesn't feel that scary. Whatever this stuff is, I just feel more *alive* than ever. Like I want to do everything, try everything, because we only get one life, don't we?"

I blinked tears away. "I don't want you to die."

She laughed. "You are funny. I don't want to die either! I want to *live*!"

Mom came out of the little bathroom, and I wiped my eyes quickly so she wouldn't see. "OK, kids," she said. "I'm off — got my cell if you need me. I'm grabbing a couple things in town and then meeting up with Mike and a few others. If you can't reach me, Julie can reach Mike. Stay here, OK? Holly, you need to rest. Play a board game or something." She smiled. "See you soon."

I tried to stretch my mouth into a smile.

The door closed. "All right," I said, and *almost* managed to keep my voice sounding normal. "I'd better go."

Imogen gave me a hug. "Knock 'em dead," she said, which didn't make me feel any better.

Joe did a fist bump. "Make sure there's nothing left of the little critters," he said in a terrible American accent.

"Please," I said. "Please don't do anything crazy. Not until I get back, all right?"

They both gave me a thumbs-up, which didn't reassure me in the slightest. "Don't worry about us. Everything's going to be fine!"

I took a deep breath. The sooner I got there, the sooner I'd be back.

I opened the door, made sure Mom was no longer in sight, and started off toward, if not certain death, then certain terror — which was almost as bad.

CHAPTER 21

The gate to the mine was padlocked, but I simply climbed over it and into the silent grounds. The tall chimney and the crumbling buildings felt eerie even in the bright sunshine of the day. There was no sign of Maverick, though a big black car was parked to one side of the building. Was that him? I headed over, but the car was empty.

I waited a bit longer, checking my watch. It was just after nine o'clock. Tours started here at ten, so I didn't have all that long to get down and do what I needed to do. Would Mav have gone down into the mine without me? He had only said, "see you there." Maybe "there" meant down in the tunnel?

I shifted from foot to foot in an agony of indecision. I hadn't wanted to come, but now that I was here, I just wanted to get it over with as quickly as possible. I couldn't afford to wait any longer. Hopefully the car was Mav's and he was already in the mine, waiting for me. If he wasn't . . . well, I would have to get going and do my job, right? It wasn't like I didn't know what to do. And every minute I was away from Imogen and Joe increased the likelihood they'd do something dangerous.

The thought galvanized me into action. I ran to the elevator shaft. Grabbing a hard hat and a head lamp from the crate, I yanked open the metal doors of the elevator and jumped inside. A thick cable hung down from the wall with two buttons — one for down, one for up. I pressed the "down" button, scrambling to get my hat on at the same time.

Nothing happened. I pressed the "up" button. Nothing.

Did they switch the electricity off in this place when they weren't using it? Or had the elevator broken? But then how would Maverick have gotten down?

I didn't have time for all this . . .

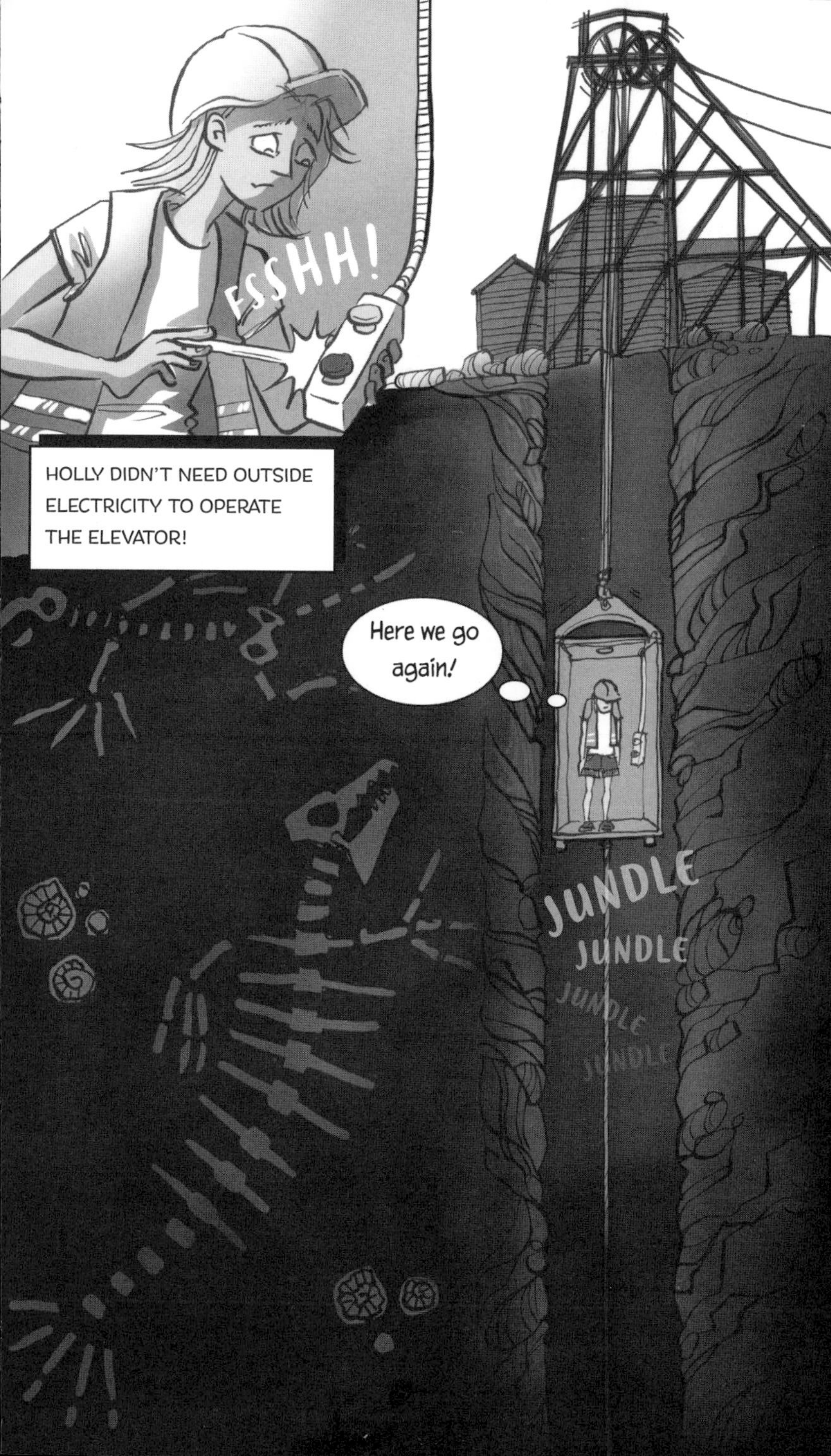
FSSHH!
HOLLY DIDN'T NEED OUTSIDE ELECTRICITY TO OPERATE THE ELEVATOR!
Here we go again!
JUNDLE
JUNDLE
JUNDLE
JUNDLE

I had forgotten just how deep the mine shaft was. It felt like FOREVER before I reached the bottom.

There was no Maverick. *Where was he? Had he decided I didn't need any help after all?*

There's no point asking yourself stupid questions, I told myself sternly. *You're on your own*, **ELECTRIGIRL**. *Get moving and get out.*

Which tunnel was it? There were two!

I chose the one on the right and headed along, trying not to think about ANYTHING AT ALL, especially not the TONS OF ROCK above my head that would kill me instantly if they fell down.

And THEN up ahead, I heard a sound. Someone was talking. I hurried toward it. Mav!

But as the voice grew louder my steps faltered, and all the hairs on my neck stood up.

It wasn't Mav.

It was another voice I knew well.

A voice that had no expression in it at all. And even though I couldn't make out the words, even though it was still only a murmur carrying through the dark, dusty air of the tunnel, I knew it instantly.

It was HER voice.

CHAPTER 22

Professor Macavity. The person I was most frightened of in the whole world. She was here, in the mine! I stopped, gasping, reaching for the walls to steady myself. My head whirled. Was Mav down here too? Had she kidnapped him? Was he — oh no — was he *working* for her all along? Was I walking into a trap?

The voice murmured on, low and insistent. I knew I had no choice. I was down here now and if I ran away . . . well, who would destroy the pixies then? I had to go on. I'd known that one day we'd meet again. Her message had promised it:

I KNOW WHO YOU ARE AND WHAT YOU ARE.

I DON'T FORGET MY ENEMIES.

ONE DAY, YOU AND I WILL MEET AGAIN, ELECTRIC GIRL

It was **Macavity** who had given me my superhero name. It was thanks to the **CyberSky** cell phone tower that I had powers in the first place: the lightning streaking across the sky that day had crashed into it and then blasted me unconscious. I still didn't know how or why.

But here she was. And this time, I wasn't imagining it.

I switched off the headlamp as I crept closer. I didn't want to be discovered until the last possible moment. I made as little noise as possible as I reached the shaft open to the sky. It was the one that had the opening to the narrow, angled tunnel where the pixies were hidden. **Macavity**'s voice echoed from that tunnel. She was in there with the pixies.

I stepped in and began to creep forward.

The **Professor's** voice was louder now, clearer. ". . . weren't ready yet. And now the whole project has had to be brought forward because some of them swarmed too early . . ."

I felt a grim satisfaction that I had already destroyed a large number of the pixies.

". . . No, the government covered everthing up. At least, I assume so. We can't wait now. The risk of discovery is too great. Send them out today — otherwise the whole experiment is wasted."

Another voice spoke — a man's. But not, to my enormous relief, Maverick's. It said, "What about the girl? Has she been infected?"

"Not as far as we can tell," **Macavity** said in that gray monotone that sent shivers down my spine. "It does not matter. It's an unfortunate coincidence that she happened to be here. My intel failed to warn me — the officer concerned has been . . . dealt with. But Holly Sparkes won't get in my way a second time."

I gasped, and then clapped a hand over my own mouth. All those times the others told me I was crazy to think that **Macavity** was obsessed with bringing me down — **HERE WAS PROOF**!

"She's just a girl," the other voice suggested.

Macavity snapped back, "She is *not* just a girl! She's an extraordinary creation." Her voice slowed. "It's a shame she isn't working for me. I have wondered whether she might be persuadable, given the right circumstances . . ."

Never! I wanted to shout. I would never work for you! You're a dangerous evil lunatic! I pressed a hand to my mouth to stop myself from making a noise.

"We could wait until the fuss has died down," the other voice said.

"No!" **Macavity** was sharp again. "I need a proper demonstration. Something big to show how people can be persuaded into mass action. The venom is strong, but the human sense of self-preservation is hard to overcome. I need to show that it only takes one person to lead the way — and then the rest will follow like sheep. Or lemmings. **You jump, I jump**, as the saying goes." An amused tone had crept into her voice.

The man hesitated before saying, "It's a lot of people to use in a demonstration."

The **Professor** made a noise of contempt. "It's necessary. Then I can sell this invention to the highest bidder. Imagine how many governments will be interested! Imagine how many dictators could take control of their countries if their population is self-destructing! The value is immeasurable."

"I'm sure you've set a price," said the other voice dryly.

There was a low bubbling noise that I'd heard once before. It made my blood run cold again.

She was laughing.

And that made me take the final steps into the cave, out of the tiny tunnel, sparks tingling around my fingers. The two figures standing in the cave, surrounded by walls of glittering pixie wings, turned in surprise.

"Hello, **Professor Macavity**," I said.

"WE MEET AGAIN."

CHAPTER 23

As far as opening lines go, it wasn't very original, I admit. But it felt right to say it. And the effect on the **Professor** was immediate. Her eyes narrowed to gray slits, and her hands tensed into fists. I imagined those square-cut nails digging into her palms. She looked exactly as I remembered her: gray suit, gray hair cut into that straight bob, gray shoes. Angles and edges; nothing soft about her at all.

"Holly Sparkes," she said, and there was almost an inflection of surprise in her voice. "Or should I say **ELECTRIGIRL**?"

"Either will do." *Yeah,* I was thinking, *I can do this. Joe would tell me to stand up to her. That's what I'm going to do!* "Call off the experiment," I said. The man standing behind her was short with a thick beard. He held an electronic tablet and looked alarmed to see me.

The **Professor** did not look alarmed. Instead, her eyebrows rose into triangular points. "I don't think so."

"People are going to **DIE**," I told her. "Do you really want their blood on your hands?"

She did that eerie bubbling laugh again. "Have you been taking lessons in superhero language? Or are you naturally overdramatic?"

My face went red. "If people die because of the pixies, it'll be your fault."

"Pixies?" Now she was really laughing. Her mouth opened wide as the horrible sound came out. "I never thought anyone would seriously believe that. My experiment has been more successful than I imagined." The laughing stopped. Her eyes narrowed. "And I can imagine a *lot*, Holly Sparkes."

"Yeah?" I said. "So can I. I can imagine you in a prison somewhere. With — with dripping walls and no toilet. And no window." I suddenly realized I was describing some kind of dungeon, or possibly Azkaban. British prisons probably weren't like that.

"Your imagination never was your strong point," said the **Professor**. "How is your clever friend, by the way?"

"Her name is Imogen," I said, feeling anger rising. "And she's absolutely fine, no thanks to you and your pixie minions."

Professor Macavity's eyes gleamed. "She's been *stung*? Interesting. I'd be fascinated to study the effect on her brain, given the changes I made on it through the cell phone —"

I was furious. "She is NOT some kind of body you can just experiment on!"

The **Professor** smiled. "Everyone is an experiment. Even you, **ELECTRIGIRL**." She gave a quick sigh. "I really don't have time to chat. Goodbye, Miss Sparkes. There's nothing you can do now. In only seconds, you'll know *exactly* what it's like to have that lust for danger . . . and then you won't be my problem anymore."

As she turned and headed to the farthest corner of the cave, the man with the beard tapped on the tablet. Instantly hundreds of eyes gleamed green in the darkness. And I heard the sound of thousands of synthetic wings unfurling.

Oh no, I thought. No you don't. Not while I'M here . . .

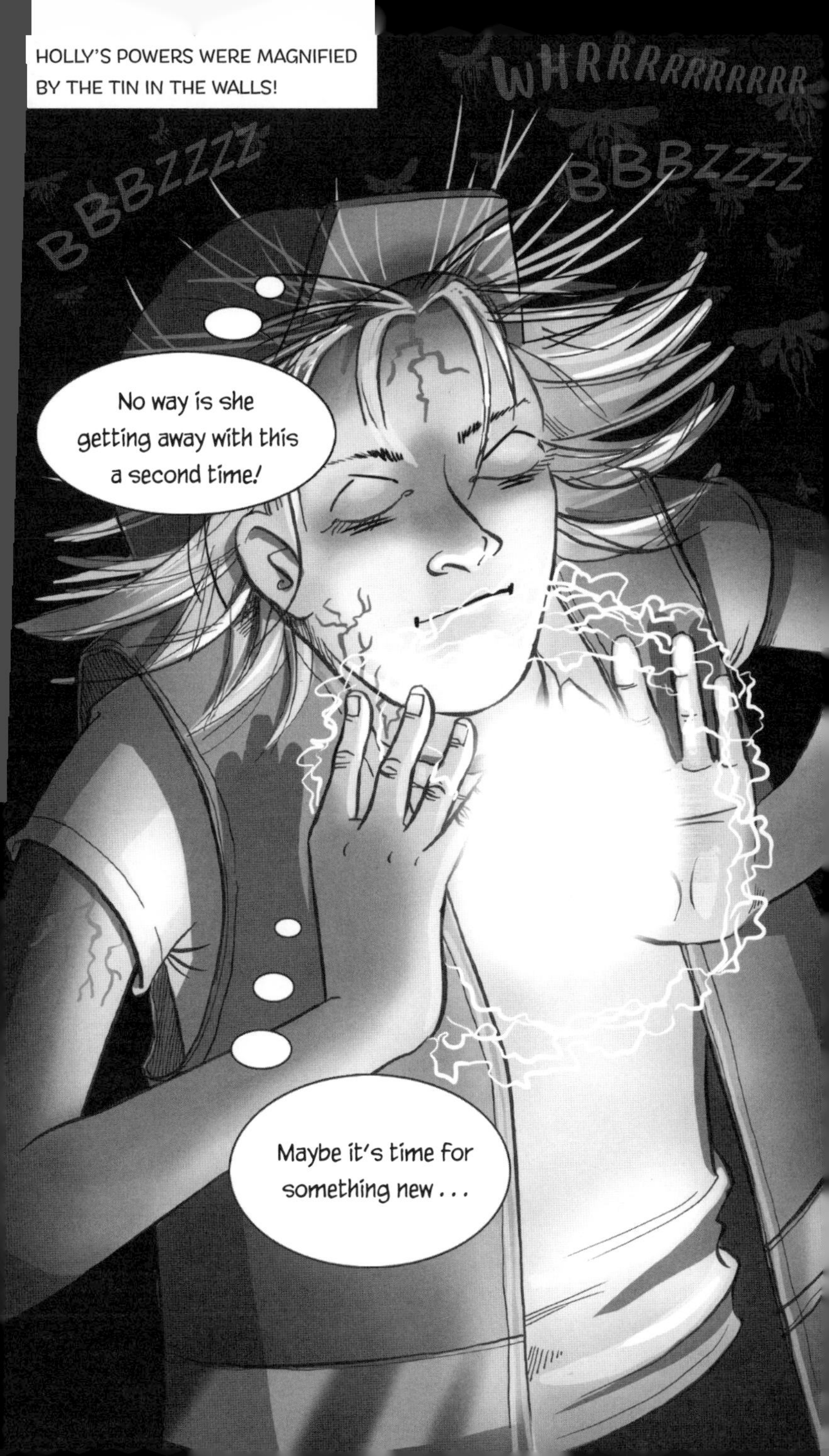
HOLLY'S POWERS WERE MAGNIFIED BY THE TIN IN THE WALLS!
WHRRRRRRRRRRR
BBBZZZZ
BBBZZZZ
No way is she getting away with this a second time!
Maybe it's time for something new . . .

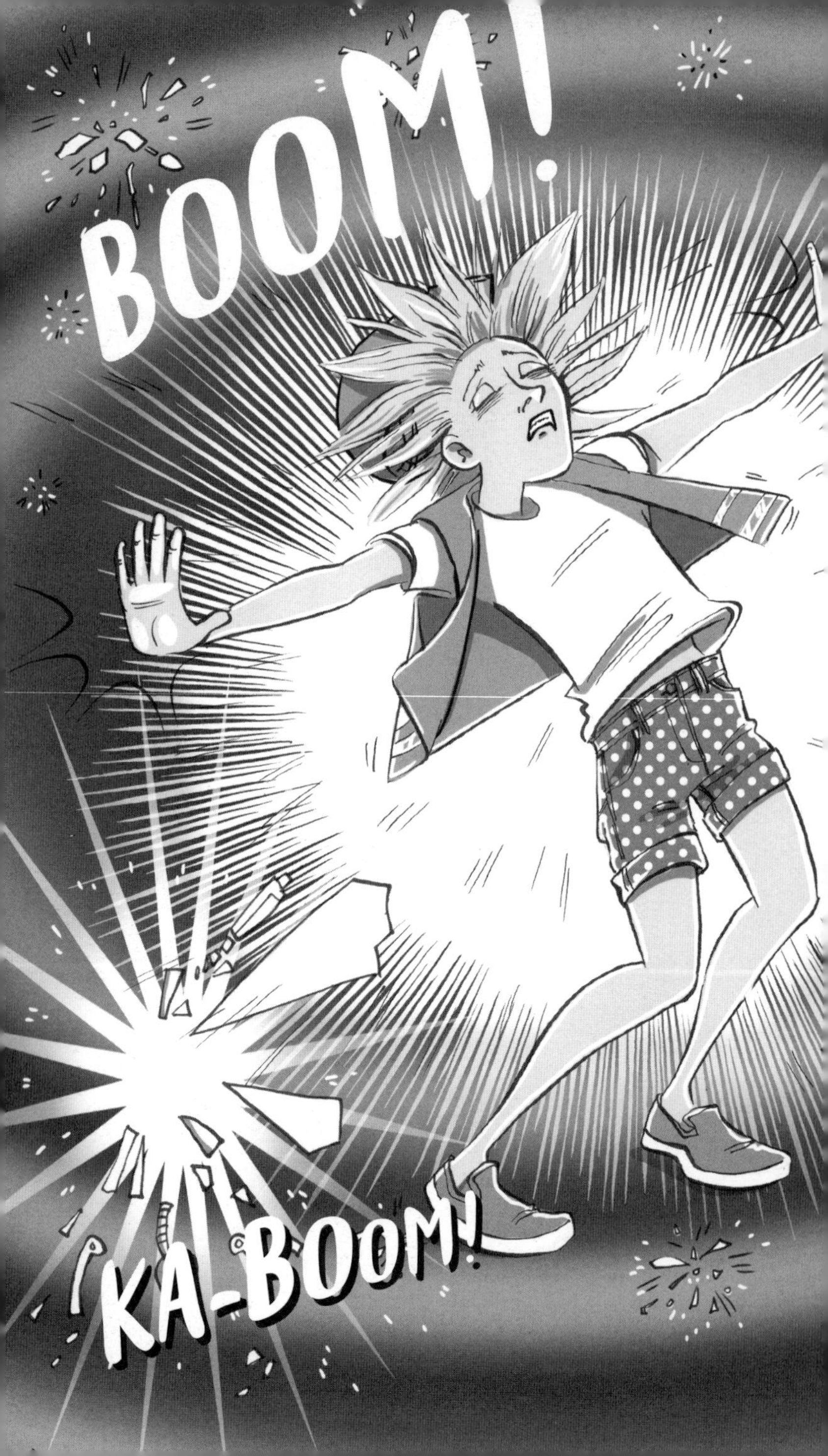
BOOM!
KA-BOOM!

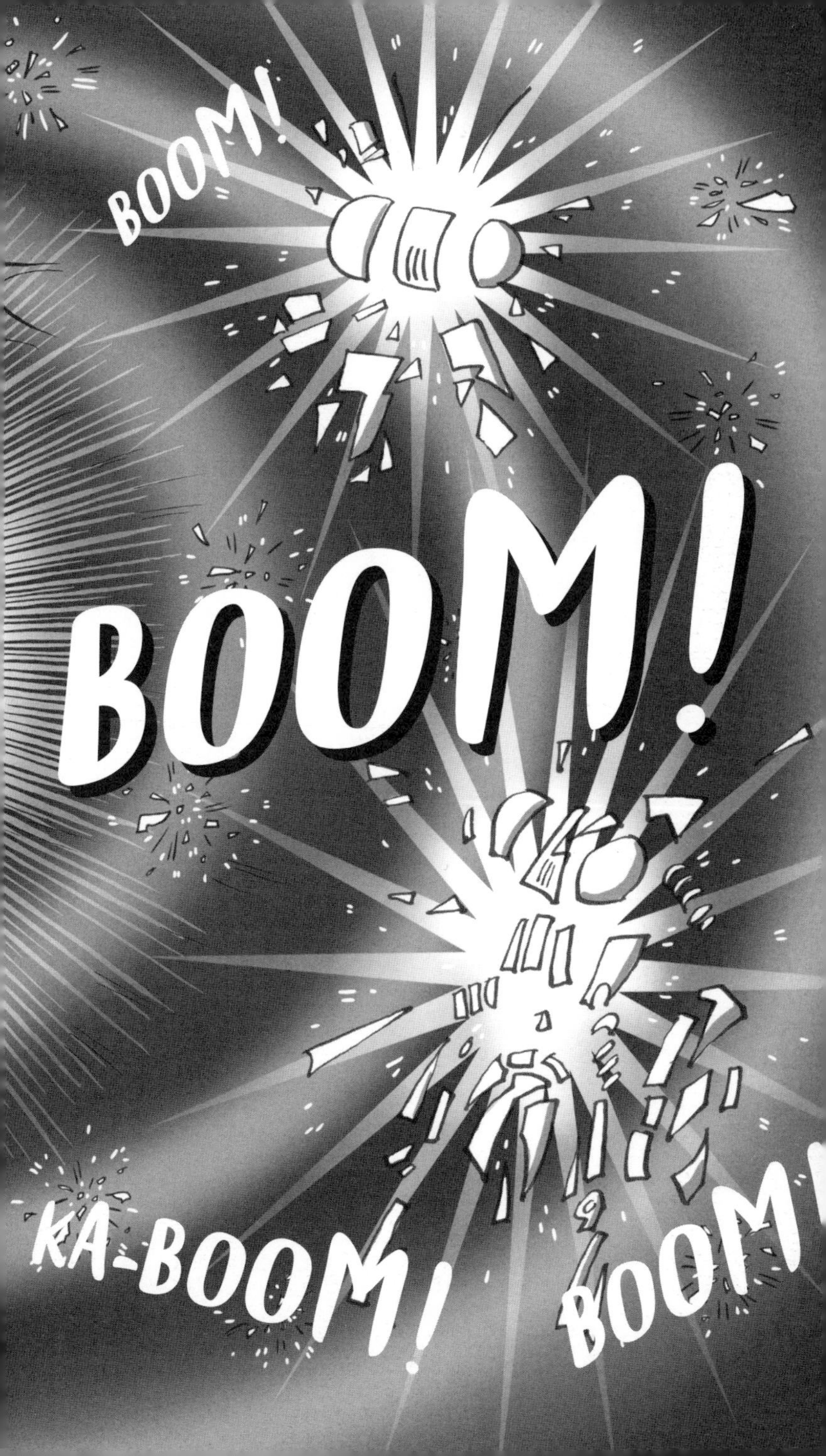
BOOM!
BOOM!
KA-BOOM!
BOOM!

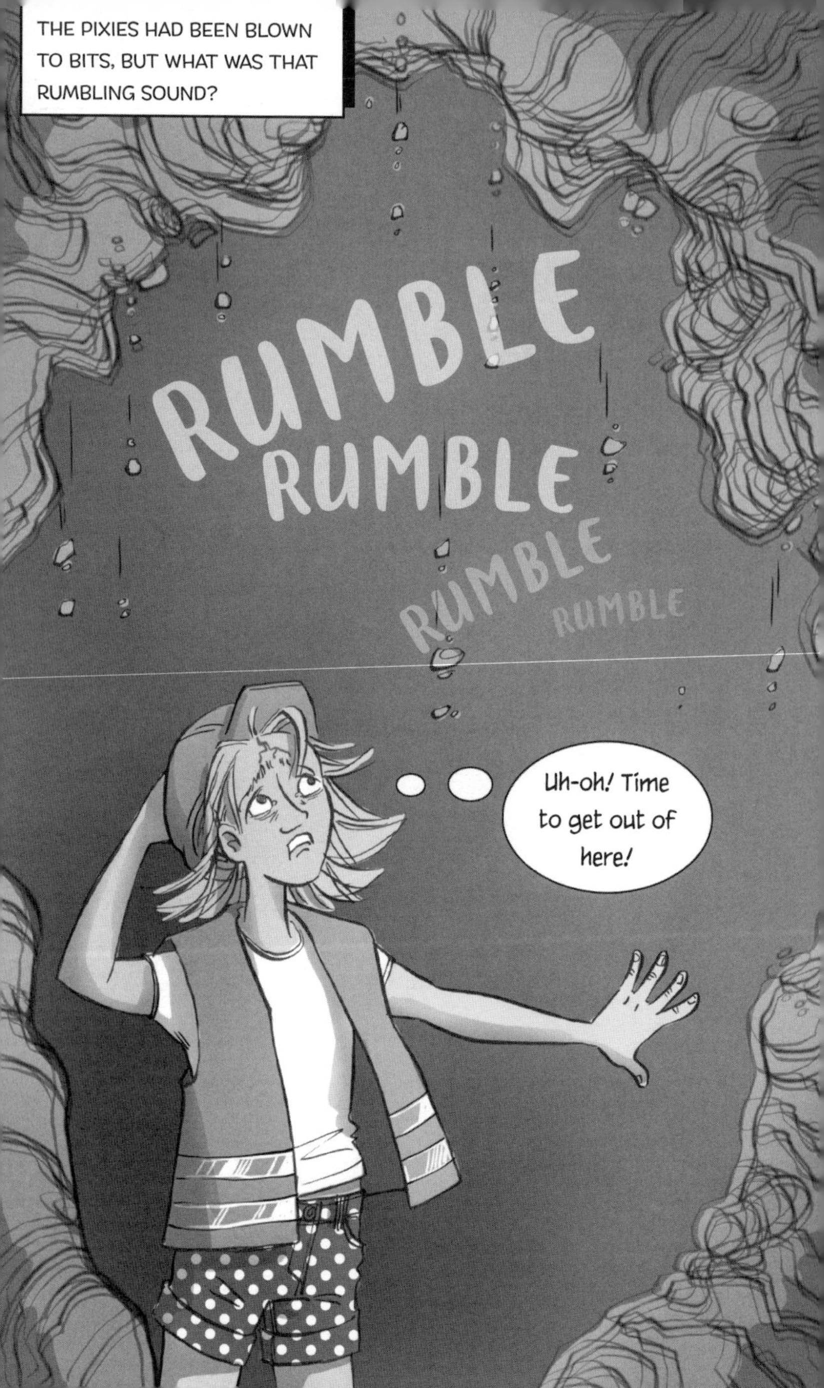
THE PIXIES HAD BEEN BLOWN TO BITS, BUT WHAT WAS THAT RUMBLING SOUND?
RUMBLE
RUMBLE
RUMBLE
RUMBLE
Uh-oh! Time to get out of here!

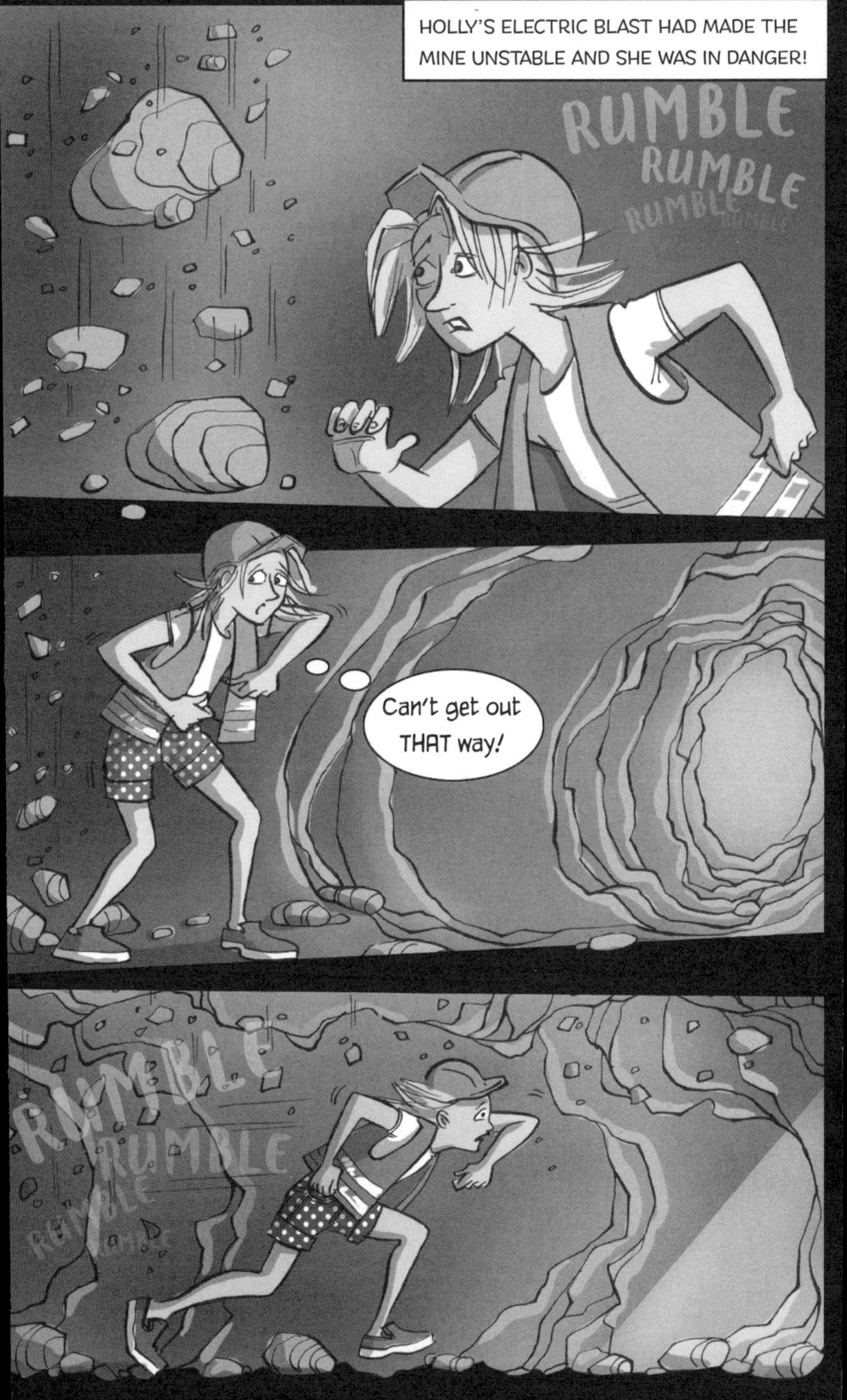
HOLLY'S ELECTRIC BLAST HAD MADE THE MINE UNSTABLE AND SHE WAS IN DANGER!
RUMBLE
RUMBLE
RUMBLE
Can't get out THAT way!
RUMBLE
RUMBLE
RUMBLE

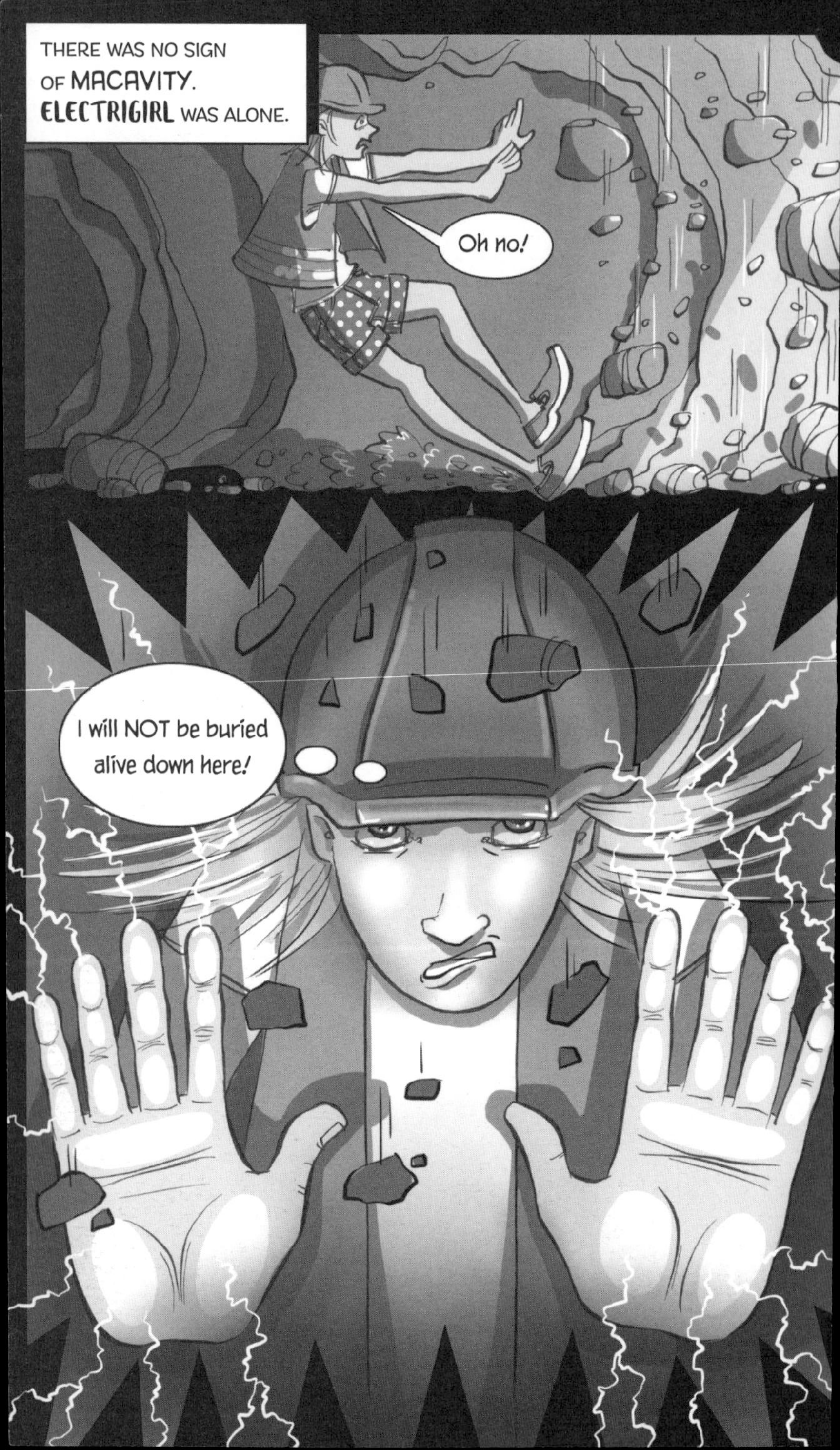
THERE WAS NO SIGN OF MACAVITY. ELECTRIGIRL WAS ALONE.
Oh no!
I will NOT be buried alive down here!

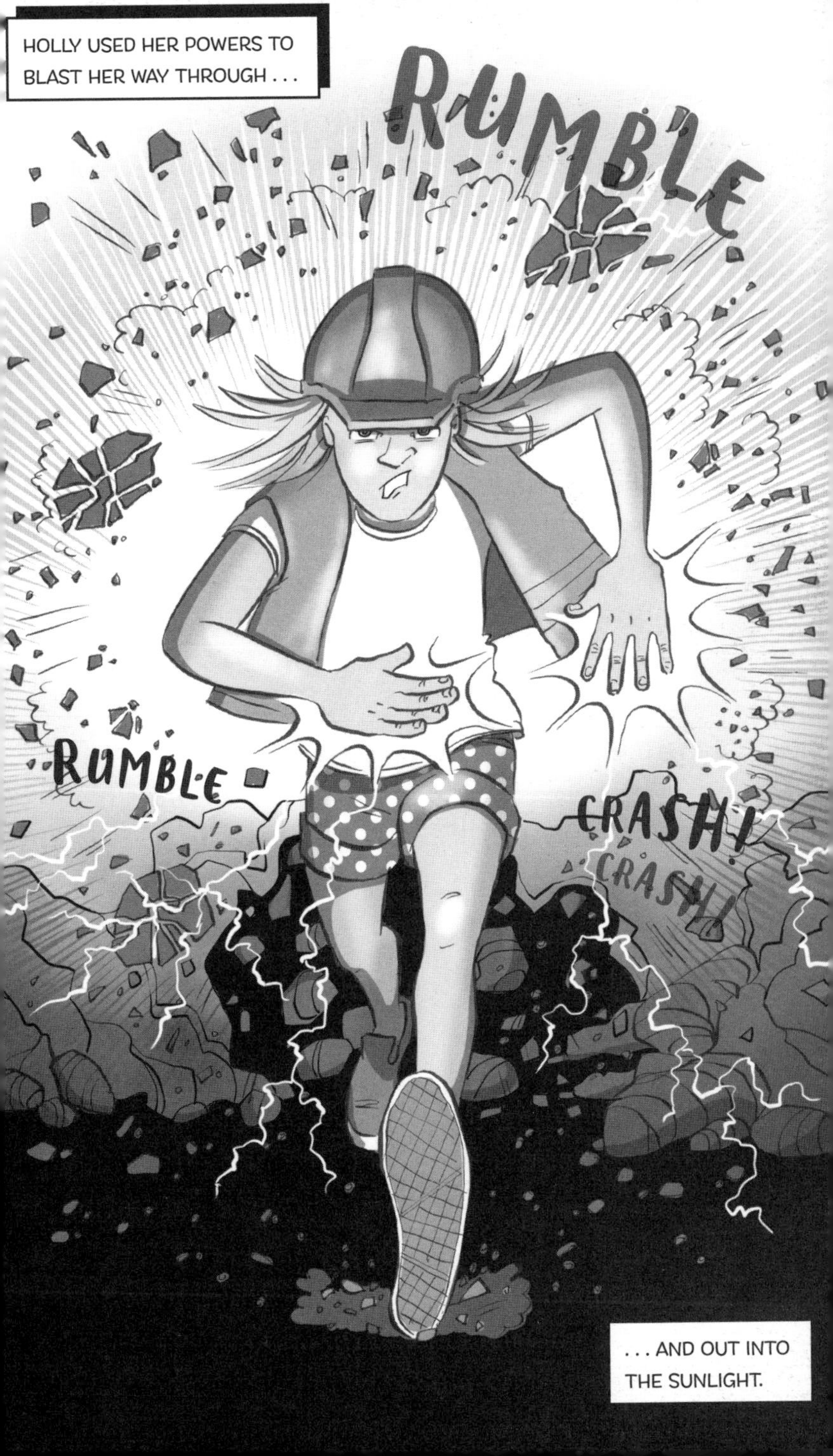
HOLLY USED HER POWERS TO
BLAST HER WAY THROUGH . . .
RUMBLE
RUMBLE
CRASH!
CRASH!
. . . AND OUT INTO
THE SUNLIGHT.

I took great gulping breaths. There was a distant rumble under my feet and a plume of dust rose from the shaft behind me. I'd made it out! My heart was racing faster than ever before and my lungs felt like they were full of dust, but I was out! And the pixies were destroyed!

For a moment I felt triumphant. And then panic gripped me. *Where was the **Professor**? Was she lying in wait for me somewhere?* I whipped around, trying to look in all directions at the same time, but there was no sign of her. This exit had brought me out in an unfamiliar place and for a moment, I wasn't sure where I was. And then I caught sight of the main building about three hundred feet away. My breath coming in ugly gasps, I set off toward it. I couldn't let **Macavity** slip through my fingers. As long as she was free, I would always be looking over my shoulder. I had to find her while I still had the chance.

But when I reached the buildings, the big black car was gone. The gate was now open, the padlock hanging clear. There was no sign at all of **Macavity**. In fact there was no sign of anyone at all. I glanced at my watch. It was after 10 a.m. Shouldn't people be here for the tour? I needed to warn Mike that the tunnel had collapsed! I also needed to find Mav — where was he? Why hadn't he come? *And* I was desperate to catch **Macavity** somehow!

I said some very rude words to myself. *What should I do now?* The best option was probably to head back to the campground. I could find Julie there and get a message to Mike about the mine. And I could also check on Joe and Imogen. Were they still safe? My feet started to run of their own accord. Every thudding step seemed to increase the panic in my chest, and I sprinted the final four hundred yards to the campground.

The little office cabin by the site gate was empty and I said another rude word to myself. No Julie, no Mike. Where WAS everyone today? I ran on to number seventeen, relieved to see that it was still standing, unscathed. But even before I reached the door, I could see the note stuck to it. "Oh no, oh no," I panted. Where were they? What had they done?

HI HOLLY

WE GOT BORED SO WE'RE GOING FOR A WALK

ALONG THE CLIFFS. DON'T WORRY, WE'RE NOT

GOING TO DO ANYTHING STUPID. NOT TIL YOU

COME ANYWAY, HAHA! SEE YOU SOON!

IMOGEN AND JOE

I had run out of rude words. They were up on the cliffs! How long would it be before the urge to do something dangerous grew too strong? Everything else flew out of my head. I had to get to them before it was too late.

I whirled toward the sea but crashed into someone, knocking us both to the ground.

"**OOF**!"

"Cameron!" I scrambled off him. "What are you doing here? I'm sorry, I have to go — my brother —"

"I have to go too!" he said, beaming. "I came to tell you — I have a mission!"

"You have — what?"

He flexed his muscles. "I am *INVINCIBOY!* People need my help!"

"What — what are you talking about?"

"The mine! It's collapsing! Mom got a call just a few minutes ago — there's a tour party trapped down there. She's on her way there right now — and I'm going to save my dad!" He turned to run.

"**NO**!" I yelled. "You can't go!" Thoughts whirled around my head. I'd gotten everything in the wrong order! I should have called the police or something before I came here — the tour party must have already been in the elevator shaft when I left. They'd been on their way down when I'd caused the rock collapse! I felt faint with horror. "The emergency services," I said to Cameron. "Has someone called them?"

Cameron laughed. "Of course! But they don't know the mines like I do. I'm going to save the day! Aren't you coming?"

"I can't," I said, feeling sick. "I have to find Imogen and Joe. And Maverick. Everyone's in danger. I can't be everywhere at once."

Cameron shrugged. "Suit yourself. I'd have thought you'd *want* to come. Seeing as your mom's down there too!"

CHAPTER 24

For a second, everything went black, and my knees buckled.

Mom — in the mine. *That* was her plan for the morning, to go down the mine? Had she told me that? Had I not been listening?

"It's all right." Cameron was starting off. "I can handle it. Leave this to me."

"No." I grabbed his arm to stop him. "No — you really shouldn't."

"They need a superhero," he said simply.

And suddenly strength flooded through me. "There's one right here," I said. "It's my job." **Macavity** thinks I can't be everywhere, huh? I'd show her! I was **ELECTRIGIRL**!

Cameron pouted. "I want to do it. I never have any fun."

"I have a job for you," I said, my mind racing. I faced him seriously. "I have something very important for you to do — a mission. Are you sure you're up to it?"

He practically grew four inches. "I'm sure! What do I have to do?"

"Imogen and Joe have gone to the cliffs," I told him. "They went for a walk, but I've thought of something much more exciting we could do. And — um — dangerous."

Cameron's eyes lit up. "What do you have in mind?"

"Trenarth Peak," I said. "It's got a really steep rock face. You said you wanted to go climbing. Well, only experienced climbers are supposed to go up there."

"That's right!" Cameron smacked a fist into his other hand. "They always say it's too dangerous for kids. Excellent idea!"

"Go and find Imogen and Joe," I told him, "and say I'll meet you all at Trenarth." Trenarth was a bus ride away. This would at least buy me some more time.

Cameron nodded, grinning. "So you're going to get the people out of the mine, right? You will make sure my dad's OK, won't you?"

I was relieved to see that the venom hadn't made Cameron completely unfeeling. "Of course I will," I said reassuringly, hoping I could deliver.

He high-fived me and set off toward the coast, yelling back, "See you there!"

"Oh!" I called back, a new idea striking me. "Get Joe to call Maverick and ask him if he wants to come too, OK?" At least that way *someone* would try to make contact with Mav!

"**OK**!" he yelled.

I took a breath and turned to face the park exit — the path I'd thudded down only minutes earlier. Time to go back.

Back to the collapsed mine, and the darkness.

The darkness that I'd hoped never to go into again.

But there were people trapped down there.

Not just people. My mom.

WOULD I GET THERE IN TIME?

CHAPTER 25

As I ran toward the mine, I could feel my powers building. If people were trapped under tons of rock, I'd need everything I could muster to rescue them. How did you rescue people trapped in mines anyway?

A siren blared, and I jumped onto the grass to avoid the fire truck racing past. If the firefighters were on their way to the mine, and if they'd been stung . . . would that make them better at their job or worse?

As I dashed through the open gates, I could see people standing around, their faces worried, some of them with cell phones clamped to their ears. Cameron's mom, Julie, was there, too — I was amazed that so many people had appeared in such a short time.

The fire truck was parked alongside one of the ruined buildings, its single wall jutting up into the sky. Two firefighters talked quietly together by the cab. I sidled closer to listen.

". . . five of them," the first one said. He was tall and handsome, with a determined expression.

"They're actually still in the elevator?" asked the second. She was shorter than the man but looked strong and fit. Her blond hair was tied back in a ponytail.

"Yeah," he said. "Lucky they hadn't yet gotten out of it. The collapse happened just as they reached the bottom, apparently. That's what Mike told me on the radio. He's the one leading the tour. Good thing they were still in the elevator, or we'd have no way of communicating. There's an alarm in it, goes straight to the emergency services."

"So they're protected by the cage," the woman said, nodding. "That was very lucky."

"They're all uninjured," the man said. "But Mike says they can't see a thing and they're covered in dust. The whole elevator is buried under rocks." He lowered his voice. "Which means the air supply is limited."

The woman paused. "How long do they have?"

He shrugged. "You know, it's impossible to say. Another hour, maybe?"

"An hour . . ." She turned and looked at the mine shaft. "But we need contractors with lifting equipment . . . specialists . . . It's not enough time."

The man caught sight of me, and his face changed. "Hello, dear, you all right?"

"My mom's down there," I said and swallowed. "Are you going to get her out?"

He smiled reassuringly. "Of course we are. We have to take it slow though. Can't risk any injury."

I swallowed again. "But . . . the air . . ."

He pressed his lips together for a moment and looked at me seriously. "How old are you?"

"Twelve."

"Well, I'm not going to lie to you. It's a tricky one. We have to get the rocks off the cage before we can lift it — and there may not be much time. We're working on a plan. There's a guy with rock-lifting equipment on his way." He gave me a nod and turned back to his colleague. Four more firefighters were gathering at the back of the engine. The woman reached into the cab for the radio.

I glanced around and took a few steps away from them. Over by the main building I could see Julie, her face streaked with dust and tears, talking to other worried-looking people. There were people everywhere — too many. How could I do anything without everyone seeing?

I couldn't help it.

MY POWERS, ALWAYS ACTIVATED BY A FOCUSED, INTENSE FEELING, SPRANG TO MY FINGERTIPS . . .

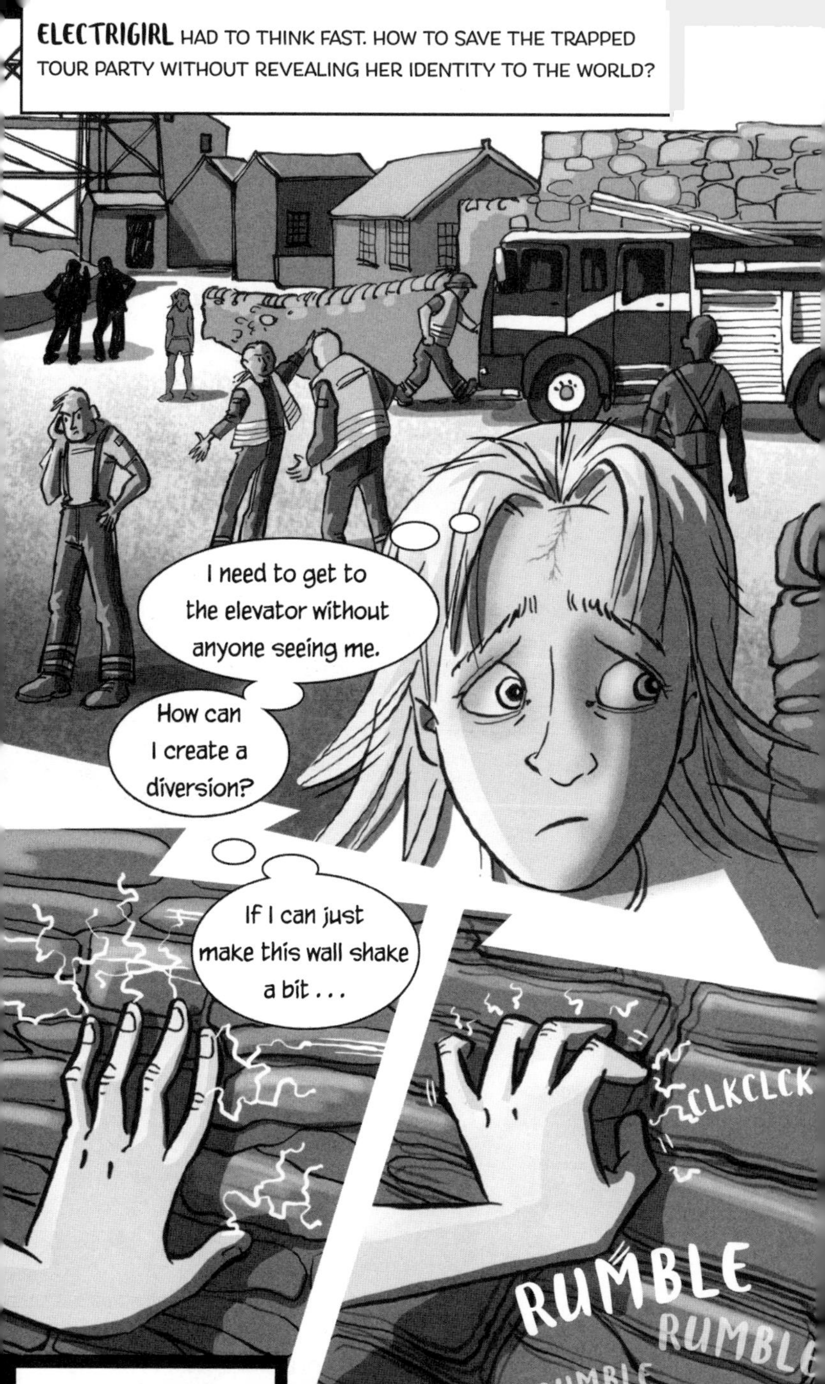
ELECTRIGIRL HAD TO THINK FAST. HOW TO SAVE THE TRAPPED TOUR PARTY WITHOUT REVEALING HER IDENTITY TO THE WORLD?
I need to get to the elevator without anyone seeing me.
How can I create a diversion?
If I can just make this wall shake a bit . . .
CLKCLCK
RUMBLE
RUMBLE
RUMBLE
RUMBLE
THAT WAS THE ANSWER!

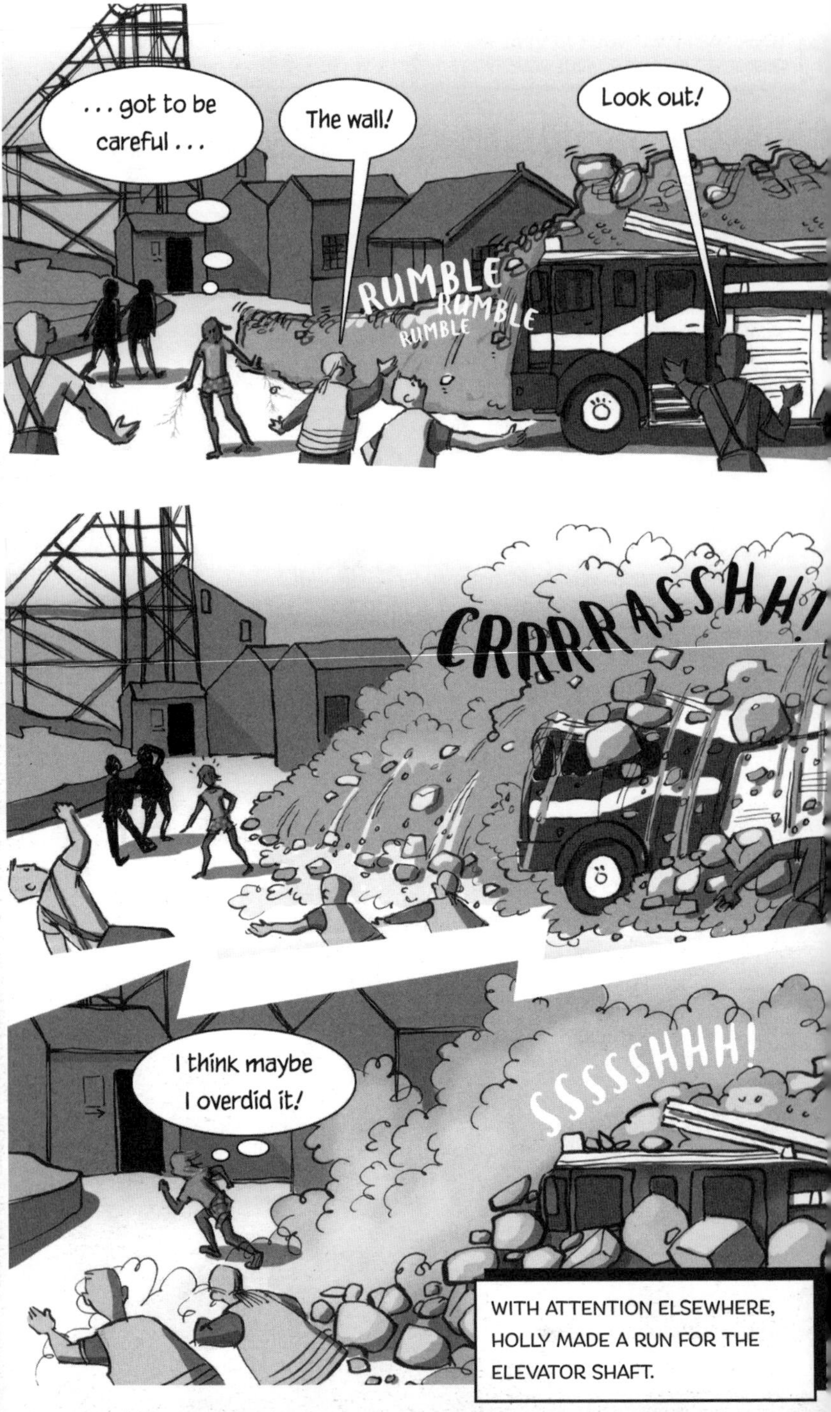
. . . got to be careful . . .
The wall!
Look out!
RUMBLE
RUMBLE
RUMBLE
CRRRRASSHH!
I think maybe I overdid it!
SSSSSHHH!
WITH ATTENTION ELSEWHERE, HOLLY MADE A RUN FOR THE ELEVATOR SHAFT.

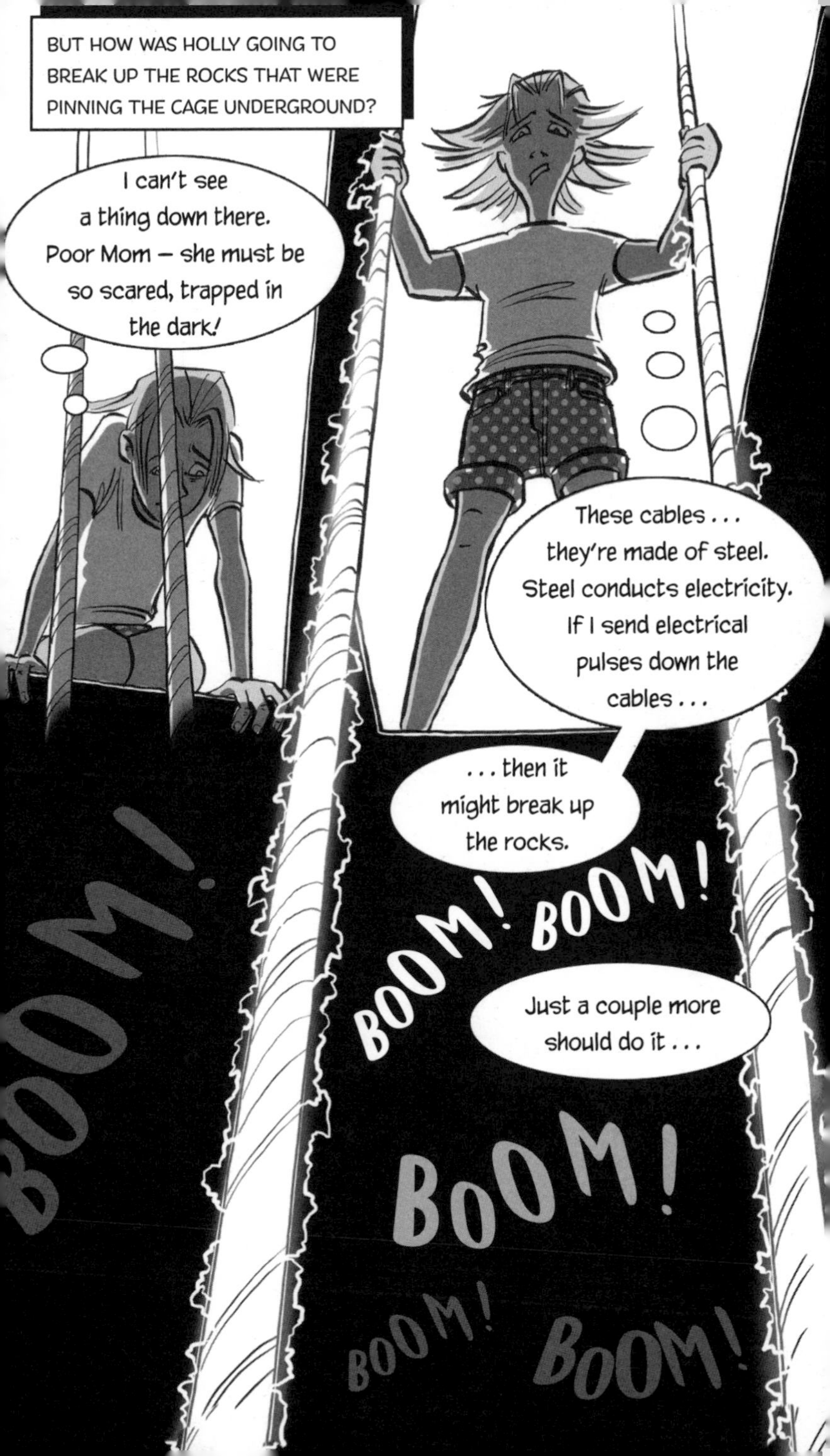

BUT HOW WAS HOLLY GOING TO BREAK UP THE ROCKS THAT WERE PINNING THE CAGE UNDERGROUND?
I can't see a thing down there. Poor Mom – she must be so scared, trapped in the dark!
These cables . . . they're made of steel. Steel conducts electricity. If I send electrical pulses down the cables . . .
. . . then it might break up the rocks.
BOOM!
BOOM! BOOM!
Just a couple more should do it . . .
BOOM!
BOOM!
BOOM!

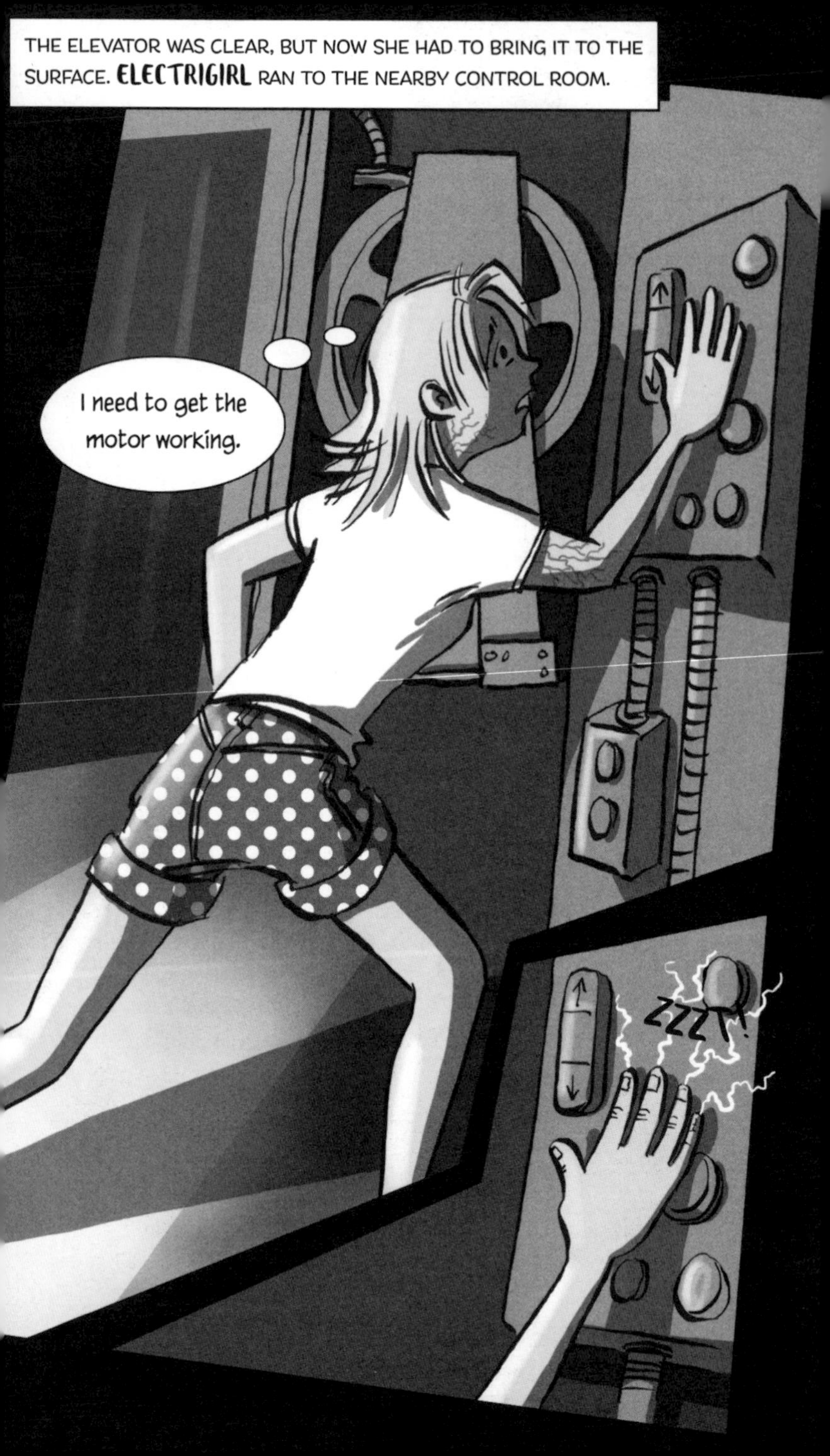
THE ELEVATOR WAS CLEAR, BUT NOW SHE HAD TO BRING IT TO THE SURFACE. ELECTRIGIRL RAN TO THE NEARBY CONTROL ROOM.
I need to get the motor working.
ZZZT!

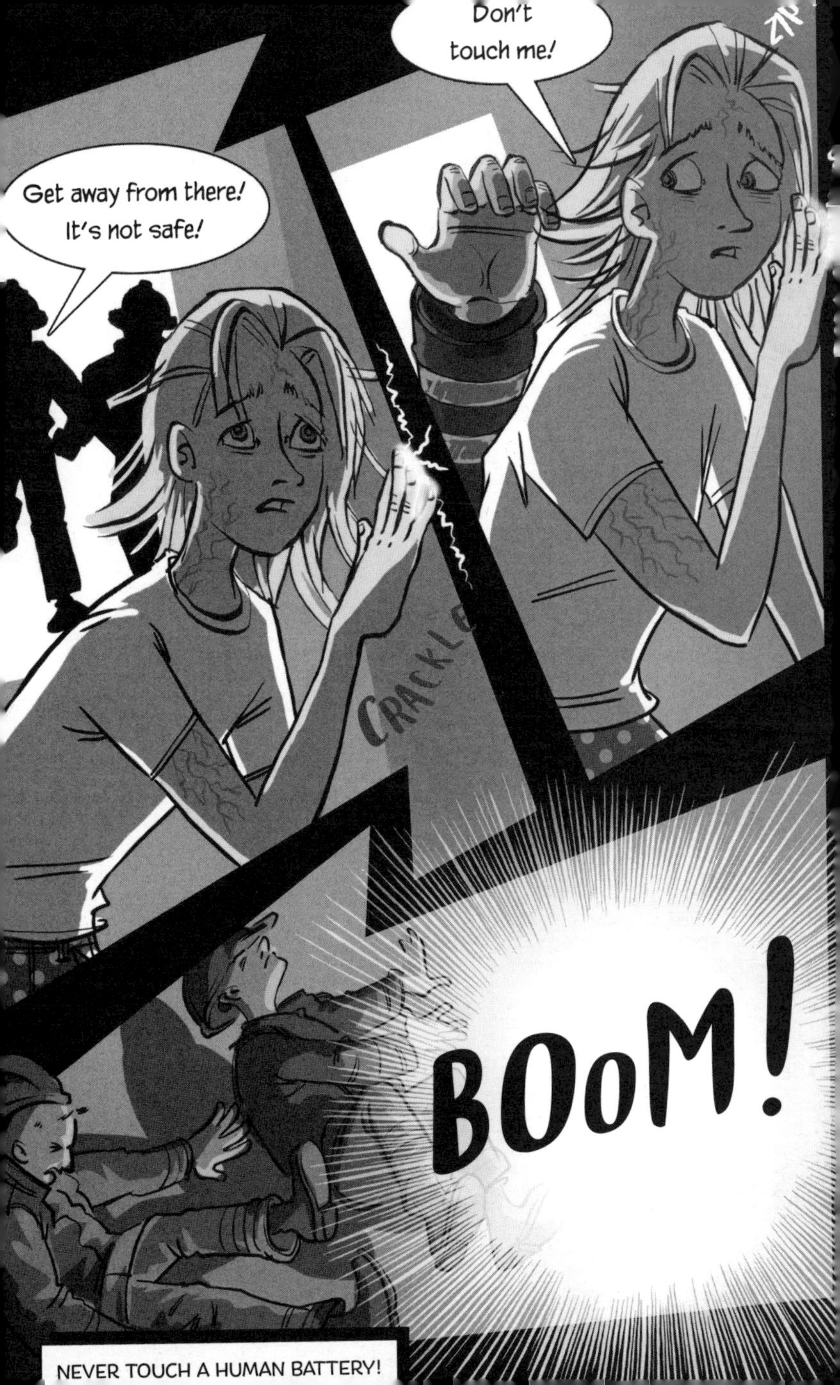
Get away from there! It's not safe!
Don't touch me!
ZIP
CRACKLE
BOOM!
NEVER TOUCH A HUMAN BATTERY!

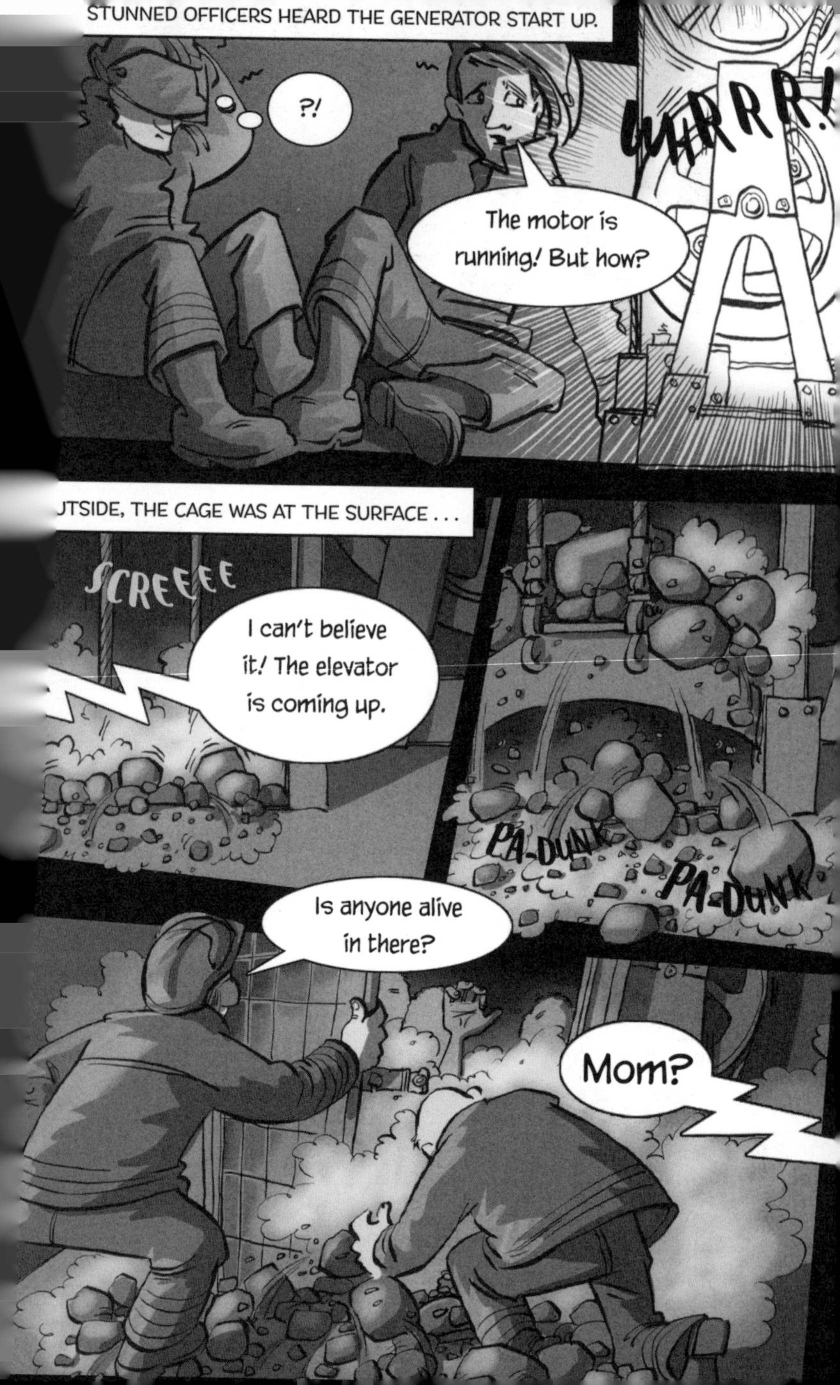
STUNNED OFFICERS HEARD THE GENERATOR START UP.
?!
The motor is running! But how?
WHRRRR!
UTSIDE, THE CAGE WAS AT THE SURFACE . . .
SCREEEE
I can't believe it! The elevator is coming up.
PA-DUNK
PA-DUNK
Is anyone alive in there?
Mom?

CHAPTER 26

The people coming out of the cage all looked identical: covered in gray dust, choking and spluttering. The firefighters were pulling them away from the mine shaft as quickly as they could, offering them water and making them sit down at a safe distance.

An ambulance squealed in through the gates, lights flashing, siren wailing.

But where was my Mom?

I gazed desperately at the gray people. One . . . two . . . three — there was Mike. Julie rushing to clasp him in her arms as he stumbled to the ground — four . . .

Five people went down, the firefighters said. Five. Where was the fifth?

And then a shout went up from near the cage. "Paramedic!" and my heart almost stopped.

A body was being pulled out from the rubble. Gray hair tumbled over the gray face. A streak of blood ran down one cheek. **MY MOM**!

My knees gave way under me and I sank unsteadily to the ground. My fingers still tingled from the after-effects of the electricity, but my powers had faded again. *Had I done that? Had breaking up the rocks caused one of them to hit my mom? Had she breathed in too much of the dust I had created?*

Was she dead?

They put her on the ground and a paramedic brought over a machine with a face mask. I guess they fitted it to her face but there were too many people in the way. All I could see were her feet. I stared at them, willing them to move.

Come on, Mom . . . Come *on* . . .

And then they twitched, convulsively, and even from here I could hear the awful coughing and retching sounds, but it didn't matter how bad it sounded because she was **ALIVE**.

My whole body started to shake.

Someone put a blanket around my shoulders. "You OK?" It was the female firefighter. She sat down and smiled at me. "Your mom's going to be OK, I'm sure. She just inhaled a lot of dust.

They'll take her to hospital — you can go too, I'm sure. Looks like I'm going to need a ride back to the station myself, seeing as our engine was just totaled." She smiled at me again. "What a day, huh?"

I tried to smile back, but my mouth was all wobbly. "Yeah."

"I'm Halina," she said. "What's your name?"

"Holly," I said automatically.

"Well, Holly," said Halina, "are you OK? Jaz and I got a really big electric shock back there when we touched you. Didn't you feel it?"

I felt my eyes open wide in alarm. Deep inside me, something went **WARNING, WARNING**! And I could practically hear Joe's voice shouting, "DON'T TELL HER ANYTHING!"

Joe! And Imogen! Had Cameron persuaded them off the cliffs? Were they on their way to Trenarth to try rock climbing?

"She's going to be OK, you said?" I slipped off the blanket and got to my feet.

Halina got up too. "Yes, but —"

"I've got to go. Please look after her."

I could hear her calling after me as I ran, but I didn't look back. Mom was *alive*, that was the important thing. Joe and Imogen might not be.

CHAPTER 27

The sun was high in the sky as I ran down the road, trying to muster every bit of strength I had left. I wasn't even sure which way I should go. The bus to Trenarth Peak left from the middle of town, but if they were still on the Polcarrow cliffs, I would waste valuable time running in the wrong direction!

Reasoning that I should check the nearest place first, I ran on toward the coast. A mile passed, then two. It was ominously quiet as my feet thudded on the paved path. Where was everyone? It was the height of summer; there should be people walking along the roads, cars, kids flying kites . . .

As the coastal path led me up to the cliffs, I discovered why. They were all there. Everyone. Hundreds of people, gathered in a huge flock on top of the dark gray rocks, which rose out of the hillside like emerging giants. They were so close to the edge — **TOO CLOSE**. I'd grown up with coastal paths. Back home in Bluehaven, my favorite place was on a hilltop overlooking the sea. But the ground at the edge wasn't safe, everyone knew that. Cliffs crumbled into the sea; if you stood on the wrong part, the earth would just slip silently from under you, and there you were, smashed on the rocks below.

I slowed to a jog, my heart thumping from the run but also from fear. There were a **LOT** of people. What were they doing here? I looked about frantically. I couldn't see Cameron — or Imogen, or Joe.

And then I heard a voice. A cold, gray voice, strangely at odds with the bright sunshine, amplified so that it boomed out across the hillside.

And my feet, having brought me to the very edge of the crowd, suddenly refused to take another step.

"Good afternoon!" the voice said. "It's wonderful to see so many of you here today. Who's ready for the thrill of their lives?"

I felt like I'd run into a brick wall. It was wrong, all wrong. The voice was **Macavity**'s, but the words sounded like something from a TV gameshow. It made my head spin. *What was she talking about?*

There was an answering murmur from somewhere near the front of the crowd.

"I said," **Macavity** repeated in her monotone, "who's ready for the thrill of their lives?"

This time the response was louder. I felt sick. This must be her great "demonstration" — but what kind of thrill was she talking about, up here on the cliffs?

Her words from the mine thudded into my head like tombstones:

You jump, I jump, as the saying goes . . .

She was going to make everyone jump off the cliffs! *That* was the demonstration of the power of the venom! But jumping from here was absolute insanity! The water below the horseshoe-shaped rocks was far too shallow!

"We won't make you sign those boring personal injury waivers today," **Macavity** went on. "Get ready for a pure adrenalin ride, from the top of the cliffs to the splash pool below. And don't forget to smile for the cameras!"

Instinctively I glanced around. Standing here and there, taller than head height, were gray metal towers, topped with speakers and video cameras, their lights blinking red. We were all being recorded!

I didn't have much time. Whatever I was going to do, I needed to do it **FAST**. I started pushing my way through the crowd. There was every type of person here: old people, small children, surfers, people in business suits, parents with shorts and sunburn. I saw sting marks on lots of them, though others were trying to hold them back.

"Don't," one girl begged her boyfriend. "Please don't — it's too dangerous."

He laughed. "Come on, where's your sense of adventure? I've always wanted to do something like this!" But he held back, I noticed. There was a flicker of doubt in his eyes.

I felt a tiny glimmer of hope. It took a lot to make people risk their lives. The venom couldn't overcome *all* human reflexes then. People weren't just jumping blindly into the water. Many of them were local; they knew perfectly well that the sea wasn't deep enough here. Jumping from this height risked serious injury, if not death. But what had the **Professor** said? *It only takes one person to lead the way — and then the rest will follow . . .*

"Who's first?" asked the **Professor** calmly. "Who's got the guts to take the first step?"

I doubled my efforts to get through the crowd, pushing and shoving. "Excuse me, can you just — coming through, sorry . . ."

I heard someone say enthusiastically, "Soon as I see the first one do it, I'm in there!"

If I could reach the **Professor** before anyone answered her challenge, maybe I'd have a chance to stop this . . .

"We have a volunteer!" **Macavity**'s voice rang out, and her usual monotone wavered in excitement. "Speak into the microphone, young man. What's your name?"

"Joe," said my brother.

I FELT ENERGY SURGE THROUGH ME.

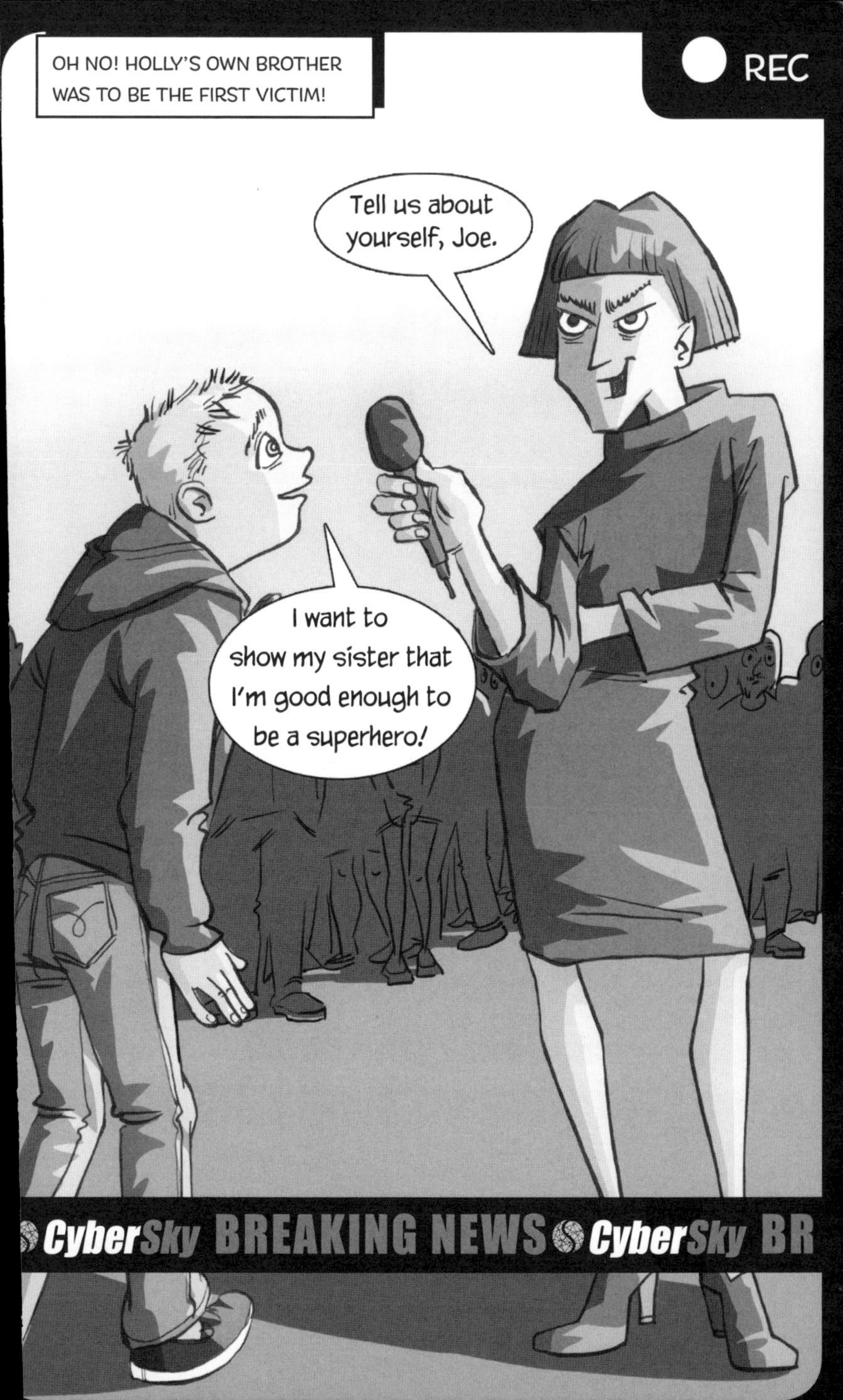
OH NO! HOLLY'S OWN BROTHER WAS TO BE THE FIRST VICTIM!
REC
Tell us about yourself, Joe.
I want to show my sister that I'm good enough to be a superhero!
CyberSky BREAKING NEWS CyberSky BR

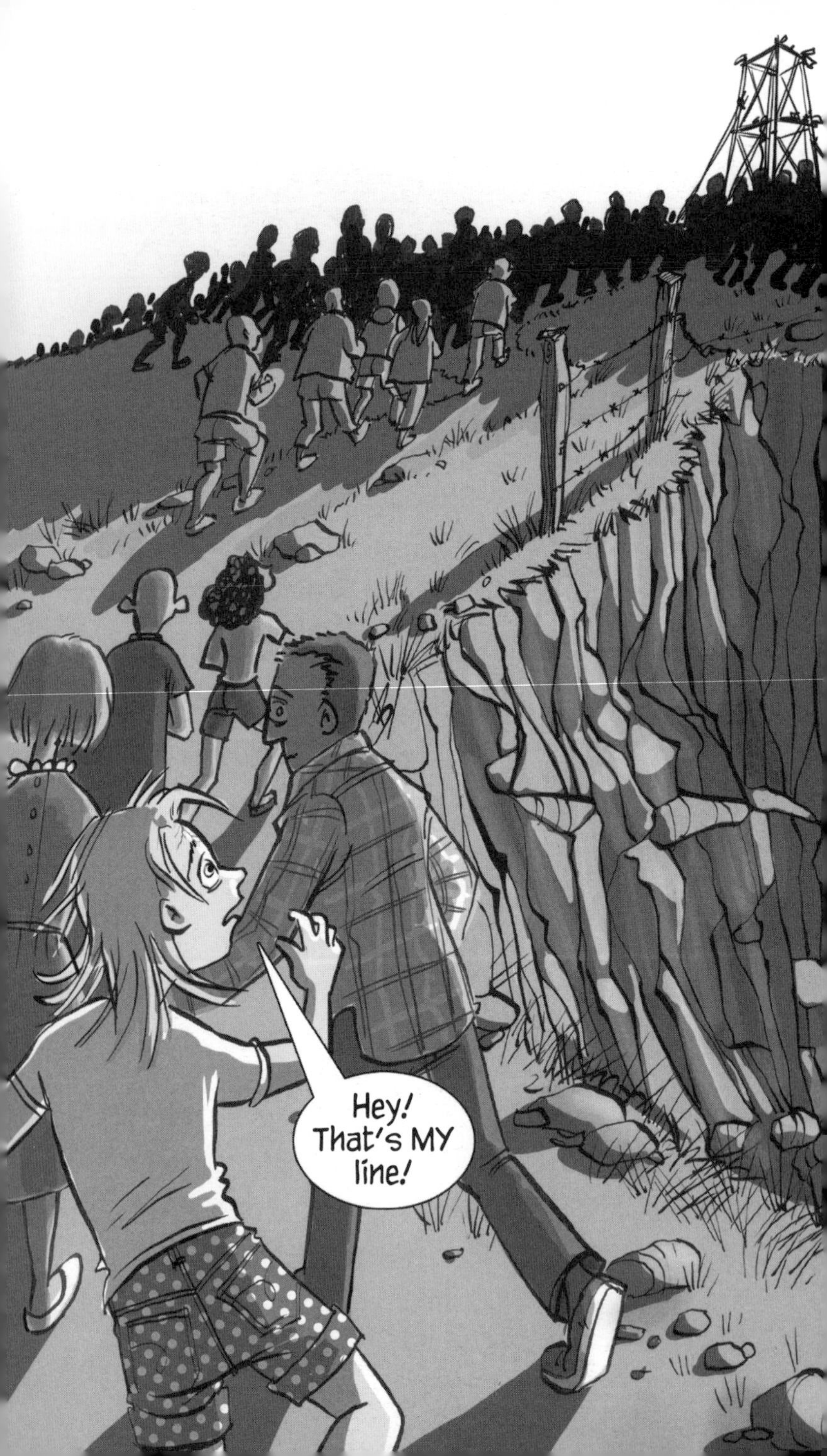
Hey! That's MY line!

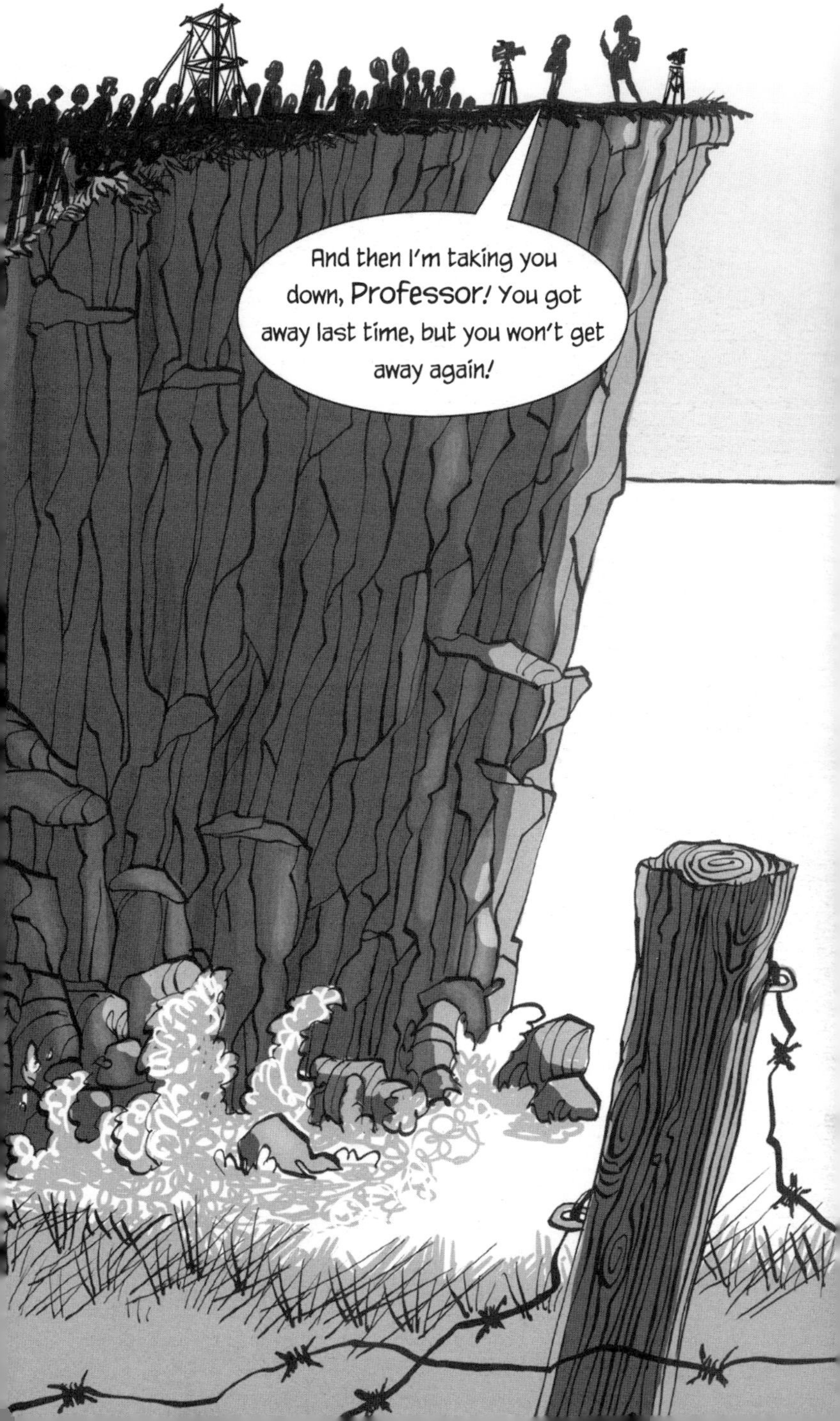
And then I'm taking you down, Professor! You got away last time, but you won't get away again!

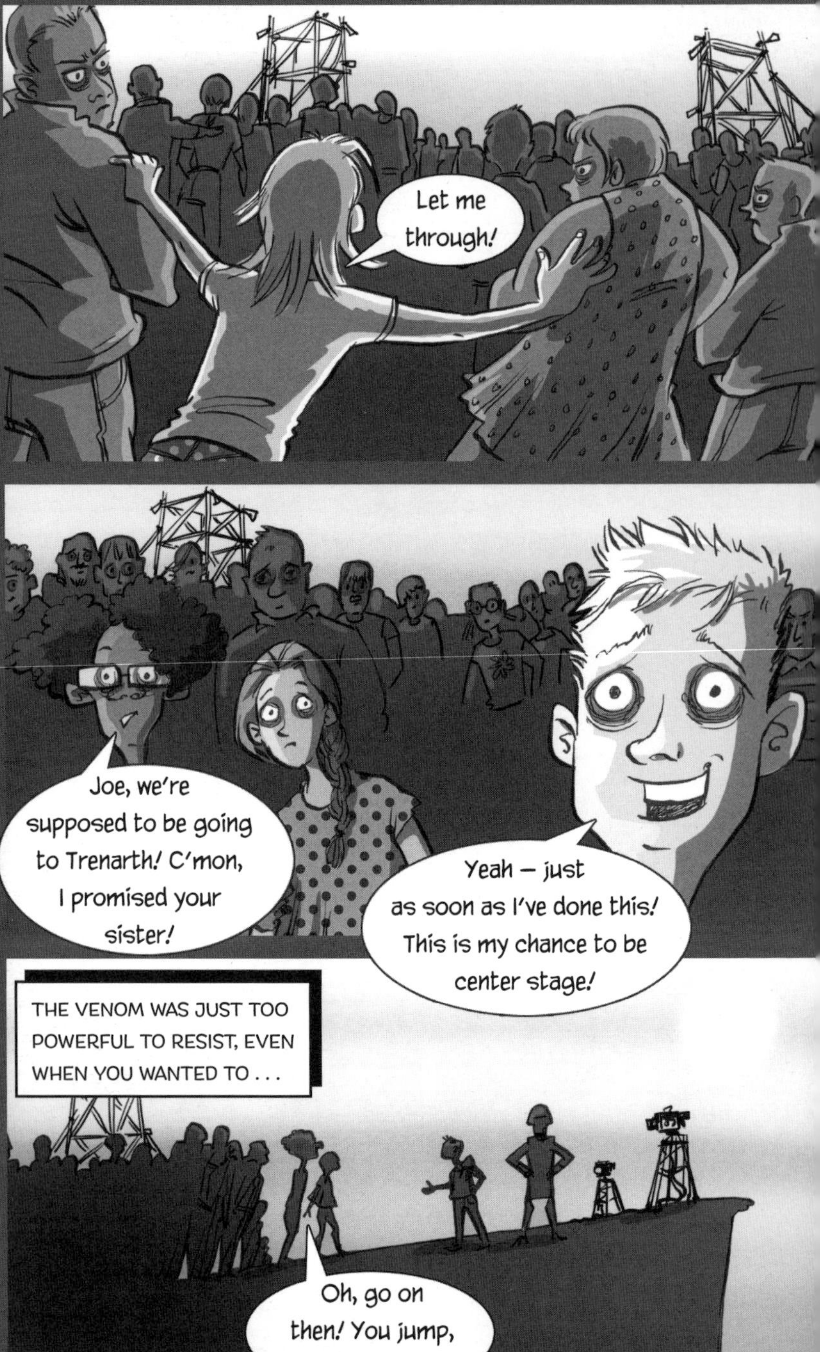
Let me through!
Joe, we're supposed to be going to Trenarth! C'mon, I promised your sister!
Yeah — just as soon as I've done this! This is my chance to be center stage!
THE VENOM WAS JUST TOO POWERFUL TO RESIST, EVEN WHEN YOU WANTED TO . . .
Oh, go on then! You jump, I'll jump!

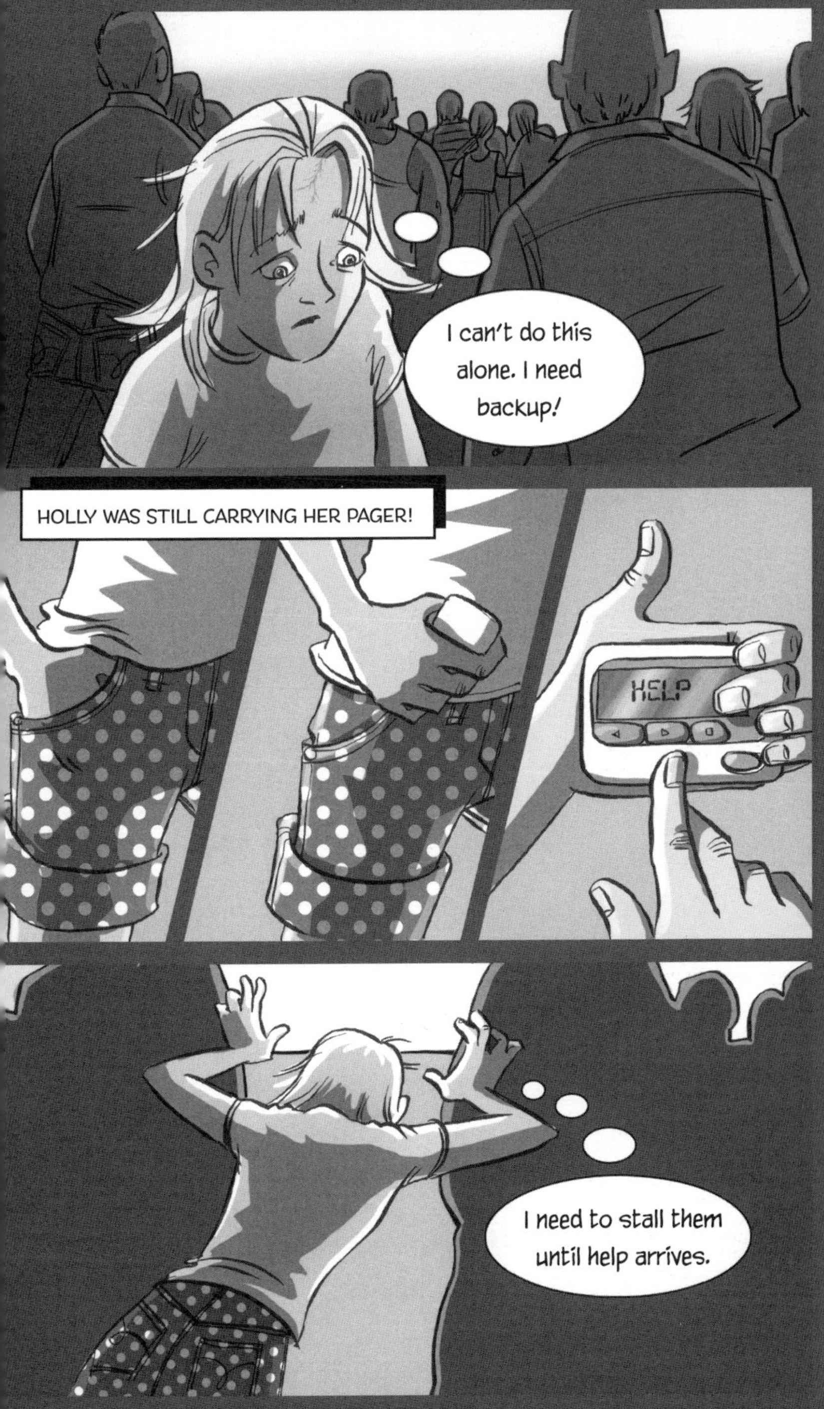
I can't do this alone. I need backup!
HOLLY WAS STILL CARRYING HER PAGER!
HELP
I need to stall them until help arrives.

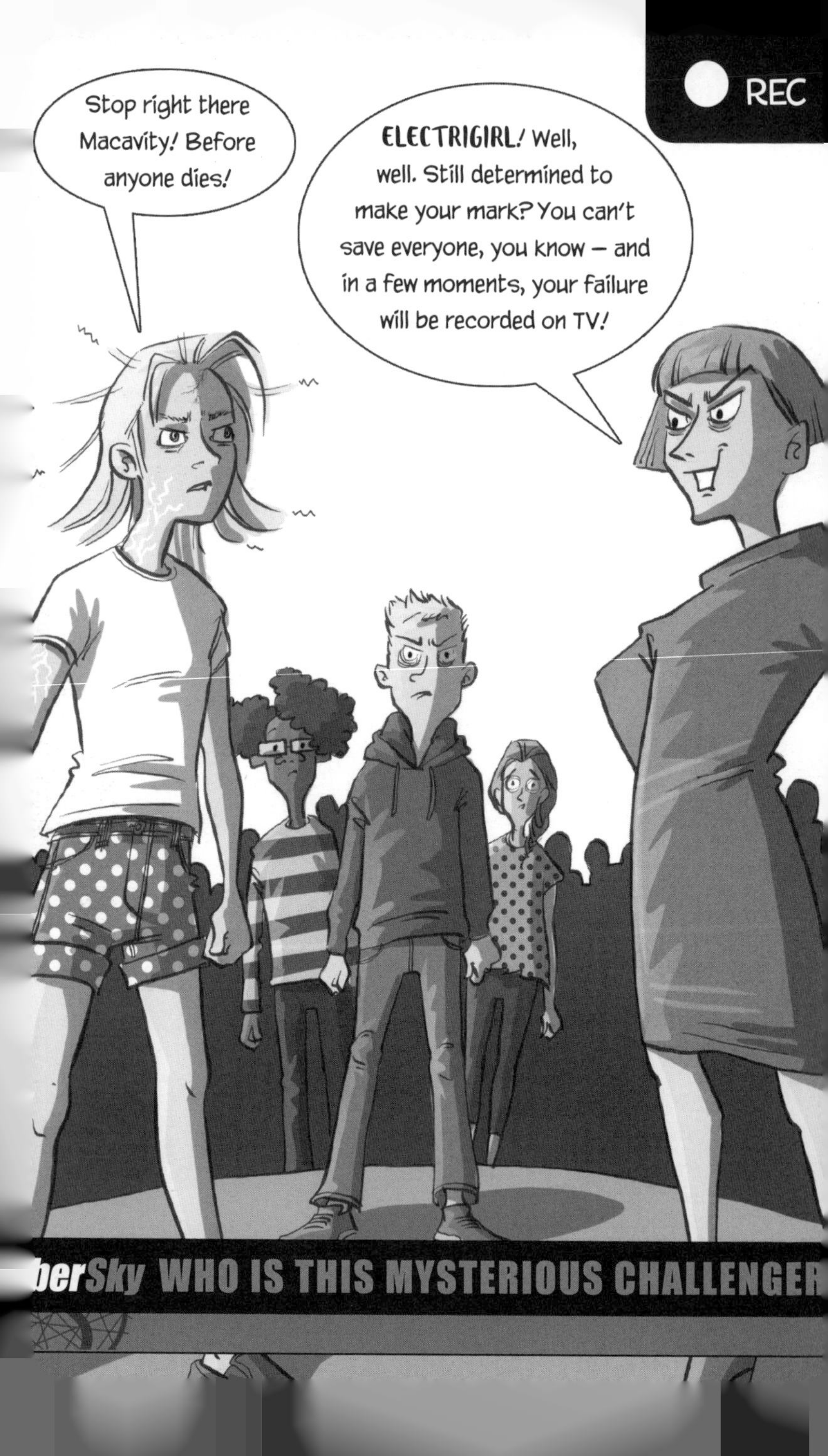
REC
Stop right there Macavity! Before anyone dies!
ELECTRIGIRL! Well, well. Still determined to make your mark? You can't save everyone, you know – and in a few moments, your failure will be recorded on TV!
berSky WHO IS THIS MYSTERIOUS CHALLENGER

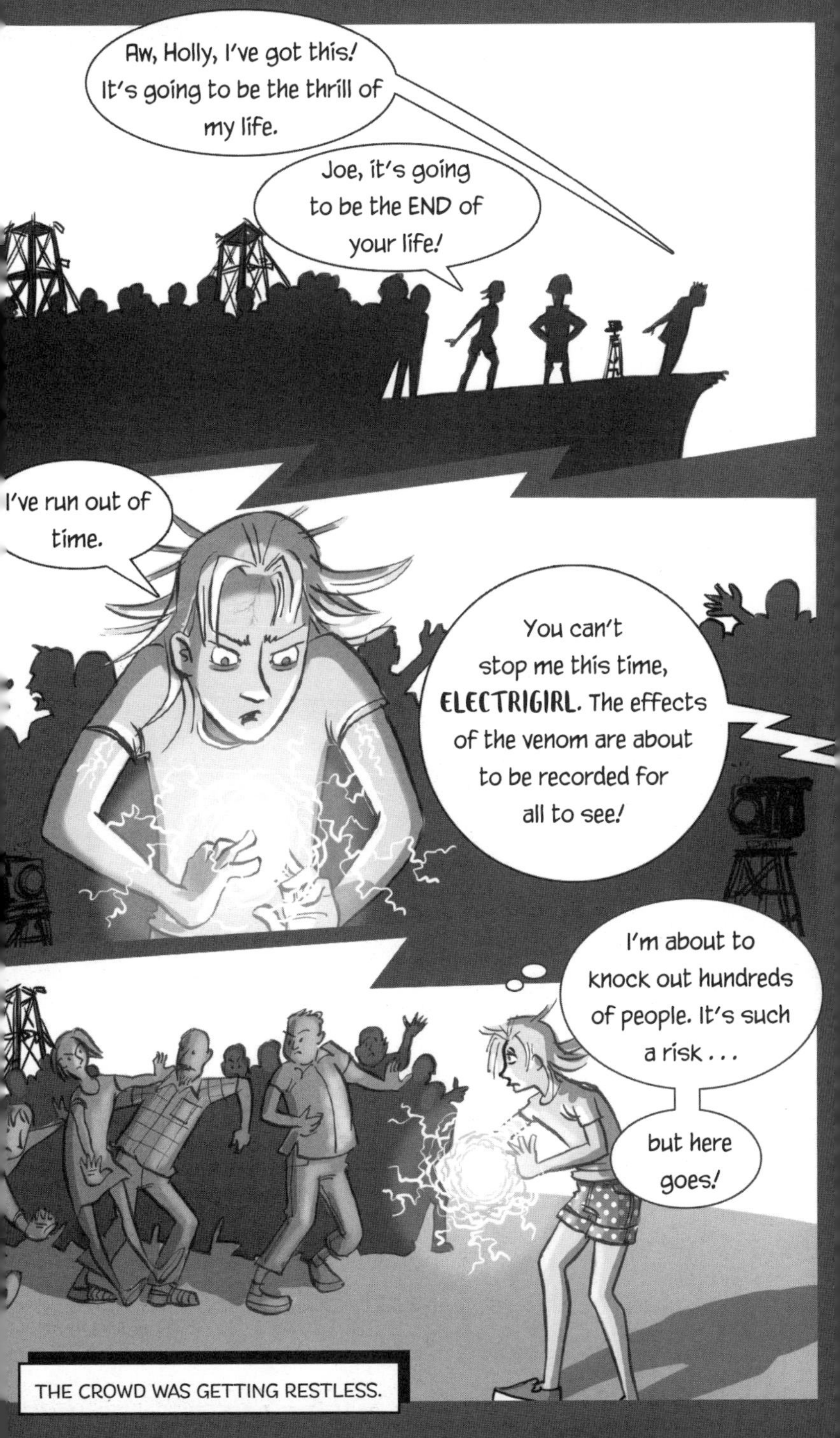
Aw, Holly, I've got this! It's going to be the thrill of my life.
Joe, it's going to be the END of your life!
I've run out of time.
You can't stop me this time, ELECTRIGIRL. The effects of the venom are about to be recorded for all to see!
I'm about to knock out hundreds of people. It's such a risk . . .
but here goes!
THE CROWD WAS GETTING RESTLESS.

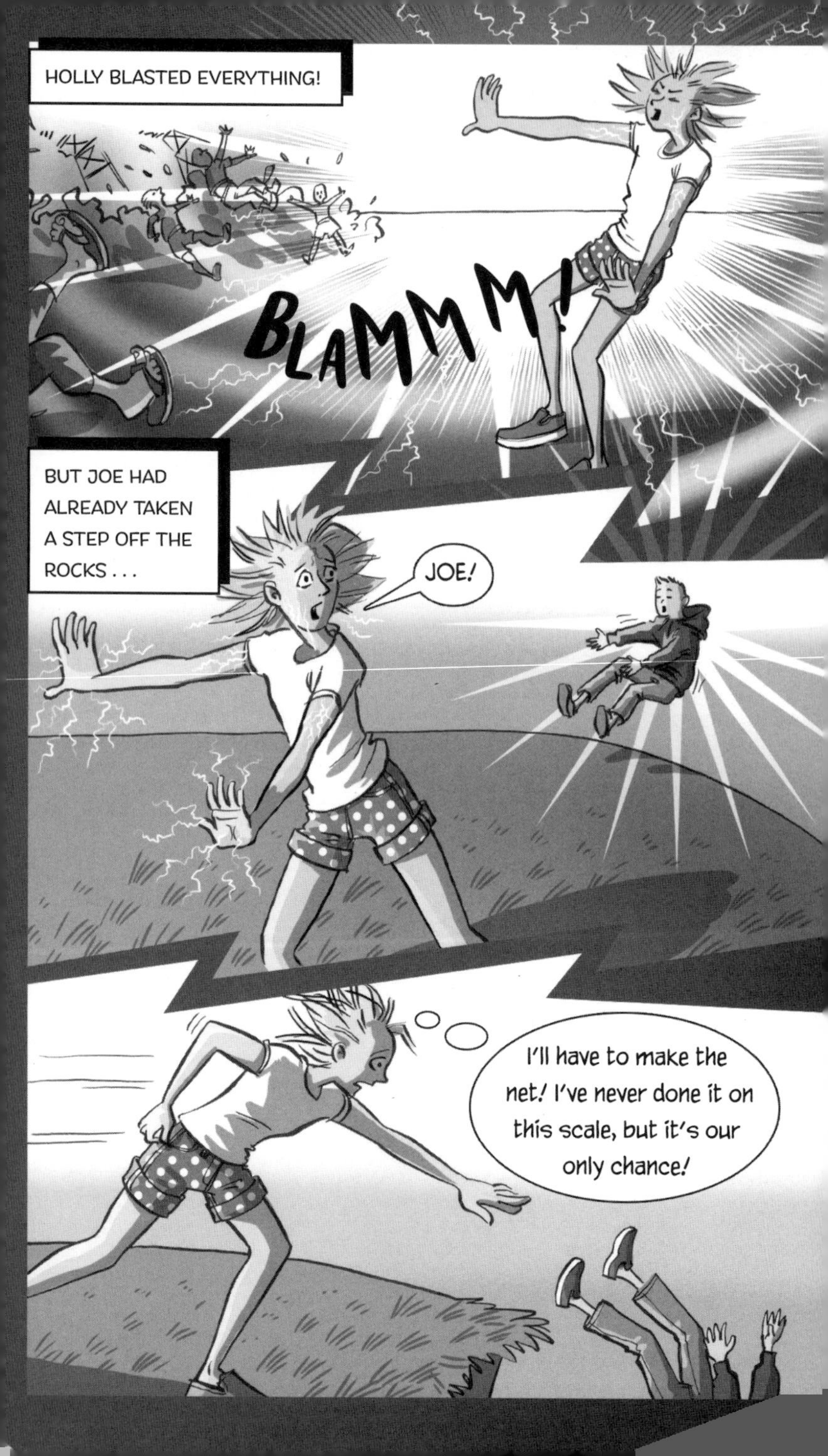
HOLLY BLASTED EVERYTHING!
BLAMMM!
BUT JOE HAD ALREADY TAKEN A STEP OFF THE ROCKS . . .
JOE!
I'll have to make the net! I've never done it on this scale, but it's our only chance!

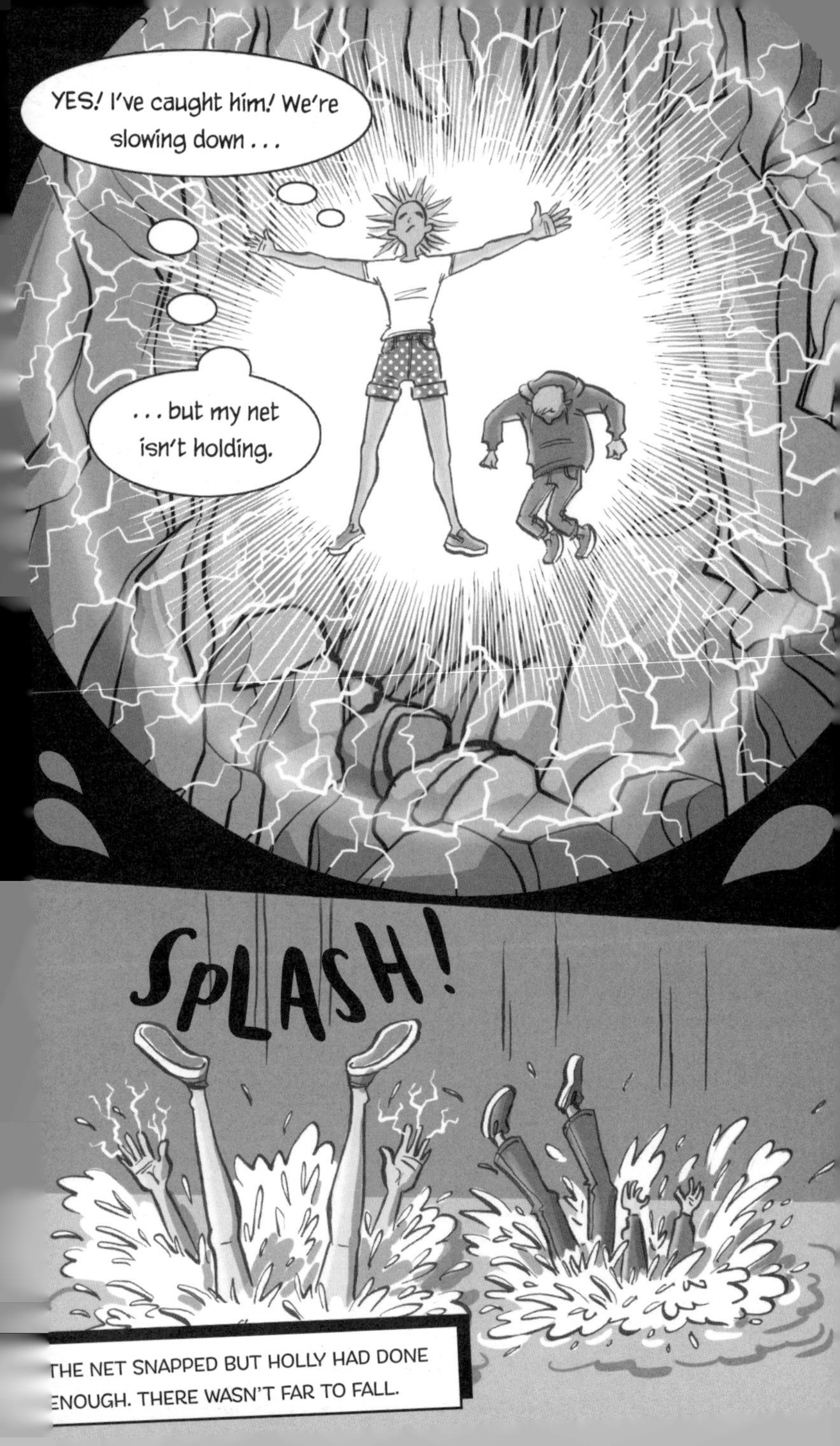

YES! I've caught him! We're slowing down . . .
. . . but my net isn't holding.
SPLASH!
THE NET SNAPPED BUT HOLLY HAD DONE ENOUGH. THERE WASN'T FAR TO FALL.

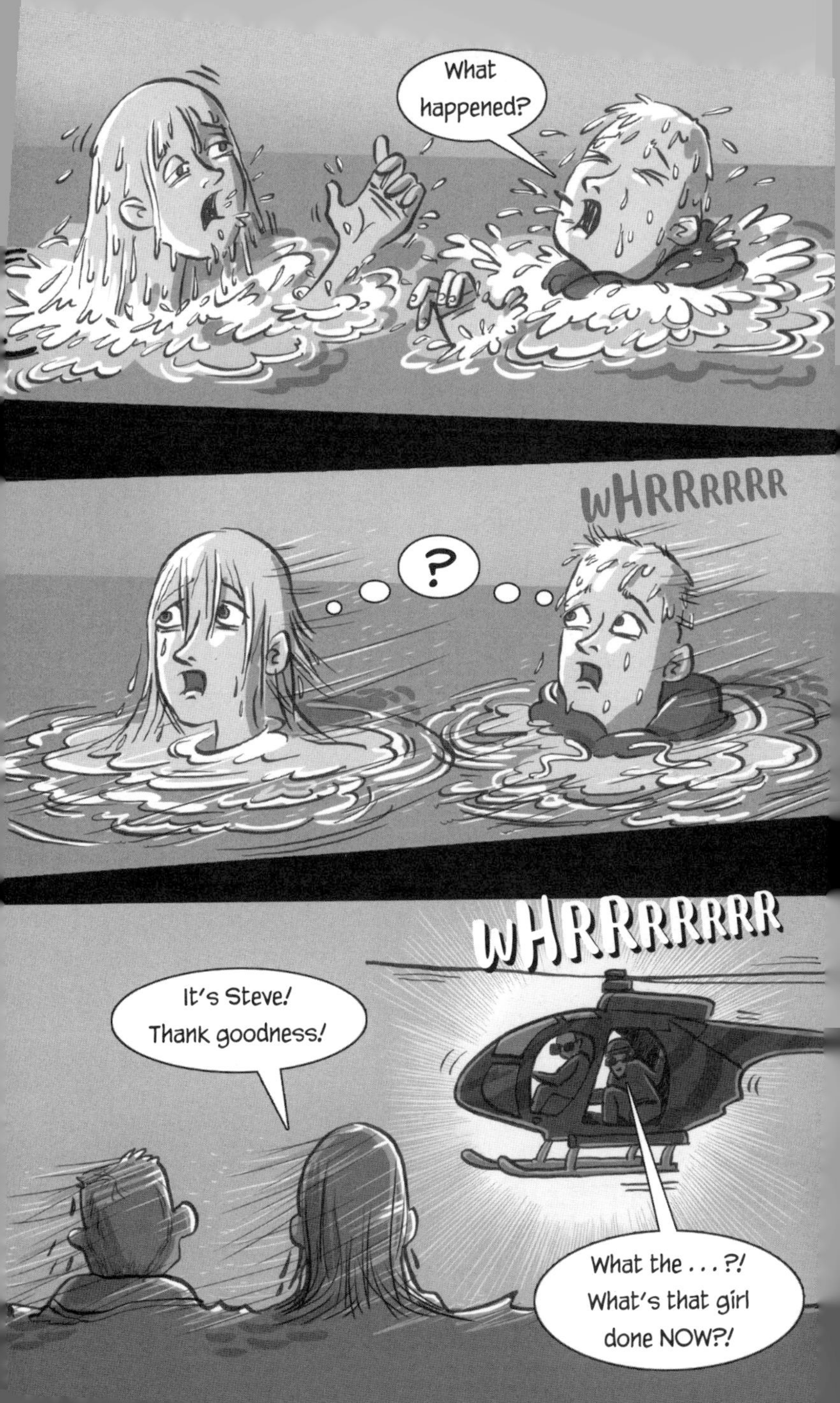
What happened?
WHRRRRRR
?
WHRRRRRRR
It's Steve! Thank goodness!
What the . . . ?! What's that girl done NOW?!

CHAPTER 28

Joe and I were airlifted out of the water, which was pretty cool. Which means, of course, utterly terrifying. Once we were inside the helicopter, Steve gave me a talking-to in the noisy cabin about knocking out so many people.

"What else could I have done?" I shouted. "They were going to jump off the cliff!"

"So electrocution was your plan," Steve shouted back sarcastically. "Perfectly safe."

"It seemed like the better option," I said, glaring at him. "How did you get here so fast anyway? I thought you were in Scotland."

"I was. Came down this morning. It's possible that the Scotland job is connected to **Macavity**."

I stared. "What? How?"

He shook his head. "Classified information, sorry. But my lab finally finished working on the antidote, so I was on my way here anyway."

"The antidote?" I felt immensely relieved. "You mean, you can turn everyone back to normal?"

Joe groaned. "It's no fun being normal — OW!" He glared at the woman withdrawing a needle from his arm.

The woman who'd picked up the pixies from the beach — Lin — stared impassively back.

"Oh, it's you," I said, feeling my face heat up in embarrassment.

She gave me a nod and the hint of a smile, slid the syringe back into a canister and then disappeared into the cockpit.

"Lin's our co-pilot," Steve said.

OMG. She could fly a *helicopter* too? "Whoaaaa," I said, awed. Cameron wanted to be Maverick? I wanted to be *Lin*!

Joe swayed. "My head feels . . . goopy."

"Have you tested this?" I asked Steve, putting my arm around my brother.

He nodded. "Yep. Just now. On him." Then he saw my face. "Of course we've tested it! And it contains just a little sedative to make the last hour seem like a dream."

"You're going to be OK," I told Joe, hoping I was right. "What about **Professor Macavity**?"

"There's a team on the ground right now," Steve said. "We're nearly there."

We landed at a safe distance from the rocks, and as soon as the door slid back, I ran toward them, ignoring my dripping hair and clothes. Not too far off, I could see a handful of people in black clothing, packs on their backs and monitoring devices in their hands. They were going from person to person on the rocks, checking pulses and pulling tiny syringes from their backpacks which they jabbed swiftly into arms and legs as they went.

"Mav!" I shouted, seeing someone I recognized.

He turned and grinned when he saw me. "Hey, kid. Sorry about this morning. I was called into the office last minute to be told off."

"For what?"

"Taking the tranq without asking." He rolled his eyes. "Honestly, it's like they want to keep all their toys to themselves! I called but no one answered your phone. I hoped you wouldn't go into the mine without me, but I guess you couldn't wait to destroy the robots, huh?"

"I thought you were down there!" I exclaimed. "I spent half the time thinking you'd been kidnapped!"

He let out a huge laugh. " Well, I can tell you this, **ELECTRIGIRL**, if I *were* kidnapped, I'd definitely count on you to rescue me." He waved an arm across the sea of people, many of whom, to my great relief, were sitting up and blinking. "You did an awesome job here. To knock out this many people and not kill them? That takes skill, girl. You saved their lives. You deserve a medal."

I blushed again, feeling so much better about it all suddenly. "Oh, I don't know about that."

"You knocked those out at the same time," Mav said, nodding toward one of the gray towers. The camera on the top was smoking gently, its lens cracked straight across. "Honestly, Holly, I don't think anyone could have done a better job."

Imogen came weaving toward me, her eyes unfocused. "Holly? Is that you?"

"Yes! Yes, it's me! Oh, Imogen!" We shared a shaky hug. "Are you OK? I'm so sorry I knocked you out!"

"Is that what happened?" Imogen rubbed her neck. "I have no idea. What were we all doing up here anyway?"

I explained. She looked appalled. "I remember everything seeming so exciting. And like nothing bad could happen to me. Even jumping off the cliff seemed like a really cool thing to do." She shuddered. "That stuff! It might have killed us all!"

"Don't worry," I told her. "Steve's brought the antidote. That's why you're not crazy anymore."

Cameron joined us. "Antidote? Antidote to what? Is that what all these people are doing with hypodermic syringes? Has it been properly tested? You can't just go around injecting people!"

I grinned. "Welcome back, Cameron."

Joe came up behind me. "We're going to have a hard time explaining this to Mom."

The world whirled. I staggered. "Mom! How could I have forgotten? We have to get to the hospital!"

"What? Why?" Joe stared at me, eyes wide. "What's happened to Mom, Holly?"

"She — down the mine! There was a rockfall! I . . ." I trailed off.

Cameron suddenly said, "My dad! He was down there too! Was he — did you get him out?"

"I got them all out," I said, my hands starting to shake. "Your dad's fine — at least, he looked like it. It was just Mom! She — we have to go now!"

"Easy." Mav caught us up. "Your mom's fine. Bump on the head and broke her wrist. Cameron, your parents are at the hospital too, but they're fine. We'll get you all over there." He signaled, and Lin came over.

"Can you get the kids to the hospital?" he asked her.

She nodded. "They've already OK'd us to land on their helipad."

Cameron went pale. "We're going in a *helicopter*? Do you know how dangerous those things are? They crash *way* more than planes."

Lin fixed him with a steely glare. "I think you'll find my safety record is immaculate."

Cameron dropped his gaze. "Oh," he mumbled. "OK."

I sighed. Could Lin be any more **AWESOME**?

"You go," Mav told me. "We'll wrap things up here."

"We certainly will," Steve agreed. "Mav's on clean-up duty for the next month."

As the four of us and Lin headed back to the helicopter, I could hear Mav complaining, "How many times! I was only *borrowing* it . . . !"

CHAPTER 29

Within minutes, Joe, Imogen, Cameron, and I were flown (after Cameron insisted that Lin did the safety checks three times) to the hospital where we met up with Mom and Cameron's parents. There may have been some crying. And it wasn't all me.

Mom had her arm put into a cast in the afternoon, and then we ate a huge meal in the hospital cafeteria because traumatic events make you very hungry.

As we were sitting in the cafeteria, I caught sight of Steve through the window and made an excuse to leave the table.

"We've dosed everyone now, we think," he told me. "It took a while, but we've got them all. And a team has been assigned to the mine, to seal it off from the public and spend time checking it for rogue robots." Then he hesitated. "There was a bit of a problem on the cliffs, though."

"A problem?" I asked. "What sort of problem?"

He gave an exasperated sigh. "We lost her. The **Professor**."

"You *what?*"

"I don't know how. The person assigned to guard her looked the other way for a moment and, well, she was gone. We're searching. She couldn't have gone far."

I didn't believe *that* for a minute. I felt slightly sick. "She's back out there again, free?'

"I'm afraid so. But listen — we've got eyes everywhere. **WE'LL FIND HER**."

"Before she finds me?" I snapped. "Like last time?"

"I know, I know. I'm sorry about that. I'm detailing two extra agents to your case. It looks like the Scotland thing might be developing, but I can't be sure yet. It might all tie up together, which makes it all the more exasperating that we've lost her. I'll know more in a few days. In the meantime, your mom can't drive because of that broken wrist."

"I know." I glanced back through the window. Mom was listening intently to Joe but her eyes were fixed on me. It made me feel a little nervous. Was she suspicious? She **CAN'T** find out about my superpowers. They had to be a secret!

"So one of my agents will also be your driver for the week."

"Huh? You mean, like a chauffeur?" I was VERY impressed.

"Yep. I figure the department can stand the expense. And I need him out of my hair for a while anyway. The kid drives me nuts."

"Who?" I asked, though I'd already guessed.

Maverick came up. "Hey!" he said. "I've got a camper next to yours. Just shout if you need me to take you anywhere. I'm going to soak up some rays." He caught Steve's eye. "Um. I mean, I've got some paperwork to catch up on."

I felt better already. "That's so cool," I said. "You can keep an eye out for **Macavity** too. Save me looking over my shoulder all the time."

He snapped his fingers. "Gotcha. Don't you worry, I won't let her go a second time!"

"A second time?" I said, puzzled.

His face froze, comically. "Oh. Steve didn't tell you? I mean . . . well . . ."

"You were the one who was supposed to be guarding her?" I said.

"Look, there was a lot going on . . ."

"I'm sure you're going to have a wonderful week," Steve said with a thin smile.

Mom, Imogen, and Joe came out the doors. "Hello," Mom said to Steve, offering her unhurt hand to shake. "I don't think we've met."

"Steve Sloane," he said, shaking her hand gently. "I work for the security services."

Mom tilted her head to one side. "Which ones?"

He smiled blandly. "The good ones."

"My husband's in the army," she said. "I hear all kinds of things. How do you know my daughter?"

I held my breath. What would Steve say?

The truth, of course. Or part of it, anyway. "We met in Bluehaven," he said, "after the accident at the **CyberSky** building."

Mom's expression cleared. "Ahh! I see. That explains it. You were the people who cleared it all up."

"That's right."

"Was it a security issue then?"

Steve smiled blandly again. "I'm afraid I can't possibly comment on that, Mrs. Sparkes. I was very sorry to hear about your accident here."

She looked ruefully down. "Yes. So inconvenient."

"My department would be very happy to help out," Steve said. "Since your accident is part of a wider investigation. I'm assigning a driver to you until your wrist is healed. In fact," he shot a sidelong glance at Maverick, "feel free to use him for any personal errands you need run, or to clean the oven, or anything else."

Mom, who had been about to protest, hesitated. "Oh. Well . . . hello."

"Hello." Maverick reached out to shake her hand. "Maverick. Good to meet you."

"*Maverick?*" she repeated. "Really?"

"Um . . .," Maverick shuffled his feet and suddenly looked about six years old. "No, it's a nickname."

"What's your **REAL** name?" Mom asked.

"It's . . . Asif."

"Well, Asif, it's a pleasure to have you along. You can keep an eye on the kids, since they can't seem to help getting into trouble."

"That's not true!" I said indignantly.

Joe was enthusiastic. "Mav's going to stay with us! Awesome!"

"Next camper over," I said.

From around the side of the building Cameron appeared with his parents. "Holly!" he said, waving. "Isn't it great that everyone is all right?" Mike, Cameron's dad, was frowning down at his phone. "The collapse of the mine is all over the news already," he said. "We're going to lose revenue."

"I'm sure we can arrange compensation," Steve said smoothly.

Mike looked surprised. "Who are you?"

"Government," said Steve. He glanced at his watch. "Time to go. Keep in touch, Mav." He nodded briefly at me and then went.

Mike held out his phone to us. "Look at this! I can't figure out if this is a spoof article or not." He grinned. "Superheroes in Polcarrow!"

A wave of fear washed over me. "Can I see?" asked Joe, sounding almost normal.

He, Imogen, and I crowded together to read . . .

POLCARROW BUGLE

SUPERGIRL SAVES VACATIONERS

Reports are coming in of a fantastical event up

on the Polcarrow cliffs earlier this morning. With no clear reason why, a large party of tourists gathered to try cliff jumping – which, as any *Bugle* reader knows, is too dangerous to attempt on this part of the coastline – but a collective attempt to jump was foiled by a freak event, caused, it appears, by a schoolgirl.

"She just came out of nowhere," said Shelley Trott, age 30. "This girl. Blasting light from her hands. I was too far off to be hit by it, but I saw them all go down like a pack of dominoes."

Neil Haigh, age 23, had a slightly different take on events. "It was a shockwave," he said. "I've felt one before. I'm in the navy. I don't know how it happened or where it came from, but it wasn't anything to do with a girl. No human can make a shockwave like that. You need a powerful generator. Trust me."

Sidney Hiller, age 73, disagreed with them both. "It was a bolt from above," he said. "God knew we were all at risk. I don't even know why I went to the cliff. My wife wanted me to come. I hate the water. I can't swim. But God was watching over us. He sent a miracle. I'll be giving extra thanks from now on."

Mandie Preston, age 40, summed it up. "I don't know what happened. Everything's a bit fuzzy. But I do know one thing. Today has been a very odd day indeed. And now I'm going home for a cup of tea and a nap."

I let out a breath. So close to discovery . . . !

"Time for a costume," Joe muttered in my ear.

I sighed. "All right, you win. But no tights. No *way*."

Imogen whispered. "I could design you something. I think it's a good idea."

"All right," I replied.

I handed the phone back to Mike. "Weird," I said. "Glad it's over now, though."

"No more weirdness," Mom said firmly, pulling me into a one-armed hug. "This is meant to be a *vacation*!"

We trooped out to the parking lot. It was a beautifully warm evening, and I couldn't believe so much had happened in just one day.

"We could have supper on the beach," Joe said.

"You've just eaten a huge meal!" I pointed out.

"So? I've got a lot of catching up to do."

Mike laughed. "Kids, huh? All the same."

"I'm not," said Cameron, offended.

Mike laughed and ruffled his hair. Cameron looked appalled at this.

"Don't worry, Cameron," Joe said, "we know you're different."

"That's why you're our friend," added Imogen. "Different is cool."

Cameron gave a wide smile. "You're my friends too. And tomorrow I'll show you my secret place. One no one knows about." His parents got into their car.

"You haven't captured a mermaid or anything, have you?" I teased.

"Of course not. Everyone knows mermaids don't exist."

"Neither do pixies," muttered Joe. Mav gave him a playful punch on the shoulder.

"Pixies!" he said. "You kids and your imaginations!"

Mom laughed with him. "People are funny, aren't they? According to one of the firefighters, you were at the mine this morning, Holly. And the firefighter said that as soon as I was brought to the surface you ran off! I told her it couldn't be you. My daughter wouldn't run off knowing I was injured, I said."

"Oh," I said.

"But then Julie came to see me," Mom went on, her tone sharpening. I looked around, frantic for an escape. "And she said she saw you there too, but she didn't see when you disappeared. And now I find out you were on top of a cliff, far too near the edge, I suspect, and caught up in some kind of bizarre stunt. Not only that, but you seem to have got yourself involved with a government agency. Your father will *not* be impressed."

"Um . . .," I said.

Mom waited for a moment, but when it was clear I wasn't going to say anything else, she said, "When we get back, I'm going to make a cup of tea. And then, Holly Sparkes, we're going to sit down together, and you're going to tell me **EXACTLY** what's been going on."

I'd faced two enormous crises today. But this was WAY bigger.

How on earth was I going to handle this one?

As Mom got into the passenger seat of the car, Imogen and Joe edged closer to me. "Don't worry," Imogen whispered. "We'll figure it out."

"Your secret identity will be safe," Joe added.

I grinned. Evil geniuses, curious moms . . .

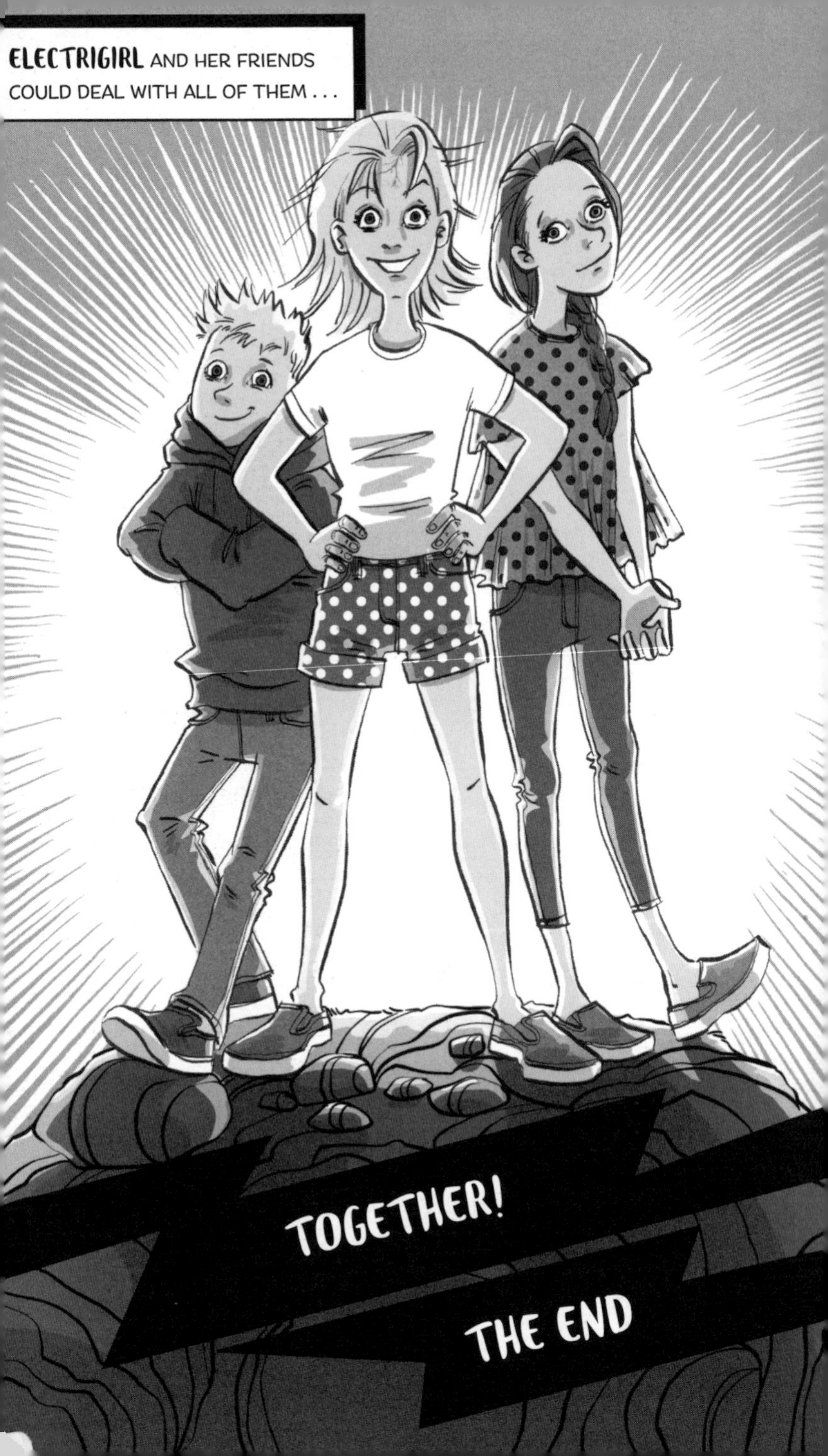
ELECTRIGIRL AND HER FRIENDS COULD DEAL WITH ALL OF THEM . . .
TOGETHER!
THE END

ABOUT THE AUTHOR

Jo Cotterill believes that superheroes are really important. They are what we can all aspire to be: people who use their powers to fight evil and help others. When she's not trying to change the world, Jo makes up stories in her very untidy office-slash-craft room, sometimes stopping to write music instead. Her other books include the Sweet Hearts series for Random House and the critically-acclaimed *Looking at the Stars*, which was nominated for the Carnegie Medal. Jo lives in Oxfordshire, England, with her husband, daughters, and two overindulged guinea pigs.

jocotterill.com

ABOUT THE ILLUSTRATOR

Cathy Brett has been a theater scenic artist, school art technician, college lecturer, fashion illustrator, packaging designer, jet-setting spotter of global trends, and style consultant to the British high street. These days she loves drawing more than anything else. Ever. Except her nieces. And cake. Drawing her nieces while eating cake would be utter bliss. Cathy lives and works in a shed-slash-studio at the bottom of a Surrey, England, garden.

cathybrett.blogspot.co.uk

CREATE A SWARM OF FLYING PIXIES USING THE POWER OF ELECTRICITY!

YOU WILL NEED:

- Balloon
- Tissue paper
- Pencil
- Scissors
- Sticky tape
- Your hair (If you haven't got any hair, a wool sweater will do)

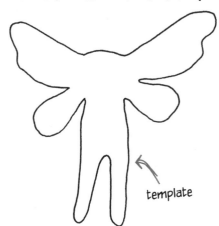

template

1. Place the tissue paper over the template of the pixie and trace it with a pencil. Then cut it out. Repeat until you have several pixies. Spread them out on the floor.

2. Blow up the balloon and tie the neck in a firm knot (an adult may be helpful here, since balloon-tying can be tricky).

3. Rub the balloon rapidly on your hair for at least ten seconds.

4. Now move the balloon slowly through the air a little way above the tissue pixies. They should leap off the ground and cling to the balloon, just like the swarm in the cave!

HOW DOES IT WORK?

When you rub the balloon against your hair, the surface of the balloon collects invisible electrons that carry tiny amounts of negative electrical charge. Positive charges are attracted to them, which is why something very light (such as tissue paper) will be pulled toward the surface of the balloon.